KNOWN TO SOCIAL SERVICES

FREYA BARRINGTON

First published in 2015 by
FARAXA

Published by
FARAXA Publishing
38 Antonio Nani Street, Rabat RBT 3047, Malta; and
P. O. Box 37, East Longmeadow, MA 01020, USA.
http://faraxapublishing.com
info@faraxapublishing.com

ISBN 978-9995782-87-0

Printed in the United States of America.

To Steve who loved me and believed.

In loving memory of Ollie and Ralph.

Acknowledgements

You know how it is: you have a challenging day at work, get home, shake your head and say, "Do you know, I could write a book." After many years of making such declarations, I have finally made good on my promise and no one is more amazed than myself. Naturally, there are people to be thanked. Top of the list is my greatest champion: my exceptional husband, Steve, who encouraged me every step of the way and never doubted that I would get this book into press. He listened patiently as I read it to him chapter by chapter, nodding, thinking and offering his balanced, creative opinions.

Next is my lovely daughter, Steff, who as a teacher was recruited to be my number one proofreader. Her eagle-eyed skills saved me more work than I care to think about. Her efforts were especially noteworthy as I know how busy she was at the time of my pleading.

I thank my dear friend, Honor, for recreating my basic idea for the book cover into something real and professional. Thanks also go to the American author and all-round good guy, James Morgan Ayres, for taking time out of his busy schedule to write the foreword for this book. To James and his uncommonly marvellous wife, ML, I thank you so very much.

Heartfelt thanks also go to Faraxa Publishing, particularly to Joanne Micallef, for the opportunity they have afforded me by publishing this book. Special, unreserved thanks also go to many friends and family who offered moral support and encouragement. Space does not permit me to mention you all by name. Last but not least, heartfelt thanks go to all my colleagues in the front line of social work. You are to be saluted.

Contents

Known to Social Services

Foreword

Freya Barrington's novel *Known to Social Services* follows Diane Foster, a dedicated social worker, taking the reader into the bleak world of the Deacon Hill estate in Millbrook and into the lives of the people living there.

This was a difficult book to read not because it is bad – it is very good – but because the characters who people its pages filled me with dismay and frustration. *Known to Social Services* was a journey into unknown territory, a place stranger than the Amazon or the Kalahari, and into a culture stranger than any I ever experienced in a half century traveling the world. Never before did I meet people like these: feckless and careless, seemingly without regard for their own wellbeing or that of others.

We meet people who are violent, uncaring and self-involved. Many stumble through life half awake. There are grimly topical subjects such as domestic violence and child abuse, along with serial paedophiles and ex-convicts who threaten the lives of many of the children in the book. There are more, much more: people trapped in a grim, grey world; a world ruled by luck, impulse, denial and immediate self-gratification.

Each day, Diane Foster enters deep into this world of misery and torment, attempting to help these people and many others whom we meet in the course of her story. Hampered by an administration inhabited by paper-shuffling, uninvolved bureaucrats, she fights daily to protect the children from rape, horror, random violence and murder. With unflinching prose, Ms Barrington shows us the unwashed dishes and dirty diapers, the musty carpets and broken down furniture of the exterior lives of these people, together with the horrifying barrenness of their interior beings. If hell is being imprisoned in the self, these people live in hell.

I would have no idea how to help these hapless, hopeless people in their desolate, existential reality. But Diane Foster does. Her dedication, courage and patience place Diane in the ranks of the saints, making Mother Teresa look like she was just going through the motions. Diane's compassion is proof that religion is not a requirement for true charity for, to her, these people may well be feckless, but they are worthy of help and she will not give up on her task to bring light into their lives. Diane is one of those quiet heroes who keep together the fragile structure of society. Her deep commitment to this mostly thankless task takes its toll on her, however, abrading her heart and wearing down her soul. In the end, she almost pays the ultimate price for her dedication.

Known to Social Services has clearly been written from life experience and rings with authenticity. Freya Barrington's first novel is a journey worth taking. It provides us with a look into the depths of society and inspires us with the story of a person who makes a difference in the lives of many. We look forward to Ms Barrington's second novel, a continuation of Diane's story and the stories of these people who are, after all, human.

James Morgan Ayres
Author, businessman, consultant, traveller.

Disclaimer

Known to Social Services is a work of fiction. While the author has drawn on her own experiences, she has done so in the broadest, most general sense. All names, characters, businesses, places, events and incidents mentioned in this book are either products of the author's imagination or used in a fictitious manner. Any resemblance to actual persons, living or dead, or actual events is purely coincidental.

KNOWN TO SOCIAL SERVICES

Chapter 1

Jodie Pearson awoke to the sound of crying. For a moment she was disoriented and unsure where she was. After a difficult, prolonged labour which necessitated a complicated emergency caesarean section, Jodie had spent almost a fortnight at *Queen's Hospital* and, for a moment, thought that she was still there. However, she soon realised that the sparsely furnished, cold, damp bedroom was in her own home at the notorious Deacon Hill estate in Millbrook, not in the clean, warm and safe hospital environment she so recently enjoyed.

The Deacon Hill estate was the place where no one in Millbrook lived by choice. It was a sprawling mismatch of high rise flats and streets of terraced houses built before the war. Also in the mix were a few pockets of pre-fab houses where some of the most troublesome families resided. There were several no-go areas on the estate where drug dens operated seemingly unchallenged by the police. Prostitutes blatantly plied their questionable trade on the corner of Carter Lane and Moorside, close to where Jodie lived. The estate was home to approximately 2000 people and while many of them were decent citizens, many were also undesirable characters with dubious reputations – characters who considered burglary and petty theft a career choice. Still, it was where Jodie had been raised. She knew nothing else.

Jodie wrinkled her nose at the smell in the bedroom: a mixture of dirty nappies, creeping damp and stale cigarette smoke. Although Jodie smoked, she did not do so in the bedroom and wished that her partner would not, either. However, that was a futile hope as Scott Taylor was not renowned for his compliance in taking advice from anyone, least of all his girlfriend.

Jodie sighed as she climbed unwillingly and gingerly out of bed. Her stomach still hurt. She was tired and emotional following the most recent baby and she wished that she could have stayed longer in the hospital.

The nurses had all been kind to her and even though Jodie had to endure visits from her nosy bitch of a social worker while she was in there, the nurses had not judged her – not like most people did, anyway.

At three weeks of age, Brandon was 20-year-old Jodie's third child and the unsuspecting half brother of four-year-old Jamie and three-year-old Courtney. Brandon was 25-year-old Scott's first baby with Jodie, although he had two other children with different women across the estate. Scott did not see these other children of his, telling Jodie that their mothers would not allow him access.

Jodie considered her new infant son. He was a small baby, born three weeks prematurely and weighing only two and half kilogrammes – a result, no doubt, of Jodie's smoking which she did not quit during her pregnancies. Brandon had his father's looks which was somewhat unfortunate because while Jodie perceived Scott to be a bit of a looker, most people agreed that he resembled an angry weasel. Brandon still had the milky, blue-eyed look of a newborn and sported a veritable shock of black hair which he had inherited from his grandfather on his mother's side. As a caesarean birth, the boy had a beautifully shaped head, free from the misshaped compression often seen in babies of a natural birth. Jodie continued studying Brandon, still awed by the perfection of all those tiny fingers and toes. She hoped that he could bring Scott closer to herself and stop him from going out so much.

Historically, Jodie never had much luck with men. She never knew her father, Bernard, since he had been unlucky enough to step into the path of a number 47 bus as he crossed the road while studying the racing post. Jodie's mother, Brenda, had shrugged upon hearing the news. Bernard and Brenda had never been close and over recent years, they had been more like housemates than husband and wife. Brenda, however, was deeply disappointed to find that Bernard had cancelled the generous life insurance he used to have, spending the money, instead, on a string of dead certs. *Story of his life,* Brenda had thought wryly as she moved on with her own life.

Jodie's first encounter with the opposite sex had occurred at the age of 10 years when her creepy uncle, Derek, explained to her that all uncles did 'this sort of thing' with their nieces, so that they would know what to do when they got a husband. He had convinced an unsuspecting Jodie that her father would have undertaken the task if he lived. Uncle Derek was a tall, thin man with close-set, piggy eyes and a thin moustache which he fancied gave him an air of sophistication. In reality, all the moustache did was to heighten his unfortunate resemblance to Hitler. Derek walked with a limp as a result of childhood polio and always smelled of cheap aftershave, cigarettes and peppermints.

Uncle Derek was the brother of Jodie's father. No one really liked him on account of his affair with Auntie Sheila who was married to the affable and genuinely pleasant Uncle Bob. This affair had scandalised the close-knit family, resulting in Derek and Sheila being ostracised for a while. Eventually, however, a lonely Uncle Bob reconciled with Sheila, while Derek wormed his way back into the family's good books.

Jodie's mother, Brenda, had eventually discovered what was going on when she grew suspicious of Uncle Derek's increasing visits to the family and his newfound enthusiasm for spending time alone with his niece. The chain of events culminated in a family feud. Unsurprisingly, Derek's half of the family felt that Jodie was nothing more than an attention-seeking liar and that the matter should be left well alone. They did, however, concede that perhaps he should stop visiting – only to avoid further allegations being made against him. The other half of the family, comprised of Brenda and her considerable platoon of brothers, felt that a public castration was a more fitting outcome. In the end, however, the indignation of Jodie's mother had got the better of her and she rang up Social Services who involved the child protection unit of the police.

All hell then broke loose. In the ensuing drama, Jodie was interviewed by the police and made a video which was used as evidence in court. She was assigned a social worker whom she saw fleetingly, who got her to do drawings and took her to McDonalds. Uncle Derek eventually ended up in prison for 18 months and was placed on the *Sex Offenders Register* for life.

The incident had generated a never-ending family rift. Derek's relations continued to blame Jodie especially when they realised that due to his status, Uncle Derek was no longer allowed unsupervised access to any child in the family. That was highly inconvenient for everyone concerned as Derek had proven himself to be a devoted and free babysitter, always more than willing to assume childcare duties for his family.

Jodie was once again at the centre of family scandal when she started dating the notorious bad boy of the Deacon Hill estate, 17-year-old Mark Vickers, who had various underage tattoos, a motor bike and a bad attitude. Mark had persuaded Jodie to return with him to his brother's flat one day, instead of going to school. He had then sat smoking spliffs and drinking beer, while Jodie sat staring out of the window at the dreary surroundings of the estate, wondering why she was there. Mark had eventually persuaded Jodie to have sex with him, although she would have preferred not to. This liaison resulted in her first pregnancy at 15 years of age which meant further uproar and involvement with Social Services. There followed endless assessments and social work visits, after which it was agreed that Jodie could keep the baby, Jamie, as long as she went to the local children's centre for support and did not allow Mark Vickers any unsupervised contact. Mark quickly lost interest in Jodie and abandoned her for the childless and unencumbered Donna Smith, leaving Jodie a single mother at only 16 years.

Jodie's next encounter followed soon afterwards. She was still living with her mother, Brenda, who had been looking after Jamie for her, so that she could go out with her mates. Jodie met an older man at *The Chunky*

Monkey, a local nightclub with a dubious reputation. This man made quite an impression on young, gullible Jodie as he owned a car. It was only a Ford Escort but, still, it was a car. There followed a messy union in the back of the said car, the result of which had been Courtney. Jodie never knew the man's name and he had never asked for hers.

Undeterred, Jodie had embarked on her current relationship with Scott Taylor and was hoping for better things. She now had her own two-bedroom council property and even though Social Services were still involved, she had become skilled at saying whatever the social worker wanted to hear.

Chapter 2

Diane Foster reached out a reluctant hand from underneath the covers to silence the alarm. Six thirty in the morning had come around and Diane yawned as she contemplated the day ahead. Her short, blonde hair – stuck on end as it always did in the morning – and her head thumped from fatigue. She had not gone to bed until almost 2.00am as she had been writing reports with deadlines that could not be extended any further.

Realising she was awake, the cat, Mojo, jumped ecstatically onto the bed. He pushed his silken face against Diane's and signalled his approval of her waking by purring in delight, flipping on his side and dabbing at her with carefully retracted, soft paws. Mojo was an Abyssinian who with his dramatic facial markings, bore a striking resemblance to the noble cats of ancient Egypt. Specifically, he was a blue Abyssinian and like all cats, knew that he was special. Diane stroked Mojo's ears absentmindedly as she became fully awake.

"Come on, you rogue," Diane scolded. "I know you want your breakfast."

Diane made her way down the stairs of her neat, one-bedroom apartment on the newly built Green Acres development located a convenient five miles from her workplace. She stopped to check the thermostat, shivered and turned it up. It was a chilly November morning and Diane was thankful for the deep pile carpets. Having responded to Mojo's polite but firm demands, Diane made a cup of her favourite Italian coffee and turned on the radio.

With Chris Evans's banter providing a pleasant background of noise, Diane stepped into the shower and felt her stomach tighten into a familiar knot as she mentally went through the visits of the impending workday.

~ ~ ~ ~ ~

At 40 years of age, Diane was a senior social worker for the local authority. She had been drawn to the job because her mother was a foster carer. From a young age, Diane had come into contact with children less fortunate than herself. She felt an affinity with the children and was determined to make them her life's work.

Diane had graduated at 24 years old and walked wide-eyed and innocent into her first job as a social worker. Within the first week on the job, she had realised that all her training was worth precisely Jack: it had not prepared her in the slightest for what lay ahead. Diane's newfound career exposed her to human behaviour that plumbed the depths of depravity and cruelty, and which she scarcely believed possible. She now knew only too well that the average man or woman in the street was blissfully unaware of what was going on around them and in their communities, and she sometimes wished that she had never taken that road.

Diane Foster was intelligent, quick-witted, resourceful and not easily deterred. While at times she despaired about her job, especially the red tape which accompanied her every move, Diane was extremely good at it and, for the most part, gained great satisfaction from her work. Diane currently had more than 20 children on her caseload, but the numbers were almost certain to increase. The children were split between several families, all of whom had come to the attention of the local authority due to child protection concerns. The information had come from a variety of sources such as schools, health visitors, police and neighbours. Concerns ranged from domestic violence, physical, emotional and sexual child abuse; to drug and alcohol misuse, mental health problems and everything in between. Most of the parents in Diane's families had experienced a poor upbringing themselves, so they had little in the way of good examples to guide them in raising their own children. Scott Taylor was a prime example.

~ ~ ~ ~ ~

Scott was a feckless n'er-do-well; a product of spectacularly bad parenting which the care system of the local authority had failed to remedy. Removed at nine years of age from his good-for-nothing, shiftless father and ineffective, alcoholic mother, an angry and ill-disciplined Scott had moved from foster home to foster home, wreaking havoc and disrupting families along the way.

Unaccustomed as he was to any routine or boundaries and being especially adverse to the word *no,* Scott did not do well. His attendance in school was sporadic and when he did attend, he required one-to-one attention and was usually sent home by lunchtime. Scott had no respect for other students and even less respect for staff. His unfortunate teaching assistant had gone off sick when Scott spat in her face and head-butted her, after she made the mistake of asking him to comply with her request to do some work.

Scott attended five different schools before being permanently excluded from the final one, after throwing a chair at the head teacher who had questioned his choice of hairstyle. Scott was then sent to a school for children with emotional and behavioural difficulties – another move of foster home. However, after an extremely unfortunate incident in which Scott decided to see how far the family cat could fall and still land on its feet (not as far as he thought, as it turned out), Scott was declared unfosterable and moved to a care home for older children. Sadly, that move only served to introduce Scott to equally damaged individuals who were only too happy to assist him in completing his initiation into the seedy side of life. By 14 years of age and despite exhaustive input from both Social Services and the youth justice system, Scott had developed into a lean, weasel-faced young man with an impressive criminal record, no scruples whatsoever and well on the depressingly inevitable path to prison.

Scott's day of reckoning had arrived when he was a spotty-faced 18-year-old. He had just burgled a house in the same area where he was sleeping on a mate's sofa and imprudently using the same address as a base for his drug dealing. Scott dealt mainly in amphetamines and cannabis – or as he preferred to call it, speed and weed – for which there was a ready market and which kept him in his own personal drug of choice: cocaine. Scott had a small network of punters which included several disillusioned housewives from the estate and more than a few teenagers from the local Deacon Hill comprehensive. His clientele were only too willing to part with their weekly benefits or daily lunch money in exchange for a temporary reprieve from the grim reality of their everyday lives. All of them were aware of Scott's ability in getting them their fix and there was a reliable, dismal stream of people beating a path to his door. Scott's mate, known to one and all on the estate as Too Smooth Jackson, was less than delighted with Scott's little arrangement under his own roof. He had, therefore, planned to relieve Scott of the sordid business and assume responsibility as that would provide him with a steady income which, unsurprisingly, he never had. Too Smooth could never have imagined the irony that his gameplan for a takeover would be expedited by the intervention of the local undercover drugs squad.

Scott had just returned from his nocturnal crime spree with a Wii Nintendo console which he could flog to his mate, Dean, for 20 quid; some cheap jewellery that he would give to his mum whom despite her maternal failures, he continued to see and an iPod which he intended to keep for himself. Half an hour later as Scott was on the phone to Dean finalising the finer details of the Wii Nintendo deal, there was a knock at the door. When Scott opened it, he found himself face to face with the police who made themselves at home and caught him red-handed with the stolen property. Scott did not go quietly, but with maximum commotion and minimum self-restraint. Dean took Scott's arrest particularly hard as he had just agreed on a good price for the Wii. Too Smooth Jackson, however, was unable to believe his stroke of good karma and immediately set about restructuring the business he unexpectedly acquired.

Chapter 3

Her morning ablutions complete, Diane chose a conventional black trousers and white shirt combo for work that day. Completing the look with a bold red cardigan and matching red shoes, Diane checked her look in a full-length mirror and despite the attractive reflection which gazed back at her, gave a heavy sigh. Although Diane had elfin good looks and a vivacious personality, she struggled with personal relationships.

~ ~ ~ ~ ~

She had been married once to her childhood sweetheart, Sam Miller. They were good together. But when Diane went to university to train for social work, she had become so engrossed in her studies that they grew apart. Diane was the first to admit that she had neglected Sam who, like most men, preferred to be the centre of her world, rather than someone who just got a look in when she had written her latest essay, completed her research into domestic violence or whatever it was that she was currently researching. So Sam had found solace with Diane's friend, Susie Pendleton, who had been their bridesmaid seven years earlier. Eventually, Diane had accepted the inevitable. She thanked God that Sam and herself did not have any children, wished him well and moved on. She still had an occasional coffee with Sam, but not with Susie. There was a limit even to Diane's ability to forgive.

After her divorce from Sam had been finalised, Diane reverted to her maiden name of Foster and did not date for a long time. She occasionally went for a drink with Carl Haines from work, but he was ridiculously overzealous and way too needy for Diane's liking. She always felt as if Carl was a case study rather than a boyfriend and she called a halt on that one before the relationship got too deep.

Diane's other serious relationship after Sam began five years ago when she had met the fabulously named Ethan Montana who as it turned out, would be the love of her life. Their paths had crossed when Diane agreed to go with her best friend, Maxine, to a jam night at the local pub. Ethan was one of the musicians who regularly got up and played *ad hoc* for an enthusiastic, discerning audience. Ethan played drums, but he could also play a mean blues guitar – Diane's weakness. He had won her over with his rendition of Robert Cray's *I Slipped Her Mind* which was Diane's all-time favourite blues track – well, it was a close call between that and *Parisian Walkways* by Gary Moore, but it did the trick. Diane was hooked.

Ethan Montana had craggy, blonde, good looks; a crooked smile and the most astonishing brown eyes which Diane likened to melted chocolate buttons. He was the same age as Diane, but had a childlike manner about him which she found irresistible. Ethan was at heart a misplaced cowboy. Although he was not from the United States of America (USA), he usually sported a cowboy hat and adopted a lazy drawl when speaking, which perfectly suited his laconic character. When Diane would fuss and worry about her cases, reports and deadlines, Ethan would raise an eyebrow: a maddening skill which Diane could not master.

"Diane," Ethan would say, drawing out her name like no one else. "You need to know when to leave it alone."

And he was right. Despite his laid back approach to life, Ethan could be energetic and spontaneous – a trait which often led to disagreements as Diane was the polar opposite by being organised and planning everything down to the finest detail.

Diane and Ethan were an item for almost five years. They had talked of marriage but, somehow, it always eluded them. Ethan had his own recording studio business, so he could pretty much please himself as to when and how often he worked. Whenever they could, Ethan and Diane would take off for weekends, indulging in their joint passion of scuba diving. It was not always easy as Diane's work constantly interrupted their lives. She always seemed to have too much to do. Ethan hated it when

Diane worked at home which she frequently did. He pointed out that firstly, she did not get paid for all the additional hours; secondly, she would certainly never get the time back; finally, no one appreciated it. He was right on all counts.

Four months ago, Ethan had surprised Diane by booking a two-week diving holiday in Oahu, Hawaii. 'Surprised' was not really a big enough word. Ethan had actually horrified Diane as her work schedule was truly frightening. She had argued that she could not possibly take two weeks out of it. However, Ethan had won her over and in the end, they stayed at a sumptuously decadent, five-star hotel and dived every day in the warm, crystal clear waters of the Pacific ocean. They explored exotic underwater shipwrecks, marvelled at the neon fish and saw some unforgettable sights. It was a heavenly experience, but one which, sadly, would not be repeated. It was as if they used up all their magic on that one holiday.

Diane knew that her work was to blame. Ethan had booked the holiday without asking her – a major issue. He did not seem to appreciate that her life was dominated by deadlines and court dates to which she absolutely had to adhere. Ethan grew tired of hearing Diane say that she simply could not take time off just yet, so he took matters into his own hands and booked the holiday. After days of argument, Ethan gave Diane an ultimatum, saying that he was going, with or without her. Diane, of course, went along, but despite having the holiday of a lifetime, she had been unable to switch off properly, fretting and worrying most of the time. Matters had come to a head one perfect, balmy evening as they sat on the hotel terrace watching the sunset after an indescribably good dinner.

"Penny for them," Ethan said as he studied Diane staring over the waters.

He caught Diane off guard and she had just consumed enough champagne to speak honestly.

"Oh, I was just thinking about DJ," she replied with a sigh.

"Who the hell is DJ?" Ethan questioned sharply.

The tone of Ethan's voice snapped Diane out of her daydream.

"Sorry, Ethan. He's a little boy in one of my families. I guess I'm just worried about him is all. Sorry. Let's have another drink."

Ethan shook his head in disbelief.

"I'm going to bed," he said with great weariness in his voice.

A wedge had been driven between them, too deeply embedded to be removed. They had limped along for a while and both of them tried to make it work, but it was terminal. Diane sensed it before she knew it. And when she became aware of it, a sadness descended upon her and clung like damp fog around her soul. There would never be another Ethan.

Ethan became increasingly more involved with a new band he formed and when the opportunity arose for him to tour Germany, Diane knew that it was all over. She cried, of course, although the tears were not exclusively for the breakdown of her relationship with Ethan which had left her exhausted and debilitated with grief. No. Diane wept at her own inability to surrender the job she knew was sucking the life out of her and which she feared would conclude with her leading a lonely, solitary existence.

Chapter 4

Diane shook off the ghosts which besieged her mind and threatened to engulf her. It was only six weeks since their breakup. She wondered briefly where Ethan was at that moment. Smiling sadly, she put on her coat for work.

Diane was at her desk by 8.00am which was not unusual. She liked to get ahead of the day before the phones started ringing at 9.00am. Diane logged onto her computer and began working her way through the long list of emails she had received in her absence from the office. She had only been gone since the afternoon of the previous day as she was out on visits, but the messages were relentless. All demanded something. A lot of messages urged her to read some new policies and procedures which seemed to change with the weather. Others declared that she had to attend training or reminded her to go to the next team meeting, warning darkly that non-attendance was not an option.

One particularly concerning email was from the domestic abuse unit of the police who notified that they had been called out to the home of Shanice and Grant Ellis at 11.00pm the previous night, due to a domestic incident. The address had a marker on it which flagged it as high risk should a call come in and which, subsequently, elicited an immediate response.

~ ~ ~ ~ ~

Shanice and Grant Ellis had four children: Tia, aged 10 years; Kaz, aged eight years; DJ, aged six years and two-year-old Darcy. All the children were subject to child protection plans due to the significant domestic violence within the relationship.

The case had already been referred to a Multi-Agency Risk Assessment Conference – MARAC for short. A MARAC meeting was generally attended by a host of relevant professionals who would discuss the risk factors within relationships when serious domestic violence was present. The purpose of the meeting was to increase the safety of potential victims and reduce the risk of repeated victimisation. The members would also be concerned with any potential risk to the general public and/or staff involved with the family. A strategy would be agreed on and each member would understand their role and responsibility to the family.

After a great deal of persuasion, Shanice had reluctantly completed the MARAC paperwork with Diane – she had managed to do that one morning at the children's school, unbeknown to Grant. Shanice had been shaking with anxiety at the thought of Grant discovering that DJ did not really have an assembly that day and would go looking for her. Shanice's case had scored 21 on the DASH (Domestic Abuse, Stalking and Honour Based Violence) risk indicator. Anything higher than a score of 14 met the criteria for MARAC. The risk to Shanice and her children was considered very high and at the top of the next MARAC agenda. Grant and Shanice both understood that if there were further incidents, the local authority would take legal advice and possibly initiate pre-proceedings to have the children removed from their care.

~ ~ ~ ~ ~

Diane sighed heavily. She knew that the issue of the Ellis family would now have to be addressed, although she had no idea how she would fit it into an already packed diary. Diane lost track of time until she heard the cheery call of Angie, the team's business support worker, when she arrived at 9.00am.

"Morning, Diane," Angie called out as she hung up her coat. "There's an urgent message in your pigeonhole from the health visitor, Hilary Williams. It came in last thing as we were all leaving."

"Thanks, Angie," said Diane over her shoulder. "I'll ring her up right now."

Diane abandoned her plans for making another cup of coffee and dialled the number. Hilary picked up the phone on the second ring.

"Ah, Diane," Hilary said briskly. "Thanks for getting back to me. I'm very concerned about Kirsty Thompson. I visited her yesterday and she was extremely low in mood. I suspect that she's suffering from postnatal depression, but she declined to complete the *Glasgow Scale* with me so I can't properly assess her. The house is in a real state and as we both know, her latest boyfriend is no help to her at all. Baby Daniel was screaming his head off, with neither of them taking any notice and when I weighed him, I noticed that he lost weight and had extremely bad nappy rash which has not been treated. I've arranged for Daniel to be seen this morning by the GP who will reiterate my advice re feeding and prescribe the appropriate cream for his nappy rash. But I thought you'd better know. Things are not great for them at the moment."

Diane scribbled furiously as Hilary spoke and immediately began planning when she could visit.

"Okay, Hilary, many thanks. I'll get out to see them asap," Diane assured as she hung up.

Diane consulted her diary. She would squeeze in an unannounced visit later that day and see for herself how things were. At only three months, Daniel was potentially very vulnerable and needed to be seen as a priority. She would write up her notes on her discussion with Hilary later on as she was due out to see Jodie Pearson and Scott Taylor at 9.30am.

~ ~ ~ ~ ~

"I'm not going to no doctor," declared 19-year-old Kirsty Thompson bitterly to her partner who lay half asleep beside her in bed.

She pushed her greasy hair back from her pinched, scowling face and continued grumbling.

"I'm not getting up at flaming nine o'clock just so some doctor can give me cream that I can get at *Superdrug*. After all, it's only a bit of a rash," Kirsty reassured herself and turned over to go back to sleep.

"Aren't you getting up to him?" asked Neil O'Grady bad-temperedly. "He's crying."

Kirsty turned back to her boyfriend of two months and wondered what she had seen in him. Neil O'Grady was 10 years her senior: an unattractive, ginger-haired man with matching ginger stubble. He had bad teeth and a temper to match. Kirsty had only gone out with Neil because he was her best mate's brother.

"Don't you think I can hear him?" Kirsty challenged sharply. "Who do you think got up to him in the middle of the night? You get up for a change!"

With that Kirsty lay back down and ignored the screams coming from the next room.

"I'm not getting up," retorted Neil. "He's not my babby. Let him cry a bit, anyway. Me mam says it's good for their lungs," he opined, focusing his attention on Kirsty.

"Oh, leave it out, Neil. Is that all you ever think about?" Kirsty bristled, pushing Neil's hands away from her body.

Neil O'Grady was a surly, disagreeable man at the best of times and not one accustomed to being denied. He acknowledged Kirsty's rejection with an open-handed slap to the back of her head, before getting out of bed to yell at her infant son who was still crying. Neil went downstairs to fetch his cigarettes and continued his diatribe, directing it at the family dog who lay cowering on a filthy blanket in the corner of an equally disgusting kitchen.

~ ~ ~ ~ ~

Jodie sat in the cold, dark bedroom, feeding Brandon his bottle. She studied her son without emotion as she reflected on how she had ended up in that situation. Her mind wandered back to the day when her boyfriend had been released from another stint in prison.

The experience had left Scott Taylor bitter and done little in the way of rehabilitating him. Scott needed a fix. He had been told that there was going to be a party at some girl's house later that night. He decided to be there, to hook up with his old mates and get back to reclaiming his territory. Top of the agenda was the unfinished business with his one-time acquaintance, Too Smooth Jackson, who had prematurely assumed jurisdiction of Scott's erstwhile, successful dominance of the Deacon Hill estate drug scene.

The party girl was none other than Jodie Pearson. Jodie had been 19 years old at the time – a sad, lonely figure. Her early life experiences had left her defeated and crushed. She may as well have had *Victim* stamped on her forehead. Jodie was not a bad-looking girl, but she was grossly overweight which added to her already inexistent self-esteem. Jodie struggled to care properly for her children, due to her lack of insight into what they required. She loved her children and had support both from the children's centre and from her own mum, but most of the time she struggled alone and knew that she was losing the fight.

Jodie had complied with the request for a party at her house as it was suggested to her by a woman from the estate, Jackie Collingsworth. Jackie had three children of her own and if Jodie was to be completely honest, she was a bit scared of Jackie – one of the main reasons she had agreed to the party. Jodie was regretting it now as there were too many people in the house. Most of them were either drunk or under the influence of some substance or another. Jodie was nervous, especially as the kids kept waking up and crying because of all the noise and loud music. She had no idea how to terminate the party, so she went upstairs wearily for the fourth time that night to try and settle the children. Jodie opened their bedroom door: the light from the landing illuminated the disturbing scene of Jackie Collingsworth in a compromising position with some youth whom Jodie did not know.

"Get out of here!" Jodie exclaimed with indignation. "This is my kid's room, for God's sake!"

Jackie stood up slowly and smoothed her clothes. She smirked as she walked past Jodie.

"Chill out, you fat bitch," Jackie said unkindly to Jodie as she waltzed back down to the party.

At least, the youth had the decency to look embarrassed as he zipped himself up and walked shamefaced past Jodie who went quickly to reassure her children that everything was okay. When she returned to the party, Jodie was met by Scott Taylor and immediately became flustered. She knew Scott through one of her brothers who did business with him, although quite what kind of business it was she did not know. Jodie had always fancied Scott even though she knew he had a bad reputation. It seemed that Jodie was doomed to spend her life attracted to the wrong sort of man. Scott put an arm around her which had a significant effect on Jodie. She felt shaky and got butterflies.

"Hiya, Scott," she said nervously. "You okay?"

Scott smiled at Jodie and she tried to ignore his bad teeth.

He replied, "I'd be better if I had a place to live."

Jodie had heard rumours that Scott had been in prison, but did not like to ask.

"Where you living now?" she asked innocently.

"Oh, you know; here and there," Scott replied vaguely. "Wouldn't mind living here with a pretty girl like you," he charmed.

And the battle was won. Jodie ceased worrying about the noise and the people. She forgot about her children upstairs, she was so flattered by the attention of Scott Taylor who presented her with a large glass of extra strong cider, while trying to get his hands down her blouse.

Jodie had eagerly agreed to Scott moving in and there she was now with his baby, but no nearer to a meaningful relationship. They did not go out together and Scott did nothing to support her with the children, which she had hoped he might. Jodie could not help feeling used.

Scott showed some passing interest in Brandon, but none in Jamie and Courtney. He spent most of his time outside the house seeing his mates – at least, that was where he said he was. Scott did not like Jodie to go out to visit her mother, so most of the time she just stayed home with the children. Jodie's mum, Brenda, would go around when she knew that Scott was not going to be there, to try and talk her daughter into kicking him out. However, Jodie did not know how. On the rare occasions when Scott was at home, the atmosphere was tense and Jodie felt that the children and herself were treading on eggshells.

Scott was unpredictable, moody and erratic – typical behaviour for someone misusing recreational drugs. He demanded good behaviour from the children and could not stand it when Brandon cried. Jamie was afraid of Scott's temper and would try as hard as he could to keep out of Scott's way. Jodie's social worker was horrified to discover that she had moved Scott into the house and became even more despairing when she learned that Jodie had given birth to Scott's baby. Still, it was done. But the social worker was always on Jodie's back, going on about her concerns about this and that. Social Services knew that Scott used drugs and expected him to 'engage' in a rehabilitation programme – which Scott refused to do. Social Services were also strongly suspicious that Scott was dealing drugs, but had no proof in that regard.

When she got pregnant with Brandon, Jodie had to attend a big meeting about her children and which she did not really understand. At the end, there had been some serious talk about what might happen if things did not improve and Jodie was told that the children were on a child protection plan. She did not know what that meant other than that she had a load more hoops to jump through. Jodie also knew that she had to keep her mouth shut whenever the social worker visited – she needed to stop telling her about how Scott could be as it only got her into trouble.

Brandon finished his bottle and whimpered, bringing Jodie out of her reverie and back to the present day. She placed him gently back into the crib that her Auntie Eileen had bought for her with the money she had got from going on the *Jeremy Kyle Show* to talk about her own brother, Derek. Jodie tiptoed through to check on Jamie and Courtney. She discovered that Jamie had wet the bed again. Jodie lifted the boy and put him in with Courtney while quickly changing the sheets. Jodie had no intention of telling Scott as she knew that he would punish Jamie as he had done the first time Scott discovered that Jamie wet the bed. Scott had pressed the boy's face against the wet sheet and called him a dirty little bastard. He then slapped Jamie hard and told Jodie not to change the bed, but to leave the wet sheets on as a lesson. Jodie had told herself that

Scott was tired and under stress that day, and reassured Jamie that it would not happen again. Jodie put Jamie back into his own bed and went back to her own. She tried snuggling up to Scott, but he grunted and pushed her away.

Chapter 5

Liam Powell woke up on the sofa. It took him a moment to focus and recall why he was there, not in his own bed. He looked around, taking in the scene in the room. Apart from the pile of clothes, dirty plates with remnants of a Chinese takeaway and overflowing ashtrays, there were three large, empty bottles of cider and several cans of *Stella*. His brother, Morris, was sleeping with his mouth wide open in the chair across the room. Liam closed his eyes against the hangover and remembered the night of drinking Morris and himself had embarked on after Morris turned up unexpectedly. As they had not seen each other in over two years, Liam had invited Morris to stay for a drink. One thing led to another and there they were.

Liam shouted to his partner, Gemma, to bring them some coffee. Upon hearing their dad's voice, six-year-old Jazmin, five-year-old Kiara and four-year-old Alfie went running through. Gemma followed with 18-month-old Kyle on her hip. Alfie leapt onto his father's knee and began bouncing up and down. Liam knocked Alfie to the floor, ignoring his indignant yelp. Then he started berating Gemma.

"What the hell did you let the kids in for, you stupid woman? Can't you see how I am?"

Gemma's response was to yell back at Liam, so another one of their famous arguments ensued. The children – except Kyle who clung to his mum, sucking furiously on his dummy – retreated back to the relative safety of their bedroom. No one noticed the eyes of Morris Powell following little Jazmin slyly out of the room.

~ ~ ~ ~ ~

Jodie Pearson was nervous.

"The social worker's coming this morning," she called up to Scott who was still in bed having his second cigarette of the day.

"So fucking what?" came the response.

"Well, I know she wants to see us both, so are you getting up? Coz she'll be here in 20 minutes."

Jodie heard a loud bang and wondered what had been thrown across the room. To say that Scott hated social workers was an understatement. He usually disappeared when they went to visit. Jodie could not blame Scott as he had been raised in care and experienced a bad time of it. However, the last time she went, Diane had insisted that Scott be there for her next visit.

Jodie turned her attention to getting the oldest children ready. She shouted to Jamie and Courtney to get dressed quickly. Unlike his youngest and newborn sibling, four-year-old Jamie was a blue-eyed blonde with curls to rival those of his sister. Jamie had an almost cherubic appearance, in sharp contrast to the harsh environment in which he was living. He was an introverted, thoughtful child who had experienced much in the way of disorder, chaos and drama during his short lifetime. His mother, while doting and affectionate, was often unavailable, spending her time with his new baby brother or, more often than not, with Scott. Jamie did not like Scott as he shouted a lot and frightened him.

Courtney ignored her mother's calls and remained in the bedroom, playing with her toys. At three years of age, the little girl already had her world pretty much sussed out. A mirror image of her older brother, Courtney had the beautiful blonde-haired, blue-eyed look which caused most adults to *ooh* and *aah* when they saw her, and bend down to ask her name. Both children's looks also had the effect of most adults looking at them first, then at their mother, wondering how on earth the latter had managed to produce two such beauties. However, where Jamie was quiet and compliant, Courtney was anything but. She had learned early in life that her mother was often distracted and did not respond unless she became loud and demanding. Courtney also understood that since Scott Taylor had come into their lives, things had changed – not for the better. She may have only been three years old, but Courtney knew what she liked and did not like – and she did not like Scott Taylor. Not one little bit.

Jodie's affection for her children was often demonstrated in her indulgence towards them. She would spend all her benefits on treats and sweets, and very rarely were either of them told *no*. To Jodie, this represented good and loving parenting She was at a loss to understand why the social worker always kept harping on the necessity of her setting boundaries and having routines. It was true that Jodie was having a bit of trouble with Courtney as the girl was often wilful and did not like to do what she was told. However, Courtney was always better when Scott was there. He seemed to have a way with her.

When Diane arrived, Scott did not appear. Diane spent some time talking to Jodie about the children and the importance of continuing to go to the children's centre and working with them in the latest parenting assessment. Jodie felt that her life had been one long assessment and she was no better off for it. She loved her kids. *Was that not enough?* It seemed not.

"Is Scott joining us?" Diane asked finally.

Jodie went upstairs to find Scott lying sullenly on the bed, smoking a joint and playing with his games console.

"Scott, she's here. Can't you just come down for a minute, then say you've got to go out or something?" pleaded Jodie. "C'mon, babes, I'm scared of them taking the kids off us if we don't go along with it."

Scott threw his game across the room, stubbed out his spliff, pushed past Jodie and stomped down the stairs to face Diane.

"Morning, Scott," said Diane cheerfully. "How are you today?"

Scott glared at Diane and lit a cigarette as Jodie re-entered the room. Diane took a deep breath.

"I've just been talking to Jodie about the dangers of smoking in front of the children, especially the baby," Diane explained. "How about smoking at the door, Scott, so the children don't breathe in smoke?"

Upon hearing Diane's suggestion, Scott smirked and took a long, pointed drag on his cigarette. Slowly, he blew the smoke into the living room, maintaining his gaze on Diane.

"And why don't you fuck off out the door altogether?" was Scott's menacing response. "We don't need you here, the kids are fine. I know worse people four doors up who are dealing drugs out their house, but you don't go to them, do you? You're just giving us a hard time. Ain't you got nothing better to do?"

With that, Scott stormed out of the house, leaving an anxious Jodie behind in the hostile atmosphere. Diane sighed.

"You know, Jodie, he's got to start cooperating with us sometime. The children are already on a child protection plan and part of the plan is that Scott visits the drug team to address his habit. It just isn't happening."

Jodie bit her lip and looked down at the floor.

"I know. I'll have a talk with him later when he's calmed down a bit," Jodie agreed, knowing it would never happen.

Then she showed Diane out.

~ ~ ~ ~ ~

Diane went from Jodie's house straight to that of Kirsty Thompson, to try and see the baby, Daniel. The curtains were all drawn, but Diane could hear signs of life inside. She knocked firmly on the front door, but other than sending the dog into a barking frenzy, got no response. She tried peering through a crack in the curtains, but the room was dark and the curtains appeared to be stuck to the window, making it impossible to see anything.

Diane went around the back, carefully avoiding a pile of broken tiles in the process and sidestepping an old mattress and fridge which were blocking the path. The backyard was a mess of weeds, rubbish and dog excrement from the family's Staffordshire bull terrier. Diane shook her head upon seeing the debris and made a mental note to discuss the health dangers of dog mess with Kirsty when she saw her next. She knocked again on the back door which had clearly been boarded up recently, although Diane did not know why. Despite knocking for several minutes, no one went to either door even though the barking of the dog reached fever pitch. Diane felt frustrated, but all she could do was put a note through the letter box, asking them to ring her up as soon as possible.

Diane then went to see Shanice and Grant Ellis about the police call out the previous night. They were home and invited her in. The house, as always, was immaculate. It was decorated and furnished to a high standard, and there was the smell of burning incense. Soft cushions were piled up on the plush sofa. The rugs on the floor were thick and luxurious. Around the walls was a collection of professionally done photographs of the family, posing happily and smiling for the camera. Diane noticed that in each one, Grant had his arms possessively around Shanice, no matter the pose. Diane had once asked to use the bathroom and found it supplied with expensive liquid soaps, soft towels and hand cream. There was even a *Yankee Candle* in there.

As usual, Shanice offered Diane coffee. The latter was not in the habit of being offered coffee and even less in the habit of accepting it, but she knew that it was safe to accept the offer over there. Shanice brought the coffee through in the usual china cup and saucer, and set it down on the handcrafted, oak coffee table in front of them. The children sat cross-legged, quietly on the floor near their parents. They were always beautifully dressed and clean. Their school attendance was perfect and the reports about their academic achievements were top class.

On many levels, one could have been impressed with such a scenario, but for Diane Foster, with her years of experience, it rang alarm bells. It was too neat; too perfect. The children were far too well-behaved and watchful. Diane spent a long time with Shanice and Grant, reiterating the concerns of the department. Grant admitted that he had been drinking the previous night as it was his birthday and a few mates had been around. He explained that one of his mates had made a pass at Shanice and he lost his temper. However, Grant and Shanice now sat hand in hand reassuring Diane that it was a one-off thing and would not happen again. Diane left Grant and Shanice to consider the possibility that the local authority take legal advice. She arranged a further visit for two days' time. But after Diane left, Grant dismissed the children with one look then turned to Shanice.

Calmly and quietly, he asked, "So you called the social, did you?"

Shanice turned pale.

"Grant," she implored, "you know it wasn't me, but the police. They have to tell them coz the kids were in the house. Please, Grant, don't!"

Her pleading fell on deaf ears. Shanice closed her eyes as Grant's fists pounded into her head and body. When it was over, Grant regarded Shanice with contempt as she lay on the floor.

"Sort yourself out," he snapped, "and clean this house up. It's a total pigsty."

Chapter 6

Morris Powell had discovered just how easy it was to coerce sex out of a girl when he was only 14 years of age. Granted, the girl in question had been his nine-year-old sister, Judith. But, still. All Morris had to do was persuade her that it was a game, then threaten to tell their parents about it, who would be angry with her for being so naughty and rude. The memory of this momentous occasion brought a smile to his meaty, unshaven face.

At 42 years old, Morris Powell was going nowhere. He was a short, balding man with an almost perfectly round paunch which he had an annoying habit of rubbing when deep in thought – which was not very often. What little hair had remained was combed over, giving him an absurd appearance like a character from a bad television comedy. However, there was nothing comical about Morris Powell. The misplaced thrill of his early sexual conquest had led to a life of licentious, debauched behaviour which resulted in him serving more than one prison sentence for the indecent assault of children – specifically, little girls under the age of 10 years.

Morris was a man of no ambition other than to target, groom and take depraved advantage of little girls. His time spent at Her Majesty's pleasure served no purpose other than to acquaint him with others of his ilk, with whom he could share his perverted preferences. One equally corrupt individual, Nigel Smathers, had introduced Morris to the novel, but as yet untested, idea of joining a church. Smathers was an oily, reptilian character with a predilection for pre-pubescent boys. He had taken warped delight in divulging his success in that particular field to Morris, boasting of his numerous conquests with choir boys – his particular favourites. Morris had sat wide-eyed at the untapped potential of such a plan.

Another inmate was Derek somebody. Morris could not remember his second name, but recalled that he looked like Hitler. Anyway, Derek had regaled Morris with tales of how easy was for him to abuse his own niece, until her mother had discovered what was going on. Morris had listened intently and taken it all in, committing it to memory so that he could relive it over and over, although in his fantasy he replaced Derek with himself. The men had made an anomalous pact to stay in touch and share more of their degenerate stories when liberated.

Once released from his latest incarceration, Morris had duly registered his whereabouts with the police: a requirement of the Sex Offenders Register of which Morris was a proud member. He had decided to move back in with his elderly mother, Gladys, so he gave her address to the probation officer. Morris felt it was a clever, cunning move. No one on the estate would suspect him of being anything other than a dutiful son, returning home to care for his old mum. It had been many years since Morris frequented the Deacon Hill estate – not without reason. He reckoned that two years was a long enough gap to dull the memories of people he had wronged and no one really noticed him, anyway.

Gladys was less than impressed with the plan of her son, but Morris had convinced her that he would be able to do her shopping and help with the gardening. The old lady had begrudgingly agreed. Morris immediately installed the internet and googled local churches, to identify what he thought might be appropriate hunting grounds. He also made contact with his brother, Liam, whom he could not stand. However, Liam lived locally and had a brood of brats among which, if Morris recalled correctly, was at least one girl. Morris rubbed his fat paunch and allowed his degenerate mind free reign.

~ ~ ~ ~ ~

Diane pulled into the petrol station, grateful for an excuse to grab a sandwich and use the toilet before going on her next visit. She was already

46

late, but got the office to ring ahead and explain, so she hoped the family would not use her lateness as an excuse to avoid the visit and go out.

Nahla and Hafiz Waleed were a Sudanese couple who lived in a neighbourhood on the outskirts of town. They had five children aged between four to 15 years. There were three boys named Raheem, Umar and Aman. There were also two girls named Zarifa and Farida. An otherwise exemplary family, Mr and Mrs Waleed had come to the attention of the local authority a few months earlier, just as schools were about to break up for the summer.

The school of seven-year-old Zarifa had reported that she confided to a friend that she was returning to Sudan in the long holidays. This friend had told her own mother who, in turn, contacted the school and reported that Zarifa had told her daughter that she was terrified. Diane knew Zarifa had good reason to be terrified as the plan was to return to their native Sudan so that she could undergo the cultural ceremony of female circumcision.

The practice of female circumcision – or female genital mutilation (FGM) as known in England – was a contentious issue for families of certain ethnic origins with a history dating back many generations. It was an illegal practice in England and one that carried with it a prison sentence for guilty parties. It was also illegal to send a permanent resident such as Zarifa back to her homeland, to undergo the procedure.

FGM was grisly and had been defined by the World Health Organisation as

> *All procedures that involve partial or total removal of the external female genitalia or other injury to the female genital organs for non-medical reasons.*

Diane knew that there were several methods of FGM, the most severe being infibulation whereby the inner and outer labia were removed and the woman's vagina was closed, leaving only a small hole for urination and menstruation. The implications for sexual activity and childbirth were almost unthinkable and often afforded the woman extreme complications and pain.

In the case of the Waleeds, the local authority and the police had intervened in their plans, causing outrage both in the family and their community. The intervention was ongoing and extremely delicate. Mr and Mrs Waleed felt that the local authority was interfering in a custom and practice of which they had no knowledge and in which they had no business. The danger was that the family would simply leave England, returning after Zarifa was circumcised, after which there was nothing anyone could do other than follow legal procedures – a long, drawn-out affair which would be of no help to little Zarifa. In light of all that, the passports of the family had been confiscated while the investigation was underway.

Diane's visit was, as usual, awkward and tense. Mr Waleed was confrontational and rude, while Mrs Waleed sat weeping at the shame of having a daughter who had not yet undergone ritual circumcision. In her eyes, such a lack reflected badly on her as a mother and seriously hampered Zarifa's chances of contracting a good marriage. Diane reiterated the agreement that both parents had signed and added that she would be visiting the children in school the following week, to speak to them on their own.

When Diane left the house, Hafiz Waleed regarded his wife seriously.

"You know what we must do," he said in a low voice.

Nahla Waleed nodded in agreement. She knew exactly what they needed to do.

Diane returned to the office just as it was closing. She was no stranger to working late and, oftentimes, Diane and the cleaner were the last to leave the building. Diane's own manager, Glenda Rogers, was still at her desk.

"Hey, stranger," Glenda called. "When are you and I going to meet for supervision?"

Diane knew that her fortnightly supervision sessions with Glenda were essential for case discussions and sharing new concerns. It was also a forum for making decisions as to the next steps for her families. However, Diane was so stretched that she had not met with Glenda for over a month.

"I know, I know," said Diane, shaking her head and getting her diary out. "How about first thing Monday morning?"

Glenda consulted her diary.

"No can do. I've got a legal meeting with Marcus Edwards. How about Tuesday afternoon?"

Diane flipped a page and frowned.

"Hmm, nope. I've got to go on some training which I can't get out of – it's mandatory. I can do Wednesday morning, but I have to rejig one of my visits."

"Okay, then. Wednesday, 9.00am, it is," said Glenda, snapping her diary shut. "Goodnight, Diane. Don't work too late," she warned, wrapping up to leave.

"Fat chance," smiled Diane, logging on to see what emails needed her attention.

It was a weary Diane Foster who finally got back to her own home at seven that night. She immediately changed into her pj's and although she knew that it was a slippery slope, she poured herself a generous glass of *Pinot Grigio* and toasted Mojo who had gone to greet her.

"What a day, Mojo," Diane sighed as she curled up on the sofa and put on the television.

Mojo purred in delight at having Diane back and began making himself comfortable on her lap in the way felines do.

"Don't get too settled," warned Diane with a laugh. "I've got to cook yet."

But within 10 minutes, she was asleep. Diane did not wake up until 10.00pm by which time she was beyond hungry. She made a cheese sandwich, drank a glass of water and went to bed.

Diane was back at work the next day by 8.00am. Her office at Cedar House was right in the centre of the estate, ideally placed for visits in walking distance. However, its location had its drawbacks. Disgruntled clients did not have far to go if they wished to take issue with any of the social workers housed there. The front desk staff had the local police station on speed dial and they were regular visitors to the building, intervening when things got out of hand.

It was an austere looking building which screamed 1960s. It had a flat roof and bars at the windows, adding to its Dickensian appearance. Inside, the building was too cold in winter and too hot in summer. There was no happy medium. Diane had a desk in the corner of the office where she could sit with her back to the wall and see everyone who came and went.

She was the first one in that morning. Diane went through the process of inputting the security code and unlocking the three doors which allowed her access. Then she dropped her bag onto the desk and made her way into the kitchen to make a customary Italian cup of coffee. Glenda entered.

"Hey, early bird," Glenda smiled. "How's it going?"

Diane returned the smile. She liked her manager who was highly experienced, fair and realistic.

Glenda Rogers was a large woman who made the most of her ample frame. She wore dramatically coloured, kaftan-type tops which billowed as she walked. Coupled with that, she would wear baggy, jazzy coloured pants, usually pairing them with jewel-encrusted sandals. Glenda may have been a generous size 24, but she was attractive and knew how to dress for effect. Her naturally auburn hair was always worn loose and fell around her shoulders in an untidy tangle of disarray. Her social work team affectionately referred to her as The Ship In Full Sail, referring to her habit of literally sailing into a room, kaftan top flowing all around. Glenda always wore the same lipstick: bright orange. The girls would laugh that you saw the lipstick before you saw Glenda. Yes, Diane liked her boss. More importantly, she respected her.

"I'm okay. Thanks, Glenda," Diane replied. "Coffee?"

Glenda laughed as she held out her cup.

"You have to ask? Hey, listen, Di. I know you're really busy, but I've got a new one which I'd like to you take a look at, if you possibly can."

Diane tried not to look too horrified at the prospect of yet another case.

Instead, she asked, "Oh? Tell me about it."

"Well, I got a call yesterday from Jane Clarke from probation. Apparently, there's a guy she's currently involved with, Malcolm Withers, who has convictions for sex offences. He's obviously on the Sex Offenders Register and has been recently released from *Stone Hall Prison* and is on probation. He openly disclosed to Jane that he is visiting a friend of his who has a family with young children. It needs looking at when you have the time. Try and go with the police if you can, in case there needs to be disclosure."

Diane nodded in agreement.

"I'll get out there this week," she replied as Glenda sailed out of the door.

Diane felt relieved to be able to go with a police officer to such a visit. Families who had contact with known sex offenders could react in many different ways. One could expect that they would all be outraged and declare their intent never to allow the person to visit again. However, Diane knew from vast experience that this was not always the case.

Often families were unwilling to believe that their friend or family member was capable of such heinous acts or they simply blamed the victim. If a family was unaware of the offences, the police would be the lead agency in sharing the information. While they did not go into great detail, the police would advise the family that the person had convictions for sexual offences against children and was, therefore, considered a danger to children. In the event that the family did not heed the warning and continued to allow the perpetrator access to children, it would be Diane's role to step in with protective measures. However, she knew that such measures did not necessarily equate to protection and that even with knowledge shared, some families would continue exposing their children to risk. Diane made a note in her diary, reminding herself to ring the child protection unit of the police, to ask them to go with her on the visit.

Chapter 7

Sharon Lewis looked out of the window of her high rise flat and surveyed the dreary view over the backs of the Stamp Lane garages. She watched in disinterest as a teenage boy threw stones at one of the many cats in the alley. Thankfully, his aim was as poor as his school attendance. *Raining again,* she mused in an absentminded way as she drank tea. Turning her head towards the rear of the flat, she called out to her six-year-old son.

"You up, Michael?"

Michael Tranter was still asleep, but his mother's shouts roused him. He sat up and rubbed the sleep from his eyes, got out of bed and went to the bathroom. Michael had a wash, brushed his teeth and got dressed without any direction or support from his mother, just as he had been doing for the past two years.

"Can I see Daddy today?" Michael asked hopefully as he entered the kitchen and got himself a dish of cornflakes.

"How should I know?" replied Sharon apathetically. "Depends on what that horrible social worker says. She'll be here in a minute – that's if she can be bothered to come on time."

Sharon opened the door to Diane who entered shaking the rain from her hair.

"Goodness, what an awful day," Diane commented pleasantly to Sharon who turned her back and walked into the living room. "Is it okay if I come through, Sharon?" Diane called after her.

"Please yourself," came the surly response.

Diane took a deep breath. This was not going to be an easy visit. She wiped her feet and followed Sharon into the cramped front room of the flat. It was simply furnished, but adequate; warm and clean. Michael ran through from the kitchen with milk around his mouth.

"Hello, Diane," he said seriously. "Can I see my daddy now?"

Diane looked at Sharon.

"No school today?" she asked pointedly.

Sharon shrugged.

"Well, I can't do everything and you were coming," she offered by way of a lame explanation.

"Well, maybe Michael could do some colouring for me in his bedroom while I talk to you?" Diane suggested.

Sharon grimaced her disapproval.

"He can stop here with me. It's his dad you're talking about."

"I appreciate that, Sharon," continued Diane in a level tone of voice, "but he's only six and it's not appropriate that he's privy to what we have to discuss. Ideally, he should be in school."

Sharon rolled her eyes and muttered something that Diane did not hear. The latter turned her attention to Michael. He was a sturdy little boy with an almost comically serious outlook on life. He gave careful consideration to everything Diane said and was clearly very intelligent.

"Hey there, soldier," said Diane in a friendly tone. "How about you go in your bedroom and draw me one of your fabulous pictures while I talk to Mummy?"

Michael frowned and considered that request for a moment.

"What if I draw a spaceship?" he asked, his blue eyes opening wide.

"Oh, wow! That would be fantastic," enthused Diane. "Would you?"

Michael nodded and went off to his room. Diane turned her attention back to Sharon.

"So?" asked Sharon the instant Michael was gone. "When can he see his dad then?"

Sharon's partner and Michael's father, Roy Tranter, was currently in *Stone Hall Prison*. He was two years into a seven-year sentence for the serious sexual abuse of his two daughters from a previous relationship. Janice and June Tranter had only come forwards as young adults once they were sure their father could no longer victimise them. He had, to their immense relief, left their mother and embarked on a new relationship with Sharon Lewis. Both girls had made a complaint to the police and after initial enquiries, the Crown Prosecution Service deemed that there was enough credibility to their allegations to take the matter to court.

Due to the many wagging tongues on the estate, the case had hit the local headlines, affording Janice and June attention the likes of which they had never previously imagined. There was a huge commotion which catapulted the women into the public eye and caused almost as many problems for them as their father's immoral deeds. After a lengthy trial lasting three weeks, Roy Tranter had been duly convicted and packed off to prison.

Eventually, the furore died down. Unable to deal with the unwanted attention, June moved away from the area and was never heard of again. Janice, however, went on to lead an unremarkably ordinary life and remained within a few streets of where she had been raised on the Deacon Hill estate.

Sharon wanted Michael to visit his father in prison, but given the nature of the offences, a risk assessment would be required.

"As I explained to you last time I came," Diane began, "I would have to complete an assessment of risk which will take several weeks. Now, last time I was here, you were reluctant to work with me in doing that, so we've reached a bit of an impasse really. Have you thought any more about it?"

Sharon stood up abruptly.

"What the hell is there to think about?" Sharon spat angrily. "Michael's been visiting him for two years now. It's only cos Roy's moved prisons that you're being awkward. It was never a problem at *Bream Cross.*"

Sharon Lewis was right. Roy Tranter had, indeed, been receiving visits from Michael at his previous prison. However, that had been agreed on in error, without any assessment of risk. It was the fault of the authorities and Sharon could not understand why after two years of visits, they had suddenly been stopped.

Sharon carried on with her castigation of Social Services, probation and the prison service in general.

"It's not as if Roy's even done anything," Sharon complained. "I mean that daughter of his, June: everyone knows she's a lying, little bitch. She only said he raped her to get back at him for leaving her mam. That means it's an alleged offence."

56

Diane tried to avoid shaking her head and sighing.

"Sharon," she said patiently, "Roy was charged and convicted. It's not an alleged offence. He was convicted of rape and not only of one daughter, but of both of them."

Sharon paced the floor.

"Yeah, well. I know he didn't do it and he'd never in a million years hurt his boy. He adores him. I get on alright with Janice. She's okay, but she just went along with her sister. Anything for attention, that one. I don't believe a word of it," said Sharon with finality.

Diane knew she would never be able to convince Sharon that Roy Tranter was guilty as charged. This made her job all the more difficult. Any parent who did not believe the conviction of a sexual offence was unable to protect any children in the house as they did not accept that there was risk. It was a phenomenon Diane had seen dozens of times. She marvelled at the way a skilled sex offender seemed able to select a certain type of woman who could be relied on to respond in that manner and protect him, over and above any children they had. All too often it gave an offender a safe, secure environment from which to continue abusing children unchallenged.

"Well," said Diane with firmness, "we're not going to get anywhere if you continue to oppose the assessment. It's entirely up to you."

Sharon was not finished. Like many of Diane's clients, she liked to create a smokescreen, pointing the finger at other people who had offences or discussing local rumours, to detract from the issue at hand.

"What about Janice, anyway?" Sharon asked, smugly. "No one says anything about her, do they? No. And there she is, shacked up with a bloke 32 years older than her. But I suppose that's okay, isn't it?"

Diane did not want to be drawn into a discussion about a family of whom she knew nothing, so she tried sidestepping it.

"I really can't comment on that, Sharon, as I've never met Michael's half-sister, Janice."

Sharon laughed sarcastically.

"Ah, well! My Roy knows her old man, Barry, and reckons he's proper dodgy. Didn't want her to marry him, but what can you do? Janice met him through her dad, so that's that, I guess."

At that point, Michael ran back through, picture in hand.

"Here, Diane," he said excitedly. "I drew this for you. Will you put it on your wall?"

Diane considered the drawing Michael had done for her and smiled.

"That's so wonderful," she congratulated. "Not only will I put it on my wall, but I'm going to put it where everyone can see it and tell them how clever you are."

Michael beamed with pride.

"You still can't see your dad," said Sharon with spite in her voice, spoiling Michael's good mood.

The boy regarded Diane. His face dropped, crestfallen.

"Diane," he said gravely, "I think I will have my picture back."

With that Michael removed the paper from Diane's hand and, slowly and deliberately, went back to his room.

"Well! Are you happy now?" crowed Sharon. "See what you did. You've proper upset the boy."

Diane counted to 10 in her head before replying.

"I'll leave it with you, Sharon. Let me know what you decide. But until the assessment is completed, Michael will not be permitted to visit his father."

Diane left the flat. As she walked down the hall, she could hear Sharon shouting after her.

"He didn't even do anything."

~ ~ ~ ~ ~

Jodie Pearson scraped the burnt bits off the toast she had just made for the breakfast of Jamie and Courtney, and spread them with margarine.

"Can I have some jam, Mummy?" asked Jamie with hope, his curls all awry.

"We ain't got none, babes," replied Jodie. "We'll get some next time we go to *Aldi* eh, when Mummy's got some pennies."

Jamie nodded and ate his toast without complaint. Courtney, however, pushed the plate away and shook her head. Her speech was delayed, but it was clear that she was not enamoured with the food that her mother presented.

"Eat it up, Courtney," encouraged Jodie, "there's a good girl."

Courtney may have been delayed in her speech, but there was one word she knew very well.

"No," she replied, pushing the plate further away and shaking her head.

It was at that unfortunate moment that Scott entered the room. Jodie instantly tried removing the plate, but he had already taken in the scene.

"Leave it there," Scott ordered. "She can eat it."

Jodie felt panic rising inside of her as she tried defending Courtney.

"Aw, it doesn't matter, babes. She's not hungry. I'll make her something in a bit," replied Jodie as casually as she could, while continuing her journey to the bin with the offending toast.

"I said, leave it!" repeated Scott, raising his voice. "Ungrateful little git can eat it now or she'll have it for dinner, tea and breakfast again tomorrow."

Upon hearing Scott's raised voice, Courtney started crying. Scott rolled his eyes and approached the little girl. Then he put his face very close to hers and muttered.

"Shut the fuck up, you little cry baby, and get it eaten."

Courtney wailed even more at that verbal abuse and tried getting off the chair to go to her mother. As she slid off, Scott reached across, grabbed the little girl by the arm, twisted her around and plonked her back into her seat.

"Sit down!" he yelled in frustration.

Courtney let out a piercing scream. Jodie knew by its tone and volume that something was badly wrong. Scott immediately became defensive.

"Stupid Mummy's girl," he complained as he left the table.

Jodie quickly went to comfort Courtney.

"What did you have to do that for?" she ventured to Scott as crossly as she dared. "You really hurt her."

Scott rounded on Jodie, his eyes blazing.

"Don't blame me, you fat slag," he fumed. "If your big baby of a daughter did as she was told, this wouldn't have happened. It's your fault. You spoil her, always letting her have her own way."

Jodie bit her lip. She knew it was futile to argue with Scott, so she picked up Courtney.

"Shh, baby," soothed Jodie. "It's okay. Daddy didn't mean it."

"Don't call me her daddy!" snapped Scott in anger. "And get her out of my sight, screaming like that."

Scott turned and put his coat on.

"Where you going?" asked Jodie anxiously.

"Out," came the curt reply.

With that Scott was gone.

Chapter 8

Diane had planned to have an office-based day. That would let her catch up on writing the numerous reports she had in hand, respond to emails and return missed phone calls. She had written a to-do list, made herself coffee and settled down to the task when the phone rang. Diane groaned inwardly and leaned back. She could see Angie trying to put the call through.

"Can you take a message, Ang?" she implored. "I really need to do some catching up here."

Angie pulled a face and shrugged.

"Sorry, Di. They said it was important," Angie replied, putting the call through.

It was the health visitor again, Hilary Williams.

"Diane," began Hilary in a business-like manner, "did you get to see Kirsty and Daniel?"

Diane spent a few minutes explaining that she had tried to visit, but no one was home so she would try again soon.

Hilary listened and continued, "Well, just so you know, I checked with the GP and Kirsty failed to keep the appointment I made her. Keep me posted, Diane. I'm somewhat concerned about this one."

Then she rang off.

"Everything okay, Di?" called her friend and colleague, Maxine, from the desk in the other corner.

Maxine Montgomery was Diane's best friend. They had gone to the same university, trained and graduated at the same time. They had much in common and Diane knew that she could rely on her in any crisis. Maxine was one of those rare friends whom one only got once in a lifetime. She was six years Diane's senior and took her role as Diane's best friend seriously. Before Maxine had introduced Diane to Ethan, they used to go out regularly for girls night – something they had not done in a while. Maxine was the perfect foil for Diane's hyperactive, super-organised personality. She was steady and, in many ways, more like Ethan – probably why Diane loved them both so much.

It was Maxine who had saved Diane's sanity when Ethan left. *Was it really only six weeks ago?* Maxine had held Diane tightly to her ample chest and rocked her like a child as Diane Foster sobbed and cried until physically exhausted. It was Maxine who had insisted that they go for a spa weekend as an antidote to the pain. It had been a diverting weekend, but did little to dull the ache of where Ethan should have been. Maxine was a constant in Diane's life: a solid, loyal friend who would always be there for her.

"Not really," replied Diane. "It's a baby I need to visit, but so far no one's been home. Usual story," she added, wryly.

"You up for lunch, later?" asked Maxine, hopefully.

"Not a chance, Maxine. Thanks all the same. I'm absolutely swamped here and will just have to work through. Maybe, next week," replied Diane, knowing she would be no less busy that week than she presently was.

~ ~ ~ ~ ~

Courtney Pearson was still screaming. Jodie knew that she needed to take her to a doctor, but was afraid to do so. She was afraid of what Scott might say. Jodie was also afraid of the possible outcome of the visit. She

64

knew deep down that Courtney was hurt badly. Jodie swallowed hard as she tried thinking of a way to explain the injury without involving Scott.

"Shh, babes," Jodie urged as she reached for *Calpol* to try and deaden some of Courtney's pain. "Shh, Mummy will take care of you. Don't cry."

Jodie hugged Courtney to herself, but it made the little girl scream all the more. Taking a deep, decisive breath, Jodie put her coat and placed Courtney and Brandon in the double buggy.

"Come on, Jamie," said Jodie to her eldest child. "Hold Mummy's hand. We're going out."

~ ~ ~ ~ ~

Diane left the office for the visits of the day. She shivered as she got into the little Morris Minor and turned the car heater up full. It was a cold, bleak December day and while the stores and homes in the area displayed their twinkling Christmas lights, Diane felt anything but festive. She did not want to think about how she would be spending her holidays. *Probably working and worrying about the children on her caseload*, she thought. Since Ethan had left, Diane found it difficult to have time on her hands, preferring to keep busy although nothing really dimmed his memory. Diane still longed for him with all her being. She pulled up at a red light and allowed her mind the luxury of a few moments dwelling on Ethan, wondering what he was doing at that instant.

As she sat there, Diane idly noticed a woman waiting to cross the road. The woman had a toddler in a pushchair, wrapped warmly in a snowsuit against the biting cold of the day. It was almost impossible to tell if the toddler was a boy or a girl underneath all the layers, but Diane could see a tiny fountain of hair on top of the child's head, suggesting it was a little girl. Diane waved the woman across, but the latter was focused on the child. She seemed to be looking for something, rummaging around in the pushchair and underneath the child's legs. Suddenly, the woman pulled the child up by the arm and delivered two full-blooded wallops to her thigh. Diane's eyes flew wide open. She could not believe what she had just seen. She sat up aghast and spoke aloud to herself.

"Oh, no. No, no! Don't do that, not in front of me," Diane groaned.

Diane knew that, no matter what, she had a responsibility to children and was thinking at top speed as to how she could intervene. It appeared that the woman was not finished, though. Realising that the lights were red, the woman began pushing the buggy across the road, but she was clearly still angry about something. She stopped in the middle of the road to shake the buggy violently while berating the child loudly. Diane looked around wildly to see if any other passers-by were witnessing this assault on the toddler, but other than an elderly man in a motorised scooter, the streets were deserted.

Diane checked her rear view mirror and was thankful that no other cars had pulled up behind her as she knew that the lights would change at any moment. Diane followed the woman's progress across the road in fascinated horror. The woman reached the pavement and her fury at the child seemed to reach a crescendo. She shook the buggy once again and to Diane's alarm, pushed it hard and let it go. The buggy flew down the street and Diane held her breath as she watched the woman give chase and grab the handles. At that point two things happened simultaneously. The lights turned green and the woman grabbed the child by the hair on top of her head, lifting the little girl bodily out of the pram a good 10 inches. Diane became incensed.

"That's it!" she exclaimed, grimly. "No way are you getting away with this!"

Diane was determined as she slammed the old car into gear to make a U-turn. She fully intended to challenge the woman and if need be call the

66

police, but she was in a one-way system and could not readily turn around. Frustrated, Diane pulled over, grabbed her mobile phone and rang the office which was literally 500 yards from where the woman was heading. The duty social worker picked up.

"Helen," barked Diane, "I need you to go straight out into the street and see if you can see a woman with a child in a buggy. You need to stop her, I don't care how. Call the police if you have to, but do *not* let her go anywhere with that child. She's just assaulted her big-time out on the street."

Diane gabbled out her story.

"I'll be back in one minute," she finally said, hanging up.

Diane was wrong. It took her over two minutes to negotiate her way through the one-way system back to the office. She ran inside and found Helen.

"Did you find her?" Diane asked breathless from exertion.

Helen looked confused.

"Di, there was no one there," replied Helen, holding up her hands in bewilderment.

"What? That's impossible! She was literally walking this way. How could you not see her?" Diane exclaimed in disbelief.

Helen continued looking at Diane in consternation.

"Honest, Di, I went straight out, but there was no one."

Diane wasted no time. She ran back to her car, leapt in and screamed out of the carpark with the rev counter indicating a startling 3000 rpm. She spent 20 minutes driving up and down the streets nearby, but it was no use. The woman was gone.

It was a disconsolate and frustrated Diane who returned to the office, her planned visit now off the agenda. She went back in and was met by the worried stares of everyone on the team. Helen had obviously relayed the story to Glenda who was part of the group.

"What happened, Di?" Glenda asked with genuine concern.

The manager had worked with Diane long enough to know that she was not given to histrionics or exaggeration. Diane recounted the incident she had just witnessed.

"If she'll do that to the child in public, Glenda, what on earth is she doing behind closed doors?" Diane finally said. "That little girl must be hurting right now and she's most definitely at risk of continuing harm."

"Well, Di, unless we can work out who she is or where she's gone, there's very little we can do," replied Glenda with sadness.

After continued discussion the team reached the conclusion that the woman must have got on a bus just before Helen exited the office. There was a bus stop right outside; it was the only possible scenario. Glenda was right: there was nothing they could do at that point; nothing at all.

Chapter 9

Kirsty Thompson turned up the television to drown out the screams emanating from upstairs.

"God, shut up!" shouted Kirsty, rolling her eyes. "I wish I never had a damn baby! No one told me they were so much trouble," she moaned to no one in particular.

Neil O'Grady had gone out to the pub after another row about Daniel's incessant crying. It was supposed to be Neil's turn to see to him, but that never seemed to happen. As the health visitor rightly reported, Kirsty had not been to the doctor. She had hidden upstairs with Neil when they heard the social worker knocking on the door, the day before. They had thought she would never leave, what with the stupid dog barking like he did. Neil had brayed him good and proper after the social worker went away.

Kirsty got up begrudgingly from the sofa and went upstairs. Daniel was bright red in the face from screaming and from the pain of his worsening nappy rash. His cries were coming in gulps and he struggled to breathe, such was his distress. Kirsty picked Daniel up roughly and took him downstairs. She offered him a cold bottle of milk which had been standing there all day, but Daniel was too distraught to drink.

"Don't have it then," snapped Kirsty in anger. "Don't say I didn't offer. You know your trouble? You don't know what you want, do you?"

All her inexperience and indifference rose to the surface.

Kirsty had not wanted a baby, but got caught pregnant during a brief fling with a lad she had known from school. Her mate, Donna, had said that she would get benefits for having a baby and be better off, so Kirsty had gone ahead with it. Initially, she had enjoyed all the fuss and attention of being pregnant. She had also managed to obtain a reasonable council house out of it too. However, Kirsty was beginning to wonder if the little extra cash and the house she had gained from having Daniel were worth it. Donna had said to try telling the social that the baby had a disability when he was older – like ADHD or something – as one got more benefits if a kid was disabled. Kirsty returned Daniel still screaming to his cot upstairs.

"Please yourself," she muttered, unkindly, while placing the protesting infant down. "I'm sure you just enjoy wasting my time."

Then Kirsty went back downstairs where she turned the television up, got herself a beer and heartily longed for the crying to stop.

~ ~ ~ ~ ~

Diane went into her supervision meeting with Glenda armed with her diary, a pen and a writing pad.

"Right," said Glenda by way of a greeting. "Who shall we start with?"

Diane began with the most recent altercation between Shanice and Grant Ellis. Glenda frowned as she gave the matter some thought.

"Well, Di, they knew the deal," said Glenda. "We made it crystal clear at the case conference that if there were any further incidents, we would have a legal meeting, so that's what needs to happen."

Diane made careful notes, detailing the actions her manager outlined, although she knew that Glenda would later give her an official copy to sign and file.

"Right," said Diane with firmness. "I'll get onto legal and organise the meeting. I'll write the pre-proceedings letter to the parents and get all the paperwork done as soon as I possibly can."

To reach such a stage meant that the local authority thought there was enough evidence to meet the threshold for further action.

At law, if a child suffered or was likely to suffer significant harm, the threshold was met and pre-proceedings could be initiated. That was the beginning of an often lengthy, legal process which, more often than not, resulted in a child being removed from their family or carers. It was often the last chance for many families to try and make the necessary changes to prevent that from happening. Contrary to popular belief, social workers did not have the authority to simply remove anyone's children without a court order, but had to follow a process defined by law. In the case of a real emergency such as where children needed to be removed from a situation immediately, social workers relied on the police who had specific powers which allowed them to remove the children, while the social workers obtained the necessary court orders to keep them safe.

The bane of every social worker's life was the tabloid press who delighted in blaming and denouncing social workers each time a child was harmed at the hands of its parents. Like all social workers, Diane knew only too well that the parents they worked with were skilled at avoiding and deceiving professionals. A child who came to harm was usually causing concern for their school, nursery, health visitor and neighbours, and in some cases just had never been brought to the attention of Social Services.

"My next worry is for Daniel Thompson," began Diane. "The health visitor has seen him and expressed some concerns and I'm having difficulty gaining access. I'm sure they're home, but they won't answer the door. Also the health visitor made the mother, Kirsty, an appointment for the doctor, but which she did not keep."

Glenda looked perturbed. She knew that Daniel was only three months old, making him particularly vulnerable.

"Okay, we'll keep trying. Meantime, write to the mum and make a date to visit this week, and stress how important it is that she is home for it. Better still, do a joint visit with Hilary if she's available."

Diane knew that it was sound practice to go on a potentially challenging visit with a colleague, not only for safety reasons, but also for confirmation of what was said to the parents. However, it made organising the visit that much more difficult as two busy professionals had to synchronise their diaries rather than one.

Almost three hours later, all the children on Diane's caseload had been discussed and her head was spinning with the additional work to her already unrealistic schedule. Before the meeting ended, Diane told Glenda that she was beginning to feel a bit swamped with work and was worried about how she would manage to meet all its demands, especially in light of the impending legal meeting which she now had to organise. Glenda was sympathetic.

"I know how you feel, Diane," she sighed, "but to whom else can I give these complex cases? I've got three workers off sick, two on maternity leave and the rest are newly qualified. You are my most senior and experienced member of staff. Without you we'd be sunk," said Glenda, shaking her head. "I'm interviewing three agency staff this week, so let's hope some of them can pick up the slack. Right, that's it. Unless there's anything else?"

Diane pulled a face.

"Only that I wish we could identify the child I saw getting assaulted in the street," Diane said. "But I guess that's a vain hope."

Glenda shook her head and agreed.

"I appreciate how you feel, Di, but you need to let that one go. I have no doubt the child will come to our attention at some point, given her mother's behaviour."

Neither Glenda nor Diane could have anticipated how true Glenda's words would prove to be.

Diane exited the meeting overwhelmed and slightly nauseous. Organising a legal meeting was not a two-minute job. As she sat back down at her desk, Angie went over to Diane looking perplexed and anxious.

"Sorry, Diane, I know you're really busy," Angie began, "but we've just had a call from the GP. Jodie Pearson was there with Courtney and she's on her way to hospital now with a suspected broken arm."

Diane closed her eyes and tried to stifle the panic which arose inside. Any child with a significant injury was a serious matter, but a child already subject to a child protection plan heightened the potential for that child coming to harm in suspicious circumstances. Diane took a deep breath before answering.

"Okay," she said finally. "Thanks, Angie. I'll go and tell Glenda, then I'll give the doctor a ring."

Glenda looked up in surprise.

"Forgot something?" she asked. Then she joked, "Or did you just miss me?"

Upon seeing the expression on Diane's face, however, Glenda grew concerned.

"What is it?" she asked quickly.

Glenda closed her eyes upon hearing the news.

"Right, well; you know what to do," she continued briskly. "You speak to the doctor. I'll ring the hospital and tell them you're on the way. Keep me posted and let me know if I need to contact the police."

Contacting the police was routine in a case where a child had sustained a non-accidental injury – NAI as it was known. First, however, Diane would need a paediatric consultant's opinion as to whether or not the injury was considered an accident.

Ten minutes later, Diane was in her car en route to *Queen's Hospital*. She reflected on her discussion with the doctor which had done little to reassure her. The doctor said that Jodie brought Courtney in and a brief examination had revealed a suspected broken arm. The doctor had then ordered a taxi and sent Jodie and her children instantly to the hospital. Jodie had apparently said that Courtney fell off a chair at breakfast-time, but she was vague and anxious.

Chapter 10

Janice Spiggot considered her reflection in the cracked, full-length mirror and breathed in. No, she could not get into her jeans yet – not so soon after having the baby. Not that it mattered, though. Janice preferred lolling about in her sloppy dressing gown for most of the day, anyway. She wrapped the grubby, familiar garment around her considerable frame and picked up six-week-old Hayley.

"What's up, gorgeous?" Janice asked before going into two-year-old Declan's room to get him up. "Declan, babby," she called, "time to get up."

At 21 years old, Janice Spiggot considered her life to be going places. She was fairly certain that she had been the envy of many of her peers when at only 18 years of age, she had married Barry Spiggot who was 50 years old at the time. There had been a lot of nasty comments on Facebook, but Janice knew that it was jealousy. Janice had known Barry since she was a little girl; he was one of her dad's best mates. Barry had been a shoulder to cry on when her dad finally went to prison.

Although Barry was a lot older than Janice, he was a hardworking man who owned his washing machine repair business. He had a nice house on the edge of the estate and away from the worst of the trouble. Barry also had a van for work and a car. Janice did not need to work like her friends. Not for her the boring checkout job at *Aldi* or the local factory; no. Janice could stay home and be a full-time mother.

Being a homemaker, however, was a skill which eluded Janice. She was unable to organise herself enough to complete even the most basic, household tasks. As a result the home environment was dirty, chaotic and untidy. Meals were never on time and always comprised of a ready-made or frozen offering. The children required a lot more of her time and attention than Janice had ever anticipated. Her days seemed to be one long round of nappy changing, feeding and washing.

Janice loved her children, but found their endless demands draining. She would leave them in their rooms for long periods of time, so that she could lie on the sofa and rest by watching television – a pastime which took up a lot of her day. Given her history, Janice felt that she had a monopoly on child abuse and all matters remotely relating to it. The highlight of her day was always the *Jeremy Kyle Show* which she watched, nodding wisely in agreement when other victims shared their sorry tales. The story of Janice had been printed in a well-known magazine and brought her the princely sum of £500. She had used most of the money to buy lottery cards and go to bingo, although some of it went on getting Barry some of that fancy bourbon he liked.

Janice put Hayley down and lifted Declan out of the bed. She immediately pulled a face: he needed changing big time. The mess had escaped from Declan's ill-fitting nappy and oozed down his leg. Janice gagged as she began dealing half-heartedly with the seepage. What Declan needed was a bath, but that would require effort – definitely not one of her strong points. Instead, she undressed Declan and made the best of it with baby wipes. Then Janice redressed the boy, ignoring the smell which still emitted from the numerous bits she had missed.

"There you go, babby," she said, satisfied with her lacklustre achievement. "Down we go."

~ ~ ~ ~ ~

When Diane arrived at the hospital, she found an agitated Jodie sitting with the children in the waiting room. Upon seeing the social worker, Jodie jumped to her feet.

"They said I had to wait until you came. Why did I have to wait? What's it got to do with you?" demanded Jodie, tearfully.

Diane tried reassuring Jodie that because her children were subject to child protection plans and had an assigned social worker, it was the norm for her to attend like that. Courtney was still crying. She was feverish and hot. Jodie was struggling to pacify the girl and attempting to respond to Jamie's demands for her to play with the toys. Brandon was also waking up and would need feeding.

"Did you bring a bottle for him, Jodie?" asked Diane.

Jodie shook her head.

"No, because I was only going to see the doctor. How did I know we'd end up here?" she sniffed.

"Don't worry, I'm sure the hospital can sort him a feed out," said Diane, calmly.

She went to ask if it was possible under the circumstances.

When she returned, Diane asked, "So, Jodie, tell me how this happened."

Jodie continued sticking to the story that Courtney had fallen off the kitchen chair at breakfast time.

"Where was Scott?" asked Diane.

Jodie looked up.

"He was there in the kitchen," she replied. "He tried to pick her up, but she was crying and wanted me."

At that point a nurse interrupted them both to explain that she was going to weigh and measure Courtney, before she was given an x-ray and taken to see the consultant. It was well over an hour later when Diane was asked to enter for a discussion with the paediatrician on duty, Dr Linda Skowinsky.

"Please, everyone, have a seat," invited the doctor. "So here we have three-year-old Courtney who, according to her mum, fell off her chair this morning which caused her to hurt her arm. Courtney does not have enough vocabulary to tell us what happened. However, having examined the x-rays of Courtney's arm, I can tell you she has a spiral fracture. This is uncommon and while it can be associated with a fall, it is more often caused by torsion. Children with spiral fractures have often had their arm pulled or twisted in some way."

Dr Skowinsky paused pointedly, looked at Jodie and said, "Tell me again, Jodie, how did this happen?"

Jodie bit her lip and looked at the floor.

"I told you. Courtney fell off her chair, then started screaming. I told you this once," Jodie repeated anxiously.

At that moment, Jamie, who was in the room and seemingly taking no notice, suddenly piped up.

"Scott did it. Didn't he, Mummy? Scott hurt Courtney when she didn't eat her toast. He's naughty."

The silence that followed was fleeting, but dramatic. All the adults turned and focused their attention on Jamie. Jodie quickly tried to cover over the boy's unexpected statement and spluttered.

"He's confused. Scott was there and he tried picking her up, but she wanted me. Scott wouldn't hurt Courtney, he loves the kids. No; it wasn't Scott, Jamie," replied Jodie, looking intently at her son who had returned to the toys on the floor.

Dr Skowinsky pursed her lips and looked at Diane.

"May I have a word with you?" the doctor said, quietly.

Jodie burst into tears.

"No, no! Why do you believe him, not me? I'm telling you, she fell. Jamie, babes, tell them she fell," pleaded Jodie.

Jamie looked surprised, but only made matters worse for his mother.

He repeated unhelpfully, "Scott's naughty, Mummy. I don't like Scott."

Jodie was escorted, still crying, out of the room to wait with a nurse. Dr Skowinsky focused her attention on Diane.

"I have to say," the doctor began gravely, "that it is my professional opinion that this is a non-accidental fracture caused by Courtney's arm being twisted or pulled by an adult. If Jamie's account is to be believed, it would provide a satisfactory explanation of how Courtney came by this injury."

By then Diane knew that the day was a complete write-off. The verdict of Dr Skowinsky about Courtney's injury meant that neither the girl nor the other two children could be permitted to return home with Jodie. The police would need to be called to investigate and if Diane was to be honest, it would create a mountain of paperwork she could well do without.

Courtney was admitted to the children's ward for blood tests, observation and treatment of her fractured arm. Further x-rays revealed that she would need to stay in the hospital for at least two nights as the consultant suspected that she could require surgery. On the way down to the ward, Jodie still tried reassuring Diane that Scott had not hurt Courtney.

Diane left Jodie with the staff nurse on the ward and went to ring Glenda, to being her up to date with the unfolding situation. It was agreed that although Jamie implicated Scott as the person who had caused Courtney's fractured arm, Jodie was denying that and the police would need to interview both parents, to hear what they had to say on the matter. Until there was further information about the incident, the local authority would have to consider all children potentially at risk of harm from both Jodie and Scott. In light of that, they would not be permitted to return home with either parent.

Diane suggested Jodie's mother, Brenda, as a potential carer for Jamie and Brandon, and also for Courtney when discharged. Diane knew that the grandmother was a rough diamond. Brenda Pearson was basically a decent person who offered Jodie endless hours of support and cared for the children on countless occasions. She was known to have no time for Scott Taylor and was vehemently opposed to Jodie's relationship with him. Diane had met Brenda many times at Jodie's home when Scott was not there. She considered her genuine, down to earth. Glenda was inclined to agree and asked Diane to contact Brenda immediately to explain the situation. In the meantime, Glenda also requested urgent police checks for Brenda and any other adults in her home before the children could go there.

Brenda Pearson reacted to the entire situation as would any normal grandmother. She was absolutely horrified.

"You know Scott did this, don't you?" Brenda said with anger in her voice. "I knew something like this would happen. He's a no-good, low-life druggie and my daughter hasn't got the brains she was born with, to stay with him. Wait till I see her!" she continued bitterly.

Diane explained to Brenda that it was not yet clear how Courtney had broken her arm, which was why none of the children could return home at that time.

"Well, you know I'll have them, Diane," Brenda agreed wearily. "You bring them here whenever you're ready. I'll go and get the beds made up, now."

Brenda gave the local authority permission to carry out whatever checks they needed to do, adding that she had nothing to hide. Diane returned to the ward and explained the plan to a still tearful Jodie. The latter hurled herself at Diane, hugging and begging her not to take her children off her.

"Jodie, calm down," reasoned Diane. "We're not taking the children off you. We're asking you to agree to them going to your mum's for a few days until we can get to the bottom of this. We just need to do some basic checks on your mum and, in the meantime, the children can go to the children's centre. Hopefully, your mum can collect them from there later tonight."

Jodie stopped crying and looked pitifully at Diane.

"So me mam can have them?" Jodie asked, hopefully.

"For now, yes," said Diane, "but I can't promise what may happen long-term, Jodie. Now, the police will want to speak to you and you need to make sure you tell them absolutely everything in detail. Most importantly, tell the truth," she said firmly.

With Jodie's agreement, Diane called on her trusted colleagues at the children's centre. Thankfully, they were always supportive in a crisis and agreed to care for Jamie and Brandon. It would only be for a few hours until Glenda had obtained the police information pertaining to Brenda Pearson and her wider family. Diane did not allow herself to contemplate a scenario where Brenda Pearson was found to have a police record, which would exclude her as a carer. She closed her mind to that thought and went back to the ward.

Chapter 11

Morris Powell sat uncomfortably and nervously in church. It was a completely alien environment for him, never having set foot in a church his whole life before that day. He was sweating profusely and not just from the excessive heat. The place was not like the churches he had seen on the telly; it was more like an old school. The building had seen better days. It smelled of calor gas mixed with fusty dampness. The walls were painted a cheery yellow, with bulky, old-style radiators painted with a thick white gloss. The carpets were red with a swirly pattern. They were made of that functional, easy clean material often found in kitchens and they were stained and worn. There was a raised kind of dais at the front and three steps up, on top of it, was a flower arrangement with lilies and green stuff. The seat Morris occupied was in one of those grey plastic chairs, the sort found in a café; they were laid out in rows of six, in a herringbone pattern, on either side of the room.

Morris had plumped for the unoriginally named *Waters of Life Church*, mainly because it was conveniently on the number 9 bus route which ran right past the door of his elderly mother's, Deacon Hill council flat. Therefore, it caused minimal disruption to his humdrum routine. Morris received a warm welcome – to be expected as the advert on the webpage of the church had assured of that. The lady at the door was a pleasant-faced, well-dressed, stick thin woman in her 50's who introduced herself as Phyllis. She greeted Morris with a big hug which took even him by surprise. Phyllis showed Morris enthusiastically to a seat near the window, apologising in advance for the heating which was, apparently, stuck on full. Phyllis then pressed a book into Morris's hand and at which he had yet to glance. Morris was more interested in scanning his new surroundings and identifying potential prey. He did not have long to wait. One by one, the families arrived – families with children. Morris smiled inwardly and made himself more comfortable.

"Is this seat taken?" asked a young woman, politely.

Morris looked up and saw an earnest-faced lady whom he guessed was around 35 years of age staring intently at him. She had three children with her of around six, eight and 10 years of age. *All girls!* he thought.

"No, no. Not at all," said Morris smoothly. "Please, be my guest. Sit down."

Morris Powell was in.

~ ~ ~ ~ ~

Jessica Jackson sprawled on the sofa, her long legs dangling over the end. She sighed theatrically. However, since that did not elicit the desired response, she turned up the volume and groaned, making a big show of looking at the clock.

"Why is she always late?" Jessica complained in a loud voice, putting emphasis on the final syllable so that it came out *lay tuh.*

Lorraine Stevenson entered from the kitchen, drying her hands on a towel and smiling patiently at Jessica.

"It's only five past three, Jess," Lorraine said, pleasantly. "Diane's only five minutes late. Why don't you put the kettle on, so she can have a cup of tea when she arrives?"

Jessica's teenage tragedy continued and she fell back into a dramatic heap of hormonal misery.

"Whaaaaat?" Jessica said, emphatically, while flicking her long brown hair. "No way! Why do I have to make her a cup of tea? That's your job."

Lorraine Stevenson rolled her eyes good-naturedly, went back into the kitchen and put the kettle on. She noticed Jessica's inhaler on the side and called through.

"Jess, have you had your inhaler today?"

There was silence in the living room.

"I'll take that as a *no*," scolded Lorraine. "C'mon, missy, you know you have to take it."

For the millionth time in her life, Lorraine questioned her decision to become a foster carer – more specifically, a foster carer specialised in providing a home for challenging and troubled teenagers. However, her doubts were only fleeting as, despite the demanding nature of her role, she would not swop it for anything. Lorraine was a rare and highly valued asset in the fostering world. Few people could aspire to the life of a foster carer with all its requirements. Fewer still could deal with the daily confrontation and defiance which were part and parcel of fostering an emotionally damaged teenager.

Lorraine was a single parent. Widowed at only 39 years of age when her beloved husband, Joe, had succumbed to cancer, Lorraine raised her own two children, Joe junior and William, alone. She had loved every minute of it. Her boys were grown up now with lives of their own and Lorraine had put her natural, level-headed, caring talents to excellent use in becoming a foster carer.

At 57 years old, Lorraine always told everyone that the teenagers kept her young and it was true. She was bang up to speed on using an iPad, iPod and iPhone. She was also computer literate. She knew all the latest boy bands and chart music, and had a pretty good grip on Trance, House, Hip Hop and other assorted kinds of music, all of which had been played at full blast in her house at some time or another. Lorraine was easy going and understanding with the young people who shared her life, but had clear and fair house rules by which they were expected to abide. Naturally, there were conflicts and disagreements, but Lorraine was a big believer in young people working things out for themselves. She would spend hours talking and negotiating with them, to identify a mutually effective solution to the day-to-day issues which arose.

Lorraine had the good sense to pick her battles wisely. She tolerated piercings, tattoos, pink, green and blue hair; and a host of things which would send most parents into a tailspin. She argued that there were far more important things for young people to worry about. Most of her charges were from the infamous Deacon Hill estate and came from abusive, neglectful families. They had contended with parents who had drug and alcohol problems, serious mental health issues; violent and abusive parents who caused them physical and emotional harm. Some of her young people had suffered sexual abuse which, in Lorraine's opinion, was the most damaging of all. No, Lorraine would not have it any other way. She loved her life and felt that she made a real difference to many young people in the area. Her own boys lived locally and often called around with their own families. With them and the three teenagers she usually had in residence, along with the tribes of friends they collected, the house was rarely quiet.

Jessica had only been with Lorraine for two weeks. It was her last chance at foster care. Diane had explained to Lorraine that if Jessica did not settle down there, it was highly likely that she would be placed in a secure unit for her own safety. Jessica was one of the many young girls Lorraine cared for and who had been sexually abused. The case of Jessica was particularly horrific.

The abuse had not come to light until Jessica was 13 years old, by which time it had been occurring for years. Prior to meeting Jessica's mother, her father, Dennis Jackson, had been in a previous relationship and imprisoned for abusing his daughter from that union. He spent three, unremorseful years in prison. When released, Dennis had struck up a relationship with Jessica's mother, Lisa – he chose well.

Lisa had learning difficulties and was poorly equipped to deal with life, much less see through the wiles of a cunning paedophile like Dennis Jackson. She had been flattered by the attention that she received from Dennis and quickly fell pregnant, agreeing to marry him. There had, of course, been social work involvement due to the previous convictions of Dennis. The social worker at the time was concerned enough to take the matter to court, fearing that Lisa would not be able to protect Jessica from her father. Dennis Jackson, however, was an intelligent, smooth-talking man who had charmed a bench of magistrates with assurances of reformation. He had joined a church and got a steady job. He had seen the error of his ways and was thoroughly ashamed of his previous conduct. He wanted to make amends and start afresh. He said that he welcomed the support of Social Services and would do anything to maintain his family. To the astonishment and disbelief of everyone involved, the magistrates had fallen for it and ruled that Jessica was to remain with her parents, with regular visits from Social Services who were to monitor the case.

The abuse had started almost immediately after the court case was over. Jessica was only two years old at the time. The following year, Lisa gave birth to a baby boy, Liam. Their father, Dennis, showed no favouritism between the two children and abused them both. Unbeknown to Lisa, he had rented another property, a house, a few streets away and took the children there regularly, telling Lisa he was taking them to the park. The house was equipped with videos and cameras. Dennis, who fancied himself a film director, would spend hours filming Jessica and her brother in vile, compromising poses. He encouraged the children's compliance by saying that they were film stars and would be famous. The children never questioned what was happening. They knew nothing else; it had always been that way. They also knew that they could not tell Mummy as it was their special secret with Daddy.

Sometimes other men would be at the house, to 'star' in the movies made. Dennis Jackson was infamous within his close-knit circle of like-minded, degenerate friends. He saw no harm in the unscrupulous, depraved exploitation of his own children and made a considerable amount of money selling his repulsive videos.

Lisa Jackson was completely ignorant as to what and to whom her husband was subjecting their children. She too was a victim of Dennis Jackson, suffering consistent beatings and emotional torture at his hands. Lisa had no one to turn to: no friends or family with whom to share her misery. Unsurprisingly, Lisa had become depressed. Dennis Jackson was at hand to administer 'medication' which he bought on the estate from a sharp-witted, weasel-faced fellow named Scott. Lisa had not known what it was, but it made her feel better. It also rendered her permanently tired and unable to meet the needs of her children. Jessica's enduring memory of her mother was of sleeping on the sofa, mouth gaping and making funny, little grunting noises. Her father would laugh at the mother and urge the children to make fun of her, calling her names. Liam was encouraged to slap his mother and boss her around – which seemed to give Dennis Jackson more pleasure than anything else.

The older she became, the more Jessica had dreaded going to the cinema – her father's nickname for the house with the video equipment. With increasing regularity, Dennis would have men waiting for her there: men whom she despised with every thread of her being. They did things to her which she could only bear if she detached herself from them and emotionally went somewhere else while it was all happening. To remain present even as an unwilling participant was too much to bear.

Jessica recalled the day things came sharply into focus for her. She was 13 years old and for the first time in her life, she had been permitted to go to her friend's house for a sleepover. Jessica and her friend had gone to bed and after the usual giggling and talking which accompanied a sleepover, the friend, worn out with all the fun, had gone to sleep. Jessica, however, had stayed awake, waiting for her friend's father to enter the room. *After all, this was what all girls' dads did at bedtime, wasn't it?* When nothing happened and she slept unmolested for the first time in memory, Jessica had become confused. She was no longer a child, but a curious teenager who began vehemently objecting to what her father was doing. A lifetime of conditioning and obedience, however, had left her powerless and impotent. Recently, she had made a feeble attempt to push her father away, but was rewarded with a stinging slap to the side of her face. Dennis had then savagely raped his daughter and made her stay in her room all night with no food or water. Liam had sneaked her a dried *Weetabix* before going to bed, which Jessica knew took a huge amount of bravery on his part. The consequences, had he been discovered, would have been terrible.

The day after the sleepover, Jessica had taken all her courage into her hands and sick with fear and shame, confided in her friend. The reaction she got confirmed what she had begun to suspect. The reality of it all hit her like a baseball bat right in the face. Jessica's response was one of total shock and it robbed her of the ability to speak – she became an elective mute. While possessing the ability to speak, Jessica simply could not. The dawning knowledge of her father's sins had rendered her catatonic. Teachers at school questioned her relentlessly.

"What's the matter, Jessica? What's wrong? Don't be silly."

And on and on and on. Eventually, Jessica was unable to contain her terrible knowledge any longer. It all exploded out of her at school one day when a particularly sympathetic teacher took her into her office and sat Jessica down.

The teacher simply said, "Tell me."

And Jessica never went home again.

Chapter 12

Back in church, Morris felt a headache coming on with the strain and effort of being pleasant. While he was a skilled manipulator, Morris was unaccustomed to having to maintain his convincing misrepresentation for so long. His face was aching from the never ending smiling as he was introduced to a seemingly uninterrupted steam of people – people whose names he had no chance of recollecting.

"Hello, nice to meet you," Morris repeated over and over, holding out his pudgy fingers to shake a multitude of hands.

Will this never end? he thought, rancorously. However, Morris knew that he would have to adopt at least a veneer of pleasantry, to inveigle his way into the congregation and gain their trust. He did not have to enjoy it, though.

Morris was already planning a treat for himself, for maintaining such a winning personality for so long. He decided that he would select a favourite video from his extensive library of child pornography when he got in and thoroughly enjoyed contemplating how he would add to it, once his plans for the church came to fruition. Morris knew just the video he would watch – he had obtained it some years ago from one of the best in the business: his old mate, Dennis Jackson.

"Friends," boomed a voice, startling Morris out of his daydream and back to the church service which was about to begin. "Friends, you are all welcome in the name of Jesus."

The voice of Pastor Alan Slater reverberated over the well-attended congregation who packed the hall. It was followed by an immediate hail of *Amen*'s and *Praise the Lord*. The church was evangelical and the congregation were known unflatteringly on the estate as The Happy Clappys.

"We welcome all our newcomers," continued Pastor Slater as he smiled down from the dais. "Please, make yourselves at home here with us. We are only too glad to have you here in our family."

Thanks, thought Morris. *I shall.*

~ ~ ~ ~ ~

Diane returned late to the office after her visit to Jessica Jackson which had, as usual, been challenging. Since entering the care of the local authority, Jessica's behaviour had deteriorated to the point of being almost unmanageable in a family home. She had run away repeatedly from her previous four foster placements and had already started associating with some of the less desirable young people on the estate. Having led such a controlled existence to date, Jessica had embraced her new-found freedom with abandon and seemed determined to participate in every possible vice available. There was no shortage of volunteers to initiate her into the underside of the Deacon Hill estate and Jessica had quickly and inevitably become embroiled in the drug scene.

The local authority worked hand-in-hand with the local police drugs squad. Diane had received intelligence from an undercover officer that Jessica offered him sexual favours in exchange for a gram of coke. However, Diane was not able to discuss this with Jessica as it had taken many months of painstaking work for the undercover squad to infiltrate the drug scene. To divulge any information received from that source would seriously compromise the police operation.

As it happened, however, Jessica's constant running away to stay with her mates had led to the breakdown of her fourth placement. This resulted in Diane being able to move Jessica to Lorraine's house. As a specialist carer for children with behavioural and emotional issues, Lorraine was a last hope for Jessica. She also lived a couple of miles away from the estate and Diane hoped that it would deter Jessica from continuing to hang out there.

It was a vain hope. Jessica still gravitated to her old haunts and Diane knew that unless the situation changed quickly, she would have to consider applying for a secure order, to place Jessica in a specialised facility for her own safety. While secure units were usually for young offenders, they offered a certain number of 'welfare beds.' These were reserved for young people who were exposing themselves to such high risk activities as to seriously threaten their health and well-being. Obtaining a secure order was almost impossible. There were numerous criteria which had to be fulfilled before a social worker could even apply for one. However, Diane knew that Jessica met the criteria and it was only a matter of time before she would be forced to follow that route.

Diane entered the office just as it was about to close. As she walked through the reception area, she noticed a woman sitting there. The woman had a child in a buggy. Diane frowned: the woman looked familiar. With a start of realisation, Diane recognised her as that woman from the traffic lights the day before. Her heart pounded as she approached the woman in question.

"Has someone seen you?" enquired Diane as casually as she could.

The woman scowled.

"I'm with my mate," she replied. "She's still in there," indicating an interview room.

"Oh, okay," said Diane going into the office, her mind working at full speed.

Thankfully, Glenda was still in her room.

"Glenda," hissed Diane with urgency. "She's here, the woman from the traffic lights. She's in reception now."

Glenda looked astonished.

"Really? Right then, let's go speak to her," Glenda replied, wasting no time.

Diane and Glenda went back to the reception area just as the woman and her friend were leaving.

"Excuse me," said Glenda, politely but firmly. "May we have a quick word with you?"

The women stopped in their tracks and turned.

"Why?" asked the older woman in a surly tone.

"Actually, it's your friend we'd like a word with," replied Glenda. "Perhaps you'd like to step in here if you don't mind?" she continued, smoothly.

The woman looked hesitant.

"What for?" she asked, stalling for time.

"I will explain myself fully if you would just come and sit down with us for a moment," Glenda encouraged.

The woman looked to her friend for a cue.

"Oh, go see what they want," said the older woman, waspishly. "You can tell me about it later," she said as she left the building.

"The reason I asked you to step in here," began Glenda once the woman was seated, "is because we need to ask you a few questions about an incident witnessed by my colleague yesterday. However, before we get to that, we just need to get a few details from you for our records."

After about 10 minutes, it was apparent that the woman, Kelly Wilson, was defensive in the extreme and reluctant to share even the most basic information. After a great deal of coaxing, Diane managed to establish that the little girl was called Ruby and was 22 months old. Ruby's father was an Egyptian, Hanif Hassan. Kelly said that Hanif did not live with them and that she did not know his address or phone number. However, as he was on Ruby's birth certificate, he had parental responsibility.

Diane knew that she would have to locate Hanif and apprise him of the situation. Kelly was only 19 years old and said that she came from Pondsford about 10 miles away. Her most recent partner was called Mohammed and Kelly explained that she had left him due to domestic violence, but claimed not to know his surname. The woman was inappropriately dressed for the cold weather, wearing only a thin dress and a cardigan. Diane could see dark bruises on her legs and noted that she presented as very low in mood and monosyllabic in her responses. After gleaning what information they could, Diane asked Kelly more questions.

"Do you know why we need to talk to you?"

Kelly shook her head.

"Well, if you cast your mind back to the traffic lights up the road at 10 o'clock yesterday, it might jog your memory," said Diane in a level voice.

Kelly screwed up her face as she thought about that. Her response was almost immediate.

"Oh," she managed.

"Yes, that's right," affirmed Diane. "I can see you remember. Can you tell me what was happening?"

Kelly looked around for inspiration, but found none.

"I smacked the baby," she offered.

Diane maintained her gaze on Kelly before responding.

"I think it was a little more serious than that, Kelly. I was in my car and saw what you did, but I'd like you to try and help me understand why that happened."

Kelly looked as if she was considering her options. Diane decided to press her point.

"Kelly, this is a very serious matter. I hope you understand, this won't just go away. You're going to need to cooperate with us in working this out."

Kelly looked at the floor.

"She lost a tenner," the woman replied in a monotone.

"Sorry?" said Diane, perplexed at what she just heard. "She lost a tenner? Can you expand a bit on that, please?"

Kelly finally appeared to understand that the game was up.

She blurted out, "I gave her a tenner to hold and she lost it and I was mad, that's all. I never usually hit her, honest."

Glenda and Diane exchanged weary glances.

"So let me understand," said Diane. "You gave Ruby a 10-pound note to hold onto and she somehow lost it. Is that correct?"

Kelly nodded with a miserable look on her face.

"Okay, I understand now. Thank you, Kelly," said Diane, patiently. "However, since Ruby has been the victim of an assault, the matter will have to be taken further. She will need to go to the hospital for a doctor to check her over. We would prefer to do this with your agreement and you will, of course, be able to go with Ruby and be there with her. Also, we will have to talk to the police who will want to interview you in relation to the matter."

Kelly looked taken aback upon hearing all that.

"No!" she exclaimed, speaking loudly for the first time. "You're gonna take her off me, aren't you?" she continued and began crying.

It took Diane and Glenda over half an hour to calm Kelly enough for her to be able to hear what they were saying. Eventually, with great reluctance, Kelly agreed to go with Diane to the hospital so that Ruby could see a consultant. Glenda rang the hospital and acknowledged that it was very late in the day to be making such a request. However, with gentle persuasion, it was agreed that Ruby should go to the children's ward at 6.30pm for a medical.

When all that was relayed to Kelly, she instantly asked if she could ring up Hanif.

"I thought you didn't know his number," responded Diane, suspiciously.

Kelly looked guilty.

"I forgot I had it," she said, lamely.

Since Hanif had parental responsibility for Ruby, he had a right to be informed. In any event, Diane would still need to speak to him. Within five minutes from the call, Diane heard an angry banging on the front door of the office which had, by then, been locked for the evening.

It was Hanif.

Chapter 13

Jessica Jackson was supposed to be in school, but had once again bunked off. She caught the bus and made the two-mile journey to Moorside on the Deacon Hill estate. Jessica looked around to make sure no one was looking, before making her familiar way to one of the houses over in a corner. She knocked on the door, biting her nails as she waited impatiently. After what seemed like an age, the door opened.

"Hey, Jodie, what's up?" said Jessica. "Is Scott about?"

Jodie looked uneasy.

"Who you with?" she asked, nervously.

Jessica rolled her eyes.

"Do I look like I'm with anyone?" she replied with sarcasm. "Maybe you think there's someone in my pocket? Jesus! Jodie, is he here or not?" Jessica demanded, rudely.

Jodie appeared to think for a moment before answering.

"Yes, he's here, but you mustn't tell anyone. Okay?"

And Jodie opened the door fully to let Jessica in.

~ ~ ~ ~ ~

Glenda and Diane looked at each other as the angry knocking continued.

"It's Hanif," said Kelly with apprehension.

Diane went to the door and after confirming that it was indeed Hanif, she let him in.

Hanif Hassan was an imposing figure. Standing over six feet tall, he strutted importantly into the interview room, ignoring Kelly and Ruby. Hanif then began pacing the floor.

"Somebody better tell me exactly why I'm here and what's going on," he shouted. "And on whose authority is my daughter here?" Hanif demanded, furiously.

Kelly's demeanour changed the minute Hanif walked into the room. She seemed to shrink in size, studied the floor and at no point made eye contact with him. Interestingly, Ruby's behaviour also became markedly different. She became very still, but in direct contrast to her mother, the little girl never took her eyes off her father, watching him intently. Diane and Glenda explained the situation to Hanif, including their plans for Ruby to have a medical. Hanif's face darkened as he listened to what Diane and Glenda had to say, then he turned to Kelly in cold fury.

"You would strike my daughter?" Hanif asked, menacingly. "You will pay for this, woman!" he exclaimed, stepping towards Kelly with his hand raised.

"No!" shouted Glenda, jumping to her feet and moving quickly in front of Kelly. "Stop this at once! I will not tolerate any violent behaviour in this office. Now, Mr Hassan, please come with me into another room and calm yourself."

Hanif lowered his hand and slowly backed away from Kelly.

"This is not over, bitch!" he hissed quietly in her direction while following Glenda out of the room.

Diane understood completely the decision of Glenda to separate Kelly and Hanif from each other. Apart from the obvious risk to Kelly, she would need to establish what Hanif's role was in Ruby's life. She would also need to obtain his contact details, to undertake checks on him.

Diane made a tearful Kelly a drink. She also gave Ruby a biscuit and some juice to keep her going until they got to the hospital. In the other room, Glenda spoke to an arrogant Hanif who refused to give his details. The only thing to which he was prepared to admit was that he lived locally, but he would not give an address. Hanif insisted on being part of the trip to the hospital and as he had parental responsibility for Ruby, Glenda could not refuse his request. One could argue that Hanif's anger was understandable, given that his ex-partner had just assaulted their child. However, Glenda had a gut feeling about Hanif Hassan and it was not a positive one.

~ ~ ~ ~ ~

Jodie went upstairs, leaving Scott alone with Jessica. She knew why Jessica was there and wanted no part of the transaction. Jodie went into the room of Jamie and Courtney, buried her head into one of Courtney's cardigans and wept bitter tears for the loss of her children. She missed them desperately and had no idea when she would get them back. Jodie knew that she was not supposed to have Scott at the house, but he had argued that as the children were not there, no one would bother. Jodie did not have the strength to resist, so when he once again presented himself at her door, she had caved in and allowed him to return.

Jodie knew that the reason Scott continued turning up had nothing to do with his feelings for her, but rather with continuing the lucrative drug business he had been running for many months out of her home. Jodie had lost count of the number of people who went to the house to see Scott 'on business.' She regularly turned a blind eye, afraid of what Scott would do if she dared to object. Since the children had gone to her mother's, Scott seemed happier and less stressed as the social worker no longer went to the house. That gave Scott free reign to peddle his wares without the risk of detection by a nosy social worker.

Downstairs, Scott was striking a deal with Jessica, a fairly new client. Naturally, the negotiations would lean heavily in his favour. Last time around, Scott had dropped Jessica a rock to give her a taste of the quality of the commodities in which he dealt. Scott had no intention of repeating that offer, but Jessica was no novice in the field, either.

"Come on, Scottie," Jessica cajoled, seductively. "Just a gram, for me. I'll pay you well," she grinned, sliding down his legs to her knees.

Scott knew that there were a dozen women on the estate who would sleep with him for a gram of coke. For an eight ball, he could command a week of sex. However, they were neither 15 years old nor were they moving south on him, promising instant gratification.

"Okay, okay," Scott agreed, "but you go first."

Jessica smiled to herself. It was too easy.

~ ~ ~ ~ ~

Diane arrived at the hospital with Hanif, Kelly and Ruby. Glenda had offered to go along, but Diane declined saying there was no point in both of them suffering a late night. She had agreed to ring Glenda the minute there was any information about Ruby's situation.

Diane was on familiar ground as to the process of a child protection medical. As expected, a nurse took blood samples from a reluctant Ruby. She then weighed and measured the little girl before ushering all three adults in to see the paediatric consultant on duty, Dr Norman Woods. Hanif had managed to contain himself well so far, but reminded Diane of a caged lion as he paced the room, hands behind his back, muttering in a foreign language and glaring at Kelly who continued staring at the floor.

Dr Woods had already listened to Diane alone, to understand why Ruby was at the hospital. He considered all the adults and calmly explained his intended actions. He asked Kelly to undress Ruby down to her pants and sit with the girl on her knee. Kelly did as she was told, although it was not easy as Ruby wriggled and protested the whole time.

As Kelly removed Ruby's long-sleeved top, Diane stifled a sharp breath. She could plainly see a host of bruises on her arms and torso. Diane had enough experience and understanding to know that the bruises were of differing ages and even to her untrained eye, one of them looked worryingly like a human bite. Dr Woods showed no emotion as he pointed to a particularly large bruise on Ruby's upper arm.

"How did she come by this?" he asked, evenly.

Kelly adopted a look of complete panic.

"I don't know," she answered.

Dr Woods nodded, wrote a few notes and moved on to the next bruise.

"And this?" he asked.

"Dunno," replied Kelly miserably.

Hanif could contain himself no longer and leapt to his feet.

"You don't know? You don't know? You stupid woman, how can you not know this? You're her mother!" he shouted.

Dr Woods raised his eyebrows.

"Mr Hassan, I will thank you to kindly take a seat and let me do my job."

The face of Hanif Hassan was a mask of rage. Diane could see the struggle he had within himself to become composed. Hanif slowly took his seat as the doctor continued. Ruby's legs were also bruised and her head was infested with lice. On being asked once again how Ruby had come by the bruises, Kelly mumbled something about the girl having fallen off a toy box.

Eventually the ordeal was over. Dr Woods asked both parents to step out of the room while he discussed his findings with Diane. A nurse accompanied Hanif and Kelly outside and sat with them, to reduce the risk of further arguments and threats.

Dr Woods removed his glasses, rubbed his eyes and shook his head.

"Well, Diane," he began, "I'm afraid there is no doubt. These bruises are not accidental. There's too many of them and none in places where children would be expected to get accidental bruises from rough-and-tumble play. The mother has no reasonable explanation and of particular concern is the one at the top of the girl's forearm which, in my opinion, is an adult bite mark. Ruby will need to be admitted tonight for a full skeletal survey and more tests. Tomorrow, we will get the police surgeon in to photograph and catalogue the injuries in detail."

Diane considered the enormity of that revelation and dreaded telling the parents. However, it was part of the doctor's role to explain his findings to Ruby's parents, so he requested that they return to the office. As Dr Woods repeated his conclusions, Hanif's temper exploded.

"No!" he shouted. "My daughter will not remain here. She will come home with me," Hanif declared in a very loud voice, tapping his chest in case there was any confusion as to intent.

"Mr Hassan," replied Dr Woods, "you do not understand. Your daughter has injuries for which we do not have a reasonable explanation. She cannot be permitted to return home tonight. Ms Foster will keep you informed of developments, but for now Ruby must remain here. I'm sure you understand and wish to cooperate."

Hanif Hassan might well have understood, but he had no desire to cooperate. Eyes blazing, he grabbed Ruby from her startled mother.

Then Hanif declared, "We leave," and strode to the door.

What followed happened rapidly. Diane instinctively jumped up to prevent Ruby from being removed. She stood in the doorway and put her hands up, palms facing, as Hanif Hassan moved towards her.

"You cannot leave," she said, firmly. "Mr Hassan, Ruby must stay here."

Diane could as well have talked to the wall. Hanif Hassan lashed out at the social worker, but thanks to her quick reflexes only struck her a glancing blow on the arm. However, it was enough to knock her out of the way. Hanif marched off with Ruby, Kelly following right behind.

Diane looked at Dr Woods who after enquiring if she was okay, wisely advised, "Let them go, Diane. They won't get far."

Diane was not hurt, but shaken. She still had her wits about her and immediately got her mobile phone out and dialled 999. As she was connected to the police, Diane followed Hanif and Kelly as they made their way to the hospital exit. Speaking to the operator, she was able to give a detailed description of both adults and of Ruby. Diane urged the operator to ask the police to hurry and was assured they had been dispatched. She was advised to wait at the entrance to the children's ward and meet the police there.

After what seemed like hours, although in reality it was only about three minutes, a squad car arrived.

"That way," called Diane immediately to the officers who stepped out of the car. "They went that way, down Blackrock Hill," she explained with urgency.

The police officer who approached Diane held up his hands.

"Don't worry, Miss," he reassured. "We have a roadblock in progress and there's a chopper in the air. They won't be going anywhere."

Diane stood open-mouthed at the impressive response her 999 call had provoked. Seeing her surprise, the officer explained.

"There's a football match on tonight and all the police cars are already in the area. When we got the call to say that a child had been abducted, it triggered a code red response and everyone was deployed straight away."

The officer was correct. Diane heard the familiar sound of a helicopter's rotor blades and within five minutes a police van pulled up. Inside was a hysterical Kelly clinging to a wide-eyed, but silent, Ruby. Hanif Hassan was in handcuffs, having been arrested for assaulting a police officer.

With Hanif on his way to the police station, Kelly and Ruby were taken to the children's ward. It took a soft-spoken police officer a full 45 minutes to talk Kelly into letting go of Ruby. Diane had managed to give Ruby a drink during her ordeal as she watched the little girl get hotter and hotter, as her mother held fast to her and refused to loosen her vice-like grip. Eventually, with promises of being allowed to remain overnight with

Ruby, Kelly finally let the girl go. Ruby had broken out in a heat rash as a result of being held tightly for so long, so nurses quickly took over and made her comfortable.

Diane had been in critical discussions with Glenda who was horrified to hear about the night's events.

"Are you sure you're okay, Diane?" the manager asked in concern after hearing that Diane had been assaulted by Hanif. "I knew I should have come with you. Now, you be sure and press charges, do you hear me?" she insisted.

Diane assured Glenda that she was fine, but extremely troubled in case one or both of the parents tried removing Ruby from the hospital. Without a court order or police protection, the staff would be powerless to prevent Ruby from being taken home. Glenda agreed.

"We can't get into court until tomorrow afternoon at the earliest," Glenda said, going into crisis intervention mode, "and that's if we're lucky. So we'll have to ask the police to use their powers to keep her safe for tonight."

The police agreed that, under the circumstances, they would use the powers invested in them to keep Ruby under their protection. It was just as well for once he had been processed, Hanif returned three hours later brandishing Ruby's passport and demanding that the nurses hand her over. He was arrested again, but would remain in custody all night long.

Chapter 14

By the time Ruby was settled in and Kelly had been persuaded to leave, it was late. Diane arrived home around midnight with instructions from Glenda not to go in the next day until at least 10 o'clock. She knew that was impossible and would be at work early, considering that she would have to go to court and get an order, to keep Ruby in the care of the local authority. *Ten o'clock,* Diane thought, wistfully. *I wish!*

She was still high on adrenaline and knew that sleep would evade her. Diane allowed herself a small glass of wine and wished with all her heart that Ethan was with her at that moment. He would have wrapped his strong arms around her, making her feel better. He would also have gone into protective mode. He would have been very angry and, no doubt, would have made threats of permanent harm to Hanif. Diane thought of how Ethan's eyes used to change colour when he was annoyed. She smiled at that memory.

Diane sighed and put all thoughts of Ethan out of her head. Instead, she spent time trying, in vain, to organise the children on her caseload into some sort of priority list. She got as far as organising the legal meeting for the Ellis family then came unstuck. Diane knew she had so many responsibilities demanding her time and attention that she was in danger of overload. She made an effort to focus and think through all the cases – really difficult with everything that had just occurred. Although hostile and resentful, the Waleed family were cooperating, so their case was not as high on her list of priorities as it had been in the previous few weeks.

Diane felt a stab of guilt as she realised that she had not seen Gemma and Liam Powell and their four children for at least two weeks. Liam's brother, Morris Powell, was a serious sex offender with convictions for offences against young children. It had reached Diane's attention through Morris's probation worker that he had been a regular visitor to the home of Gemma and Liam. The couple were aware of the convictions of

Morris, but did not believe him guilty. That made it impossible for them to effectively protect their children from potentially becoming victims as they did not believe he was capable of such heinous acts. Diane knew that a follow-up visit was required in the very near future, to make sure Morris Powell was no longer visiting.

On the subject of sex offenders, there was also the new case involving Malcolm Withers which Glenda had given her the other day. Diane knew that she needed to contact the child protection unit of the police and arrange a visit soon. It was all piling up into one big mess. When Diane finally fell into bed it was almost 2.00am. She went into an immediate, exhausted sleep.

~ ~ ~ ~ ~

Shanice Ellis picked herself up off the floor and went to the bathroom. The face which stared back at her was not her own. She had a black eye and a cut lip. Her nose was bleeding and a clump of hair was missing from the side of her head. Shanice touched her face and wept. She knew that she was trapped and rued the day she had met Grant Ellis.

Shanice had been a successful beautician with a good job in a salon in the nearby town of Blenton. Grant's sister, Louise, had been a regular visitor to the salon and introduced her to Grant. Shanice had been impressed with his 6' 2" frame and rugged good looks, not to mention his charm. As an added bonus, he ran a construction business and was not short of money.

Grant had been loving and attentive to Shanice when they first met. He swept her off her feet, showered her with gifts and flowers, and took her to dinner every few nights. It was a whirlwind romance and he had proposed to her at midnight one Christmas Eve. Shanice had said *yes,* never suspecting that her fairy-tale romance would evolve into a nightmare.

The changes had initially been so small as to be almost insignificant: a complaint about her cooking, followed by a teasing laugh and an accusation that she was sulking. A comment about how Shanice was dressed for an evening out, accompanied by a seemingly innocent suggestion of how she might prefer to dress when she went out with him. Then came the objection to her working, with the argument that she did not need to work as Grant provided a good living for them both. Eventually, but reluctantly, Shanice had given up her job and devoted herself to being a full-time home-maker. Grant then started openly disapproving of her regular visits to her mother who lived 10 miles away, stating that it was taking up too much of her time. The same argument was used to curtail Shanice's trips into town for coffee with friends. Worn down by constant criticism, Grant had finally succeeded in isolating Shanice, then announced that he was ready to start a family – the final nail in the coffin.

Grant's first assault had occurred when Shanice was pregnant with Tia. She had been tired due to severe morning sickness. Grant made sexual advances, but Shanice said *no* – what followed changed everything forever. Grant attacked Shanice with such ferocity that she had feared for her life. After he finished, Shanice lay in shock on the bedroom floor, shaking and covered in her own blood. Grant had dragged Shanice to her feet and told her to go and get cleaned up.

"Don't ever make me do that again," he warned.

Grant had, of course, done it again – repeatedly. Shanice did not dare tell anyone, not even her own mother, for fear of what Grant could do. However, the walls were thin and the neighbours called the police on them more than one occasion, eventually leading to the intervention of Social Services.

Grant had been furious at that and blamed Shanice. She tried desperately to put on a brave face, but knew that she was reaching breaking point.

111

Grant also started picking on the children. Only the previous week, he had hit their six-year-old son, DJ, across the back of the head when the latter failed to answer his father's question quickly enough. Shanice studied her battered face and wept some more.

~ ~ ~ ~ ~

It was 8.30am and a tired, weary Diane hoped to catch Kirsty Thompson at home before she went to work. However, all the curtains were drawn again and there were no signs of life, apart from the inevitable barking of the dog which Diane fancied were more subdued than those of the other day. The social worker left another note, saying that she would return the next day at 2.00pm. In a way, Diane was relieved that Kirsty was not home as she had an unenviable amount of work waiting for her.

First on the agenda was to prepare all the necessary paperwork to apply for the court order for Ruby. Although the girl was currently safe in the hospital under police protection, the latter would expire after 72 hours and alternative measures for Ruby's safety were necessary. The local authority intended to apply for an interim care order which would give them shared parental responsibility for Ruby, allowing them to make decisions such as to where and with whom she could live. If the court agreed, the interim order would last a maximum of eight weeks and thereafter be renewed every 28 days.

That was, however, a temporary order. If it was deemed untenable for Ruby to remain with her family, such an order would become a full-blown care order which would, in practice, lead eventually to Ruby's adoption, but not before a lengthy legal process took place and which could take up to 12 months. However, before making such a grave and irreversible decision, Diane knew that the court would quite rightly demand lengthy and detailed reports. Some of those would come from the local authority and some from experts such as psychologists or psychiatrists agreed upon by the court. There would inevitably be a parenting assessment of both parents, to establish their suitability to continue caring for Ruby. Diane would be expected to locate as many family members as she possibly could, to see if they wished to put themselves forwards as potential carers. She would have to undertake viability assessments which could be highly complex minefields, requiring great tact and skill on the part of the assessor. The danger of placing a child within his or her own family was that the family member might collude with the parents, allowing them unsupervised access and placing the child at ongoing risk of additional harm.

The police would be asked to share any information they had on either parent. That would include a national search of all police databases in case Hanif or Kelly had lived elsewhere and committed criminal offences in other areas. Diane would need to undertake checks with other local authority areas where the parents had lived, to establish whether or not they were known to them and, if so, why. Also importantly, she needed to find out if either Hanif or Kelly had other children living elsewhere as they would similarly have to be considered at risk.

Diane tried not to allow panic to rise within her as she realised just how much she had to do on that one case alone. She knew with gut-wrenching certainty that all her other cases would suffer as a result. Visits would have to be cancelled. Children whom she was supposed to see would not be seen until the next week or the week after. Diane pushed all these thoughts away from her mind and concentrated on the job at hand.

Diane's first phone call was to the legal department of the local authority, to ask them to make the necessary arrangements with the court and give them a brief synopsis of the reasons for the urgent application. She spoke to Marcus Edwards: a serious, up-and-coming young solicitor who was rapidly gaining a reputation for being a formidable opponent in the courtroom. Marcus listened intently to what Diane had to say before speaking.

"Well, Diane," Marcus said, crisply. "It is highly apparent that the threshold criteria have been met in this case. Leave it with me and I'll do what I can to get it before a judge today."

Diane smiled at his efficiency. She had no doubt that the matter would be in court before the close of that business day. Diane was about to request police checks on Hanif and Kelly when an ashen-faced Glenda suddenly appeared.

"Diane," said Glenda, quietly. "You need to come into my office, please."

Diane felt a chill. Rarely had she seen Glenda so upset. Once in the office, she realised that it must be really serious as the police were also present.

"What's going on?" Diane asked, unable to wait for someone to speak.

A poker-faced officer who introduced himself as Detective Sergeant Martin Bell told Diane without ceremony that they suspected that Nahla Waleed had somehow managed to leave the country with Zarifa, possibly as long as two days before. Diane's mouth dropped open as she let out a cry.

"No!" she exclaimed with vehemence. "No, no, no! How could this happen? You have their passports," she said almost accusingly to DS Bell.

The explanation was almost too incredible to be true. Bell explained that they thought Nahla had used her own sister's passport to travel – they were identical twins – as the daughter of the latter was the same age as Zarifa and also on the passport. If an official had not looked too closely, she could have got through. Mr Waleed had been arrested as an accessory to the fact and the remaining children were placed under police protection.

"We need foster placements for the other four children," said Glenda, bringing Diane out of the trance-like state into which she had gone. "Unfortunately, Diane, we will have to do this right now as at this moment in time, the children are at the police station which, of course, is not acceptable."

DS Bell raised his eyebrows.

"You're not kidding. It's *not* acceptable," he told the manager. "They can't stay with us, Glenda. They're going to have to come here. We can't babysit four kids – that's your job."

Glenda raised her hands in protest, but knew that he was right.

"Okay," she replied, tersely. "Bring them here and we'll get one of our family workers to sit with them in the contact room."

Glenda knew that it was not an ideal solution, but there was nothing else they could do under the circumstances.

"Diane," prompted Glenda. "Foster placements?"

"What?" said Diane, absently.

Her mind was still reeling from the awful news.

"Oh, yes, of course; foster placements. I'll get on it," Diane responded.

Glenda moved to her desk and began making the relevant phone calls.

"Given the emergency, we'll need to get into court for an EPO and hope to get a recovery order too," Glenda said in her usual, business-like manner, "which I'm confident we'll get, but you need to get onto legal as a priority," she added almost apologetically. "Ask Helen to help you with all the paperwork for the foster placements. She's on duty today."

Diane left Martin Bell talking to Glenda about their plan of action. They would involve Interpol and hope to pick up Nahla and Zarifa before any harm came to the girl, but it was a vain hope. Diane tried not to think about the horrors which awaited the little girl.

The EPO was an emergency protection order which was necessary to place the remaining children in foster care. It would only last for eight days, after which they would apply for an interim care order. Hopefully, the court would issue the EPO without too much debate since it was a genuine emergency. They would also be asked to attach a recovery order, to order the return of Zarifa to England – if and when she was found.

Diane went straight to work. Once again, she phoned up the legal department of the local authority and spoke to the lawyer.

"Hey, Marcus," Diane began, "you're not going to believe this. We've got another emergency which needs immediate attention. It's going to have to take priority over Ruby."

Diane gave Marcus the bald facts of the case which, once again, he agreed were more than enough to request a court order.

"You don't do things by halves, do you, Diane?" Marcus said without a hint of sarcasm as he hung up.

Diane then followed Glenda's suggestion and asked her colleague, Helen, to assist in filling out the paperwork for the remaining four Waleed children. That was no small task as each child required their own individual application. The forms were understandably detailed and among other things, they had to input all the children's routines, likes and dislikes, as well as any medical, religious, cultural, emotional or

116

behavioural needs. Diane was expected to know if they posed a risk to any potential carer. She also had to know about their criminal histories, if any. As Diane did not have all that information about the children, a lot of those details would have to be left out under the proviso *to be added at a later date*. All that would cause understandable frustration for the fostering team who would use the information in the forms to make the best possible match with families who would care for the children. Most importantly, there had to be medical consent usually given by a parent. However, under the circumstances, the area manager of the local authority would sign – if they got the court order.

As Helen began filling out the forms, Diane rang up the fostering team who specialised in identifying foster placements for children.

"We won't be able to place them together," warned her colleague.

"I didn't think for a minute that you would," said Diane with understanding.

Placing children together was nigh on impossible due to the lack of suitable family placements. Most people who fostered wanted one or, at the most, two children. Sadly, most people only wanted to foster babies or young children. Finding someone who could care for three or more children from the same family was almost unheard of.

Diane knew that by law, she had a duty to see if the children could be placed within their own family before considering foster carers. She would make enquiries whether there was, for example, a suitable aunt or grandmother. However, as it was highly likely that the entire family had colluded in Nahla Waleed's flight from England, Diane had no intention of involving them and hoped that the judge would see it in the same way.

Chapter 15

Nahla Waleed had bundled her daughter into a taxi and urged her to hurry up. It was just after midnight and Zarifa had been woken from a deep sleep by her mother's voice compelling her to get up. She was hastily dressed and pushed into the waiting taxi before she had the time to ask where they were going. Her father had kissed her on the forehead and bid her goodbye, telling her to be a good girl for her mother.

Nahla now sat beside Zarifa in the taxi. She was restless and uneasy; a light sheen of sweat was visible on her upper lip. Nahla had left the minimum time to get to the airport on schedule for the long trip to Khartoum. There would be a stopover in Istanbul which would be the critical time. If the authorities realised that she had fled England, they would deduce that she was taking that particular route into Sudan – she feared that would be where her plans could come to a premature finale.

Nahla Waleed had been vigorously encouraged by her husband to make the trip to Sudan, so that their daughter could undergo the necessary ritual ceremony so important to their culture. However, Nahla had also found a zealous accomplice in her sister, Faheema. As identical twins, they had taken each other's part many times over the years. As the cleverer twin, Faheema had doubled for Nahla in oral tests in school, with teachers being none the wiser. On other occasions, Faheema and Nahla had fooled even their own parents when either one of them had a date and needed to escape for a few hours. However, the game plan at hand was by far their most ambitious attempt at subterfuge, yet Nahla was truly afraid that it was doomed to failure.

Putting those fears away from her mind, Nahla focused on the mission ahead. She could not contemplate the notion of failure. She would simply have to get Zarifa to Sudan as the alternative was unthinkable. Nahla shook her head to dispel the notion. She would never live to bear the shame of having a daughter who would be considered unmarriageable in their culture unless she underwent the ceremony of circumcision. Nahla and Faheema had undergone the ritual together – only fitting, given their relationship. It was not a day Nahla wished to dwell on and she trembled at the sheer memory of it. However, she knew that her daughter, Zarifa, would have to endure it or be shunned and reviled by her own community. No, Nahla knew that she needed to succeed and spoke sharply to the driver, urging him on.

~ ~ ~ ~ ~

"Time to go, Di," called Glenda from the door.

Diane glanced at the clock and groaned. *Was it really 12 o'clock, already?* She knew that Glenda was right. They had to leave right away, to make the short trip to the county courthouse for the scheduled 2.00pm hearing about the four Waleed children.

It had been agreed by senior management that due to Ruby's current status under police protection and safe in the hospital, her case would be put before the court the following day, allowing them additional time to prepare for the more urgent matter of the Waleed children. By sheer hard work and determination, Diane and Helen had managed to complete all the paperwork and secure foster placements for all four children. It was nothing short of miraculous. Naturally, the children would be separated, but Diane was amazed that they pulled it off at all. She had managed to keep the two youngest children together, but the older two boys would be placed individually. It was the best they could have hoped for and she was counting on the judge agreeing. There was little choice, given there was absolutely nowhere else to place them and the children were, at that moment, seated in the family room at Cedar House.

Diane's role in court was fairly simple. The case would be put before His Honour, Judge William Glendinning, by the solicitor of the local authority, Marcus Edwards. Diane would only have to give evidence if the judge required it or was unclear on some point. Mr Waleed was also present, accompanied by two grim-faced police officers who sat at the rear of the courtroom. He was represented by an equally stern-faced barrister, Ashraf Hakim, who had been hired hastily and at great cost to Waleed's affluent brother.

Ashraf Hakim sat by his client, consulted his leather-bound notebook and leaned over to whisper something. Waleed nodded. However, he seemed to be in a daze, not really comprehending what was being said.

"All rise," came the commanding voice of the clerk of the court as Judge Glendinning swept into the room.

"Here we go," thought Diane as she respectfully rose to her feet.

~ ~ ~ ~ ~

Six-year-old DJ Ellis woke up to the all-too-familiar sound of raised voices. He pulled the duvet over his head and tried not to listen. However, the voices grew louder and were more urgent than usual.

DJ was afraid. He crept out of bed and went quietly into his big sister's room. Ten-year-old Tia was also awake and trying to ignore the all-too-familiar, raging argument taking place downstairs in the neat and tidy front room of their home. In the bedroom next door, eight-year-old Kaz and two-year-old Darcy slept on unawares.

Tia sat up quickly when DJ entered her room.

"What are you doing?" she hissed in fear. "Go back to bed. You'll be for it if Dad sees you."

DJ considered that for a moment. Until recently, his father had been his hero. Daddy always had time to play football with DJ and listen to him read and everything. However, lately Daddy was different – as if he was always cross. That confused DJ who did not know what he had done to make his dad so angry.

DJ's bewilderment had peaked the previous week when out of the blue, he felt a sharp pain across the back of his head and realised in horror that his dad had actually hit him. Tears blurred his eyes as he sought an explanation for the assault. However, Grant had just shouted at DJ and sent him back to his room. The boy was still none the wiser as to why he had been hit and the experience had left him feeling anxious and sad. Like all his siblings, DJ knew that Daddy hit Mummy, but that was something no one ever talked about – well, no one apart from Grant who told them sternly that they were *never* to talk to anyone, especially the social worker, about anything that happened at home. His warning that they would be taken away and never see Mummy and Daddy again was an effective silencer.

"I know," said DJ, "but I'm scared, Tia. What's going on?"

As the oldest child, Tia felt a crushing responsibility to keep her younger siblings safe and protected from the worst of what she knew went on in the house. Tia had walked in on her mother more than once after Grant had beaten up Shanice. She had seen for herself the damage he repeatedly did, not only physically, but emotionally. Her mother had often sobbed in pain as she tried to hide the bruises from Tia. Mummy had hugged her tightly and told her daughter how much she loved her.

Shanice kept saying, "I'm so sorry, Tia. I'm so sorry, it was never meant to be like this," over and over again.

Tia had a constantly funny feeling in her tummy which at her tender age, she did not recognise as stress.

"Okay, we'll go to the top of the stairs, but that's all," agreed Tia in hushed tones. "Don't make a sound," she warned.

DJ nodded solemnly and followed Tia along the landing. He hunkered down beside her and peered through the balustrade.

Grant and Shanice Ellis were in the living room, oblivious to the furtive, unseen audience above. Grant had been drinking and was grabbing Shanice by the hair. He had taken offence when she objected to his putting on the football on television, asking if they could perhaps watch a movie together.

"You need to learn, woman!" Grant raged without reason as he grabbed his wife. "I pay the bills in this house. I'll be the one to decide what gets watched, not you!"

Shanice opened her mouth to deliver her customary apology, but before she had time to speak, Grant slapped her across the mouth and grabbed her hair. Shanice tasted the sharp, metallic blood which sprang from her tongue as she bit it. Perhaps it was the fact that she was so tired – or perhaps she had just plain had enough. Something in Shanice gave way. She felt something within her snap and for the first time in years, found herself thinking clearly – crystal clear. Shanice pulled free from Grant's drunken, grasping hands and moved as though on automatic pilot. It was like an out-of-body experience as she went into the kitchen. Shanice watched herself from afar as she opened the cutlery drawer and returned to the lounge where Grant continued berating her.

"Don't you fucking walk away from me, you whore!" he roared. "My mother was right, I never should have married you!"

It was the last insult Grant Ellis would ever utter. Despite Tia's warnings to keep silent, DJ could not help himself.

"Daddy!" he cried piteously as he witnessed the unfolding drama.

Tia stared in abject terror and put her hand on her own mouth to stifle the scream as she watched her mother bring her arm down – again and again and again.

~ ~ ~ ~ ~

"Your Honour, if I may?" Marcus began in polished tones. "Today, the local authority is seeking emergency protection orders in the matter of 15-year-old Raheem, 13-year-old Umar, nine-year-old Aman and four-year-old Farida Waleed."

Marcus then spent a few succinct minutes detailing Nahla Waleed's suspected flight from England and the impending ceremony which awaited Zarifa in Sudan, were she not to be recovered. Judge Glendinning adopted a sombre look as he listened intently to the lawyer's delivery.

"As Mr Hafiz Waleed is being held in custody, Your Honour, and with no suitable family members identified, the local authority has managed to secure foster placements for all four children as of today and requests the court's agreement to proceed in this matter," Marcus concluded.

Judge Glendinning looked at counsel for Mr Waleed.

"Mr Hakim?" he enquired, inviting the opposing barrister to make his arguments.

"Yes, Your Honour," began Ashraf Hakim, consulting his notebook. "At this point in time, the local authority do not have a shred of evidence to substantiate their argument that Nahla Waleed actually fled the country. While I concede that her sister, Faheema, has indeed taken a flight to Khartoum as indicated by passport records, the actual whereabouts of Nahla Waleed and her daughter, Zarifa, are unclear. It appears to me that the local authority has acted prematurely in this matter and I invite the court to reject their application and return these four traumatised children back into the care of their loving father. Your Honour, all the children are, as we speak, seated in the area office of the local authority and must be wondering what is happening. It is untenable," he concluded, stiffly.

"Your Honour," rebutted Marcus Edwards with great conviction, "it is the opinion of the police and the local authority that Nahla Waleed used her sister's passport to flee the country. As an identical twin, this is an incredible, but entirely plausible, explanation. The local authority and the police have been involved with Mr and Mrs Waleed with the sole purpose of preventing Zarifa from being taken to Sudan for the barbaric ritual ceremony of female genital circumcision. I conclude that in the absence of Mrs Waleed and Zarifa, the only explanation as to where they might be at this moment is Sudan. If this is not the case, I would invite my learned colleague to offer an alternative explanation as to the whereabouts of Mrs Waleed and her daughter."

"Counsel," asked Judge Glendinning, his eyebrows raised as he focussed on Mr Waleed's barrister, "I'm sure you are about to explain to this court exactly where Mrs Waleed and her daughter are?"

Ashraf Hakim wavered for the first time – a hesitation not wasted on Marcus Edwards. Seizing the opportunity, the latter stood up.

"Your Honour, may I?" Marcus asked, respectfully.

The judge inclined his head.

"I wish somebody would," he agreed, sardonically.

"Your Honour, I suggest that Mr Hakim is fully aware of Mrs Waleed's and Zarifa's real location which I fear is not in this country. I would, therefore, invite the court to put an end to this charade and agree with the petition to place all four children in an immediate place of safety until the police have further investigated the matter. As we speak, they are in urgent discussions with Interpol who are employing all available resources into locating this child."

Judge Glendinning fixed both legal representatives with a level gaze.

"Gentlemen," he said finally, "the court will take a 30 minute recess while I give consideration to this grave matter."

With that the judge stood up and strode determinedly out of the court. The clerk was taken off guard by the judge's sudden departure. He delivered a belated *All rise* just as the judge reached the door.

True to his word, Judge Glendinning returned 30 minutes later. All eyes were fastened on him for his judgement.

"It is the decision of this court," the judge said solemnly, "that unless Nahla and Zarifa Waleed are presented to this court within one hour, the local authority will be granted emergency protection orders in respect of 15-year-old Raheem, 13-year-old Umar, nine-year-old Aman and four-year-old Farida Waleed. All four children will then be placed in the care of the local authority while further investigations are undertaken."

The judge paused for four seconds then added soberly to a startled looking counsel, "You heard me, Mr Hakim. One hour."

And Judge Glendinning was gone. Diane turned to Marcus and looked at him with incredulity.

"So what? We wait?" she said in amazement.

Diane had never heard a judgement like it before. Marcus adopted a mournful look.

126

"It would seem so," he lamented. "The judge has basically called their bluff and given the barrister and Mr Waleed the opportunity to make good on their assurance that they are still in the country. If, as we suspect, they have fled, then you get your order. Meantime, the children sit tight."

Diane phoned the decision through to an astonished Glenda.

"Well, okay," said Glenda. "I guess we just have to wait, but I feel for those kids."

Ashram Hakim hurried his client into a private anteroom for urgent discussion. The two police officers waited outside. Diane got herself a strong cup of coffee from the court's vending machine and joined Marcus in a separate room where they sat and waited.

"I know she's not in England," said Diane with certainty, sipping her coffee and pulling a face at the vending machine taste. "I know it, they know it and the judge knows it."

Marcus nodded.

"I'm sure you're right, Diane," he agreed, "but Judge Glendinning is nobody's fool and he has thrown down the gauntlet. Hakim is right in saying that we don't actually have any firm evidence to prove that Mrs Waleed has actually taken Zarifa out of the country. But the judge isn't going to risk delaying her recovery for long, which is why he made the unusual judgement."

For Diane, the wait was almost intolerable. After 45 minutes, a smug-looking Ashram Hakim knocked on their door and asked to speak to Marcus.

"I have succeeded in locating Nahla Waleed," Hakim said with undisguised satisfaction. "She is, as we speak, on her way to court. It is my intention to request a 30 minute extension on the judge's one hour window, to allow her to get here."

Diane's mouth dropped open.

"What?" she exclaimed. "You found her? What about Zarifa?"

Ashram Hakim looked at Diane with great contempt, ignored her and addressed Marcus.

"The child also," he said and strode out of the room.

Under the circumstances, Judge Glendinning agreed to wait for Mrs Waleed and Zarifa to arrive. It was with great anticipation that Diane and Marcus waited to be called back into the courtroom. Finally, the time arrived and everyone was instructed by an increasingly flustered clerk to reassemble.

As soon as Diane went in, she scanned the courtroom. Sure enough, there was a woman, with a child of Zarifa's age, seated next to Ashram Hakim. However, Diane could not see the child's face as the mother had covered her head with a scarf which obscured it. The social worker became immediately suspicious. *Something was not right. But, surely, they wouldn't try . . . no, it was too far-fetched!*

"Mr Hakim," boomed Judge Glendinning with a trace of skepticism, "it would appear that you have managed to pull the proverbial rabbit out of the hat. Am I to understand that this is Nahla Waleed and that this child is Zarifa Waleed?"

Ashram Hakim stood up to address the judge.

"Indeed it is, Your Honour. As it turns out, Mrs Waleed went to visit her cousin in the adjoining town, but failed to tell her husband where she had

128

gone. However, after several phone calls within the family, we managed to find them safe and sound."

Diane continued staring at the woman and the child. She knew that she was being played and her mind worked overtime. Inspired, she leaned over to Marcus and whispered something. The latter nodded and stood up.

"Your Honour," Marcus began, "Ms Foster is the allocated social worker for this family and with the court's permission, I request that she be permitted to address Mrs Waleed."

Judge Glendinning thought for a moment.

"Mr Edwards, as I understand it, you are acting counsel for the local authority. If there are any questions for Mrs Waleed, you may ask them."

"Of course, Your Honour," said Marcus. "Mrs Waleed, could you please tell the court what arrangements Ms Foster made with you the last time she saw you? Specifically, when is her next visit to be?" he asked, pleasantly.

The woman looked nervously at Ashram Hakim, then at the floor.

"Mrs Waleed," prompted the judge, "please answer the question."

The woman sought inspiration from the ceiling and the walls of the courtroom.

"I cannot recall," she said.

Marcus continued, "Well, perhaps you can recall what was discussed between you and Ms Foster on her last visit to you? Surely, that has not slipped your mind?" he pressed.

Again the woman looked anxiously at Mr Hakim and shook her head.

"I cannot bring these details to mind," she replied, angrily. "She comes to my house and tells me what I can and cannot do, that is all I know."

Marcus raised his eyebrows theatrically.

"Your Honour," Marcus said, "it is the opinion of the local authority that this woman is not Nahla Waleed, neither is this child Zarifa Waleed. It is our strong opinion that this is Nahla Waleed's twin sister who has been a co-conspirator, scheming and plotting to enable her sister to flee to Sudan. I strongly suggest that this is Faheema Waleed, the one whom the police suspect has given Nahla Waleed her passport. This child is her own daughter who is of similar age and appearance to Zarifa. Your Honour, the entire family has colluded together with the sole purpose of duping the police and the local authority, with the intent of subjecting a seven-year-old child to an act of unimaginable, unnecessary cruelty."

Judge Glendinning adopted a look of restrained anger.

"Counsel," he said with sharpness to Ashram Hakim, "explain yourself. Is this correct?"

Ashram Hakim tried to continue with the charade.

"Your Honour," responded Hakim in wounded tones, "I can assure you that my colleague's imagination is getting the better of him. All this talk of subterfuge and plots is distressing for my clients. You can see here before you Mrs Nahla Waleed and Zarifa, and I implore the court to be done with this nonsense and dismiss this application."

Diane was rapidly running out of patience. She had met Nahla Waleed's twin sister and her own children on more than one occasion. Despite the risk of being in contempt of court, Diane called out.

"Tahani."

Immediately, the child looked at Diane despite the mother's quick hand of restraint. The interaction was not wasted on the judge who followed it up.

"Tahani, is it?" said Judge Glendinning directly to the child. Then he added, "Be quiet, madam," to the mother who was attempting to shush the little girl. "Tahani. Is that your name?" he asked the little girl, kindly.

At seven years old and in the face of such a stern, important grown-up, the child nodded. It was over.

"Mr Hakim," said the judge. "In my chambers. *Now!*"

Chapter 16

Diane was dreaming about Ethan when the sound of the alarm interrupted her rudely. He had been making love to her and it took Diane some time to realise that it was just a dream, it felt so real. His touch had been almost tangible and she fought back the tears which threatened, which she knew resulted from her emotional state.

Diane was exhausted and completely overwhelmed with the avalanche of work she still had to complete. This day would be no different. She forced herself to get up and complete her morning routine. Mojo was highly offended to be passed over and meowed indignantly as Diane left the house without her usual, cheery salutation. She drove to work on autopilot with an all-too-familiar, thumping headache and a knot at the base of her stomach. Mojo retired to his bed in an aloof feline sulk. He would ignore Diane for the next two days in retribution.

The previous night had been harrowing. After the debacle in court which could have come straight out of a soap on television, Diane and Helen had taken the four Waleed children to their foster placements. It had, as usual, been traumatic both for the children and the social workers. It was never easy taking children away from the care of their parents and placing them in the homes of total strangers. In an ideal world, the children would have gone to a family member, but in light of the collusion within the family, the judge had wholeheartedly agreed with the local authority that there was too great a risk of the entire family fleeing England in a misplaced show of solidarity.

Helen had taken the two older boys to separate placements. Fifteen-year-old Raheem showed incredible maturity and self-restraint. He retained his composure and was polite and well-mannered. Raheem's concern was for his younger siblings. He wept and clung to them when they had to leave the office and urged them to be good. All the children cried and asked to go with Raheem. It had been immensely difficult to restore calm once Raheem and Umar left with Helen. Diane could not help thinking that despite their failings, Mr and Mrs Waleed must have done something right in raising such children who were all a credit to them.

Helen took Raheem to John and Deborah Young, a middle-aged couple who specialised in caring for teenagers. Raheem's dignified behaviour continued as he thanked the couple for taking him into their home and made no fuss when Helen left. He did, however, hug his brother, assure him of his love and urge him to display good behaviour in honour of their parents.

Helen then made her final stop of the night at the home of Cindy Plummer. Cindy was a 35-year-old, single carer approved for just one child up to the age of 13 years. According to the approval, Cindy could only care for girls, but due to the lack of suitable placements, the area manager had agreed that she could care for Umar. It was further agreed that it would be a temporary measure. The local authority would continue trying to identify a more suitable placement for Umar, but that would take time. The boy had been understandably detached and somewhat embarrassed at being cared for by a single woman. Helen did her best to reassure him, but given Umar's dignified silence, she felt that it was in vain. Helen left Cindy trying to engage Umar in a discussion as to what he might like to eat and what he liked to watch on television. Helen did not envy Cindy one bit and made her weary way home.

While Helen was busy with the two older boys, Diane took Aman and Farida to Tom and Pat Pendleton, a kind and homely couple in their 50's. The Pendletons had just moved a six-year-old Somali child on to an adoptive placement, so they had some experience caring for a child of another culture. Tom and Pat were approved for two children up to the age of 10 years. However, due to their previous child moving to an adoptive placement, they had not taken a second child in so as not to disrupt him. Diane knew how lucky Social Services had been in the timing of this placement. People like the Pendletons never had space and to find a home with two spaces available was almost unheard of.

The couple welcomed the frightened, younger Waleed siblings with open arms. Diane stayed until the children had seen their individual bedrooms and were given something to eat and drink. As usual, she had ascertained ahead of time what food the children liked and disliked. As the family were devout Muslims, the Pendletons and the other foster carers had been made aware of the dietary and cultural issues which they would need to observe and respect. When it was time to go, Aman remained withdrawn and silent, refusing to speak. However, four-year-old Farida ran to Diane and held onto her tightly.

"It's okay, Farida," Diane said softly. "Tom and Pat will take good care of you. I will come and see you soon and arrange for you to see Daddy as soon as possible."

Whenever children were placed in foster care, the local authority had a duty to promote contact between the children and their parents unless the circumstances were particularly extreme. The contact was always supervised by professionals and usually took place at a children's centre or similar venue. Organising contact was one of the biggest headaches for a social worker as many things needed to be coordinated prior to taking place. Then, inevitably, the parents would not turn up or arrive late, upsetting the children. In addition, there was the problem of parents trying to secretly discuss things with the children, coaching them what to say to social workers or threatening them with what could happen if they told anyone what was really going on in the home.

Diane knew that more often than not, children did not tell their full stories until they were away from the full-time care of their parents and feeling safe. For Diane, organising contact for four children in three different placements was one more, unenviable task to add to her ever-growing to-do list. She forced herself to stop thinking about the Waleeds and turned her focus to the day ahead.

~ ~ ~ ~ ~

Throughout the morning, Angie consistently interrupted Diane with messages which the latter had to decline unless they related to Ruby. She had far too much to do without being drawn into other, potentially time-consuming scenarios.

"Duty will have to deal with it," called out Diane to Angie as another call came through. "If I don't get this paperwork finished for Ruby, I'm in danger of not getting it into court on time," she explained.

"It's the hospital about Courtney Pearson," Angie called back. "They want to know if she can be discharged to her grandmother."

Diane groaned. She had forgotten that Courtney was due for discharge that very day.

"Can you tell them I'll ring them in about 10 minutes, Ang? I just need to confirm it all, thanks."

Diane knew that the police checks on Brenda Pearson and her family had been okay, but she needed to make sure that the grandmother had everything required to care for all three children. Courtney needed an operation to straighten out her arm and would require specialised care. It all had to be checked out before Courtney could join her brothers with their grandmother.

Ten minutes later, Angie called again.

"Diane, I'm so sorry, but you need to take this one," Angie said, putting the call through without hesitation.

136

Diane raised her eyebrows, wondering how her day could get any worse. The voice at the other end of the phone was, once again, from the hospital. For a moment, Diane thought it was about Courtney and frowned in frustration as she had already said that she would ring them back in 10 minutes time. However, it was not about Courtney. It was the nurse from A & E – Accident and Emergency. The colour drained from Diane's face as she listened to what the nurse was saying.

At 12.30am that day, Shanice Ellis had stabbed her husband, Grant. He was pronounced dead on arrival. Shanice was, of course, arrested and the children, two of whom had unfortunately witnessed the attack, were currently with their grandmother.

Diane almost dropped the phone. The breath went out of her as she listened in disbelief to what she was hearing. Her colleagues quickly realised that something extreme had occurred. All of them stopped what they were doing and waited silently for Diane to finish the call. When she hung up, the social worker could not prevent tears from welling up in her eyes as she broke the appalling news to the rest of the team.

What followed was a blur. The police rang up Diane not long after the hospital and advised her that Shanice had been arrested and charged with murder. She remained in custody. The children were with Shanice's mother, Mary Gardener.

Diane would have to visit them and the police needed to formally interview Tia and DJ who had witnessed the terrible, tragic incident. The social worker did not have space in her head or her heart to fully allow what had happened to take root and overwhelm her. She simply had to focus on getting through the rest of the day and would deal with her emotions when she got home. For that moment, Diane just filed them all away like an unwanted email.

~ ~ ~ ~ ~

A crowd of grandmothers gathered in the yard. They were a formidable group, with their wizened, wrinkled features turned to leather by a thousand suns. A fat, yellow moon hung in the sky, suspended in animated relief – an unwilling accomplice lighting up the scene below. Zarifa lay docile on a simple, makeshift bed, below which burned acrid incense in a cracked clay pot. Her hands and feet were stained with henna which had been applied the previous evening. Zarifa's own grandmother stepped forward and it was clear from the murmurings of the group that she was held in high esteem as the matriarch of the clan.

Grandmother employed the help of two other women from the tribe to support Zarifa's torso, while two others held her legs apart. Out of the darkness, another old woman approached and as the most important person there apart from Zarifa's grandmother, the women respectfully made way. Then, in silence, the woman took a sharpened piece of glass and, quickly and efficiently, cut away the clitoris and labia minora of the helpless child. With a shriek of triumph, the woman hurled the rejected tissue into a fire across the yard like the trimmings from a chicken breast. They hissed as if in disapproval of the primeval act as they shriveled and died.

The old woman staunched the flow of blood with a cloth, then selected a needle and thread from her basic kit. She bent over in concentration, clucking to herself as she crudely sewed Zarifa's outer labia together, leaving a small opening at the vulva. Finally, she selected a sharp twig and poked it into the remaining aperture to keep it open. The ceremony was over.

Zarifa seemed to be experiencing more shock than pain. Her head swam from the adrenaline of the experience. She was thirsty, but no one offered her a drink. Her legs had been tied from hip to ankle and would remain so for the next three weeks, to allow the wound to heal.

Zarifa knew that she should not even be there. Her mother had borrowed her aunt's passport and they had managed to avoid detection on their flight to Sudan. Zarifa was scared that she would be in trouble when she returned to England. She knew that the social worker kept returning to the house, to tell her parents off for trying to bring her to this special ceremony, but the girl had not truly appreciated what all the fuss was about. Now, in a world of shock and pain, Zarifa came full circle to understanding how truly abhorrent the endeavour had all been.

Amid loud, ceremonial ululations, Zarifa was lifted high, taken outside and invested with ritual jewelry and perfumes. She was anointed with cosmetic pastes to protect her from attack by malignant spirits and the evil eye. She was given a bright, new dress to wear, a bridal shawl and her family's gold. Zarifa's relatives appeared and sprinkled guests with as much cologne as they would at a wedding.

All that did nothing to dull the pain. Zarifa feared that she would be sick all over her new dress, but the thought of the disgrace it would bring caused her to swallow deeply and focus on something else. Her mother, Nahla, smiled and nodded her thanks to the well-wishers who turned out for the occasion. It was, indeed, a momentous day as a newly circumcised girl, Zarifa, had just been rendered marriageable – and Millbrook Social Services were a world away. Zarifa turned her head so that her mother would not see her shame. Then she let the tears flow.

~ ~ ~ ~ ~

"You out again, Di?" asked Vicky Waring absent-mindedly from where she sat studying her computer screen as she saw Diane putting her coat on.

Vicky was one of the newly qualified social workers in the office and had only been in the post for three months. She had far too many cases to manage and already felt completely out of her depth. Diane had found

Vicky in the ladies toilets during her second week on the job, all alone and crying inconsolably. Vicky had confided in Diane that she did not think she was cut out for the job. Diane hugged her and tried to be as encouraging as possible, offering support if Vicky needed it. Vicky rallied, but Diane could see that her heart was not in it. She predicted that Vicky would not be there in six months' time. Diane tried not to think of the additional work that would result if Vicky or any of the other social workers left.

"Yes, I'm off to try and catch Kirsty Thompson at home again, although I know she's avoiding me," said Diane. "I meant to go at 2.00pm today, but I'm in court then, so just want to nip over and see if I can catch her."

Diane was still reeling from the news about Grant Ellis and felt as if she was on autopilot for the rest of the day. It seemed unreal and try as she might to push it to the back of her mind, it all threatened to engulf her. She tried not to think about Tia and DJ, and how they must have felt to see their mother kill their father. Diane knew that the lives of the entire family had been forever altered by that fateful event. She shook herself out of her state and moved for the door. Other cases were demanding her attention.

Diane pulled up once again outside the home of Kirsty Thompson. It was 10 o'clock. While Diane had arranged to be there at 2.00pm, she hoped to catch Kirsty and have a discussion with her about Daniel and the concerns raised by the health visitor. However, as she got to the door, Diane realised that nothing had changed. The curtains remained closed and apart from the usual barking of the dog, no one opened the door. It was getting very worrying and Diane knew that more direct action was needed. She once again left a note, explaining that she was unable to visit at 2.00pm as planned and would be in touch. The social worker knew that she would have to write a strong letter to Kirsty, explaining the possible consequences of her continued avoidance. However, that would have to wait as, for the moment, she had a heavy workload to address.

Diane returned to the office and made a final check on the paperwork for Ruby's court case which was scheduled for 2.00pm. She checked her watch and decided that there was enough time to ring probation, to try and organise a visit to the family who were being visited by Malcolm Withers. Thankfully, Jane Clarke was in the office and she told Diane that the names of the parents were Barry and Janice Spiggot. Diane then rang her colleague, Jill Fletcher, at the child protection unit of the police, who agreed to do a joint visit with her the following day.

Diane busied herself with the task of re-reading the paperwork for Ruby's court hearing, now only a few hours away. She would meet Marcus again and hoped that the matter would be heard by the eminently sensible Judge Glendinning who had made a positive decision the previous day for the Waleed children. Diane had found it relatively simple to find a foster placement for Ruby – one little girl of 22 months was not too difficult to place. Foster carers, Joe and Sandra Prentiss, were on standby for that day and understood that once Diane had secured the order, they were to meet her at the hospital where Ruby was ready for discharge. Marcus was going to argue that the parents should not be permitted to go and say their goodbyes, citing the trouble they had caused on the night of the medical as a reason.

Seeing that there was nothing left to do in relation to Ruby, Diane set about writing a very strongly worded letter to Kirsty Thompson. She outlined her concerns and stressed the need for Kirsty to ensure that she was at home for the next visit which Diane organised for three days hence. The social worker also stated that if Kirsty were to remain unavailable to discuss the concerns in regard to Daniel, the local authority would seriously consider taking legal advice.

A statement like that usually had an effect in one of two ways. Either the parent or parents would get on the phone, ranting and raging about how Social Services dared to threaten them, or there would be a tearful phone call and a promise to be at home for the next scheduled visit. However, unbeknown to Diane at that stage, her letter would elicit neither response from Kirsty.

With another half hour to spare before leaving for court, Diane rang up Gemma Powell and arranged a visit for the following day. This meant another busy day of visits as she was also going with the police to see the Spiggots. *No rest for the wicked,* thought Diane.

"Boy, I must have been really bad at some point," she said aloud to no one in particular.

With that she put her coat on and set off for court.

Diane met Marcus in the anteroom of the court. Sitting together, they poured over the last details of Ruby's case. Diane had seen Hanif Hassan and Kelly Wilson outside, although they were not together.

"I do not foresee any problems," said Marcus peering over the glasses perched at the end of his nose. "The case is very straightforward. With Dr Woods's medical evidence, the judge will have little choice but to make the order, at least until further assessment has taken place," he said, briskly.

Diane knew that Marcus had a lot of cases in court that day and did not need any delays in the Ruby Wilson hearing. It should not take long. The local authority was only applying for an interim care order not an EPO, so it was more planned and had less 'blue flashing lights' attached to it.

Both solicitors of Hanif and Kelly had been in to speak to Marcus and accepted that there was absolutely no chance of Ruby going home with either parent at that stage. They had, therefore, been going over the details of potential family members who could care for Ruby, to prevent her from being taken into the care of the local authority. However, without viability assessments, any prospective family carers would have to wait. All parties agreed that if the order was made, Ruby would go to Joe and Sandra Prentiss.

Eventually, the clerk instructed all the involved parties to enter the courtroom. Diane was mightily relieved to see the familiar, craggy face of Judge William Glendinning. She fancied that he winked at her as he entered, but then told herself that she was only imagining it.

As anticipated, it was a no-contest hearing. Both solicitors had advised Ruby's parents to save their arguments for a later date and to concede to Ruby going into the care of the local authority. Hanif's solicitor had used every ounce of his skill and tact to get his client to agree to that, whereas a puffy-eyed Kelly had cried a lot but gone along with the suggestion of her own solicitor. Judge Glendinning made the order that would last 28 days, then be renewed as a matter of course unless the local authority advised the court otherwise. The judge, however, also ordered viability assessments on one of Kelly's aunts and another on Hanif's sister, both of whom had put themselves forward as potential carers for Ruby.

Diane winced at the thought of the additional work the judgement created, but acknowledged that if Ruby could be safely cared for within her own family, it was better than remaining in the care of strangers. Judge Glendinning also ordered psychological assessments of both parents and additionally ordered the local children's centre to undertake parenting assessments of Hanif and Kelly. The judge set a further date for a hearing and that was it; the court was adjourned. Marcus agreed to wait for a printout of the order for Diane to take with her to the hospital, while the social worker said that she would go and call both Glenda and the foster carers with the news.

Finally! thought Diane with relief as she left the court and got her phone out. *Finally, something's gone according to plan.* Diane stepped outside for privacy and stood in a sheltered corner of the building, out of the bitingly cold winds. She dialled Joe and Sandra Prentiss to tell them the news.

Diane was engrossed in her discussion with Sandra when she suddenly became aware of a figure approaching her and realised, to her horror, that it was Hanif Hassan. The social worker cursed her lack of foresight. Usually, after a hearing in which there were aggressive or particularly challenging parents, Diane would not leave court alone and always kept her wits about her. However, on that day she had been so intent on letting the foster carers know the plan that she was lacking in awareness for her own safety.

Diane spoke quickly and quietly to the foster carer.

"Sandra, listen carefully. I am being approached by a man called Hanif Hassan. He's Ruby's father. If this line goes dead, please call 999 immediately and ask the police to attend the county courthouse and give them Hassan's name," she said urgently.

Diane could almost hear Sandra taking in the information.

"Oh, Diane, be careful," Sandra said, anxiously.

Diane turned her attention to the approaching man.

"Mr Hassan," she said as brightly as she could. "I am just on the phone, but will be happy to speak to you in a few moments if you don't mind waiting. Perhaps you would be warmer inside where I will join you presently."

Hanif showed no intention of returning inside. Diane knew that she was trapped in a corner and that no one, apart from Sandra who was five miles away, knew where she was. Diane braced for the inevitable, but at that exact moment, she heard a familiar, mournful voice speak.

"Mr Hassan," said the voice with forlorn authority, "the exit is this way."

It was Marcus. He had come out of the building at the right moment and instantly took in the unfolding situation. Hanif Hassan hesitated for a slight moment, then fixing Diane with a threatening stare, he made a sweeping, cut-throat motion across his throat with the flat of his hand. Then he turned around slowly and walked away. Diane froze on the spot, then heard a small voice squawking.

"Diane, Diane! Are you there?"

It was Sandra.

"Yes, I'm here, Sandra. The panic is over for another day. See you at the hospital," replied Diane with relief.

The social worker walked over to Marcus and gave him a hug – which was akin to hugging an ironing board.

"You're a lifesaver!" she exclaimed with heartfelt thanks.

Marcus stood stiffly with his arms by his side. He was not accustomed to being hugged.

"I anticipated you could run into a little trouble out here," Marcus said, woefully, "so I took the liberty of following you. It appears that, once again, my judgement was accurate."

Diane laughed.

"Oh, Marcus, are you actually making a joke there?"

Marcus looked crestfallen.

"Diane, I assure you," he continued gravely, "I do not consider this funny in any way. Now, if you'll excuse me, I have other cases waiting for my attention."

And he was gone.

Diane went up to the hospital and spent an hour with Joe and Sandra Prentiss as they were introduced to Ruby. They had got her a toy rabbit and on seeing it, Ruby's eyes widened and she clutched it to herself much in the same way her mother had held onto her a few nights before. The girl then smiled shyly at the couple and when the time arrived for her to go with them, she went without a fuss. Ruby looked clean and well cared for. Thanks to the nurses, she was now also free of head lice. The skeletal survey did not highlight any injuries of concern, although she had been covered in bruises.

"I'll be in touch about the first review," explained Diane to Joe and Sandra. "It will be sometime next week and I'll ring you tomorrow to see how it's gone overnight. Many thanks to you both and let me know if you need anything."

Diane watched Joe strap Ruby into their car and off they went. *That's one more safe and sound,* she thought. Then Diane drove back to the office, to deal with the never ending emails.

Chapter 17

"Thanks for meeting me, Jill," Diane told the police officer.

DC Jill Fletcher smiled.

"No problem, Di. Always glad to help our colleagues on the front lines."

Diane and Jill were en route to Janice and Barry Spiggot through a short car journey. Diane took the opportunity of asking Jill for more details about the case and its accompanying concerns.

"Well," Jill began, studying her notebook. "It would appear that your man, Malcolm Withers, has been going for tea with the family. He made no secret of it and openly told his probation officer, so I'm not sure what the deal is here. It's not clear how he knows the family, so we'll have to do a bit of digging."

Diane nodded.

"Okay, I'll let you lead the way. Are you happy to disclose to them if they're unaware of all this?"

"Oh, yes; no problem. We'll give them the basics and the rest is up to them."

"Remind me," said Diane. "What was he convicted of, again?"

Jill consulted her notes once more while biting her lip.

"Hmm, two counts of gross indecency against a male child of nine and one count of sexual assault against a female child of four. They were brother and sister, so it wouldn't appear that he has any particular gender preference."

There was silence while Jill continued reading and picking out the salient points to share with Diane.

"Oh, here we are. He had volunteered as a babysitter for his neighbour. She was a single parent who was struggling to get to work in the evenings and, of course, here comes good old Malcolm to help out. They always manage to find a vulnerable mother, don't they?" said Jill, finally.

Diane and Jill arrived a few minutes later at the family home of the Spiggots on the outskirts of the estate. Janice Spiggot opened the door and Diane was immediately struck by the overpowering smell of dirty nappies. She concentrated on keeping a straight face and held out a hand in greeting.

"Janice?" she said. "I'm Diane Foster, the social worker who rang you to arrange this visit. This is my colleague, Jill Fletcher. Jill is with the police. Is it okay if we come in and talk to you?"

Janice had a little boy on her hip and Diane could hear the cries of a fairly new baby in the house. Distracted by the cries of the latter, Janice turned her back and went inside.

She called out, "Come in," as she left Diane and Jill.

Once inside, the smell intensified. Diane looked around in despair at the untidy, dirty interior of the home. Both Diane and Jill were then met by the disconcerting sight of Barry Spiggot who stood in the living room, his arms folded and face glowering.

Barry was a small man, no more than five feet six in height. He was, however, stocky and bull-like in appearance. His image was accentuated by a perfectly bald head. Diane could not help thinking that he reminded her of a nightclub bouncer. Shaking the thought from her mind, Diane repeated the ceremony of greeting and proffered her hand. It was ignored. Barry Spiggot turned to his young wife.

"Get me a coffee," he ordered with bluntness.

Then Barry turned back to the two women. It was clear that he had something to get off his chest. With Janice out of the room, he cleared his throat and began.

"I don't know what this is all about, but it had better be good. I don't want Social Services involved with my kids – poking your noses in where it's none of your business and finding fault with everyone."

Diane had been in a similar position many times in her career and knew that she needed to stop him as quickly as possible.

"Mr Spiggot," she interjected, "if we could all sit down and discuss this together, you will soon realise that we are not here to criticise you or your wife. We're here to talk about a serious matter of which you may not be aware."

The expression on Barry's face changed slightly.

"You better sit down then," he agreed, begrudgingly.

They all waited until Janice returned with Barry's drink. Then Jill began.

"It has come to our attention that a person called Malcolm Withers has been visiting your home. Is that correct?"

Janice and Barry exchanged glances.

"What of it?" said Barry, roughly.

"Before I get to that, may I ask how you know Mr Withers?" continued Jill, smoothly.

The face of Barry Spiggot clouded over with annoyance.

"He's a mate, alright?! I know him through work. We used to move washing machines together a few years back. Now, you better tell me what this is about."

Jill made a show of consulting her papers before continuing.

"Mr and Mrs Spiggot," she began, "I need to ask if you are aware that Malcolm Withers has convictions for offences against children."

Barry stood up angrily and began pacing the room.

"Oh, I see; that's what this is all about. It's a load of nonsense! Yes, we know about it and it's rubbish. I've known Malcolm for years, he'd never harm a kiddie. Those kids were put up to it by their mother when Malcolm said he didn't want to go out with her. She was being spiteful, that's all there was to it, and now he's got a record for something he didn't do. When will this stop following him around, so he can get on with his life?" Barry finished with bitterness in his voice.

"Mr Spiggot," said Jill, seriously. "Mr Withers was convicted of offences against two young children and pleaded guilty. What you or anyone else feels about that is, quite honestly, immaterial. Mr Withers is a convicted sex offender and our concern today is that your children are kept safe from any potential risk which Mr Withers may pose. Do you understand?"

Barry Spiggot continued pacing up and down.

"Oh, I understand all right!" he declared, raising his voice. "I understand that this is a witch-hunt and that a good man is being persecuted for something he didn't do. I don't give a toss what you lot say. I know the truth and the courts don't always get it right."

Diane sighed inwardly. It was going to be awkward. In an effort to interrupt Barry Spiggot's soapbox speech, she spoke up.

"What do you think about this, Janice?" said Diane, directing her question to a distracted Janice who was battling to bottle-feed the baby.

Janice looked anxiously at her husband.

"I think the same as Barry," she replied, nervously. "I mean, Malcolm's alright and he's always really good with our kids. Isn't he, Barry?"

Barry looked at his young wife with disdain.

"Of course, he's alright! Why wouldn't he be? Hey, see to your son, will you? He's into mischief," Barry added, indicating Declan who was gravitating towards the overflowing rubbish bin.

Janice broke off from feeding Hayley and laboured over to Declan.

"No, babby," Janice said, half-heartedly. "That's dirty."

Then she guided Declan over to the settee, to sit beside her, and carried on with her attempts to feed Hayley. Barry made no move to assist his wife, but continued his diatribe.

"I'm telling you right now: Malcolm Withers will always be welcome in this house and I don't care what anyone says, so you'd better do whatever it is you need to do. This is my house and I'll say what goes," Barry said with finality.

"Mr Spiggot," responded Diane, "unfortunately, if you continue to allow Mr Withers access to your children while denying that he is a potential risk to them, you will leave us no choice but to convene an initial child protection case conference. This means that a group of professionals will meet to decide whether or not Hayley and Declan need to be subject to a child protection plan, to safeguard them from any potential risk of harm from Mr Withers."

Barry Spiggot immediately turned on Diane.

"Get out!" he said in a menacing tone. "Both of you, out of my house and don't come back!"

Both women sat still. Jill continued where Diane had left off.

"Mr Spiggot, you need to understand the gravity of the situation you're creating here," Jill explained, patiently. "As you do not seem to accept that Mr Withers is a potential risk to your children, you are, in effect, indicating to us that you would not be in a position to protect them should he reoffend. I'm sure you would not wish either Declan or Hayley to become a victim of any sort of abuse, but your refusal to acknowledge the criminal history of Mr Withers is leaving them vulnerable and open to exactly such a scenario."

Barry Spiggot was having none of it.

"I said, get out!" he repeated, angrily.

Then he went to the front door and opened it. Diane and Jill had no choice but to leave. As they went, Diane tried one more time.

"Mr Spiggot, you are, unfortunately, going to force the local authority's hand here as we simply cannot allow your children to be at risk. I'm afraid that while you've every right to ask us to leave, this is far from over. Please consider what has been said here today as I will need to come back."

Barry Spiggot sneered at both women and delivered a parting shot.

"I don't want to see either of you here, at this house, ever again!"

With that he slammed the door. In the car, Jill grinned at Diane. In an attempt to lighten the mood, Jill spoke first.

"Well, that went well," she said, brightly.

Diane laughed, but she knew that it was far from funny and was not looking forward to her next visit which she knew would have to be in a very short time.

Chapter 18

Morris Powell was feeling good. He regarded his reflection in the cracked mirror as he straightened his tie. It was Sunday – which meant church, and church meant an unfamiliar tie and jacket. Morris carefully combed over the remaining remnant of his thin, wispy hair and put an ingratiating smile on his face. *Perfect*, he thought. *How can I fail?*

"I'm off to church, Mother," Morris called out to his elderly mother, Gladys, who sat in her easy-chair by the window.

"Up to no good, if you ask me," mumbled the old lady.

At 84 years of age, she was nobody's fool. Gladys knew what her son was and she was highly suspicious about his joining a church. She knew full well that Morris had been in prison and had been told the reason why by people on the estate. Morris had told his mother that he was framed and vehemently denied ever having done anything wrong. But unbeknown to Morris, his sister, Judith, his first victim, had long ago told their mother what Morris had done to her as a child, although they never spoke of it to him.

Gladys knew that Morris was a wrong 'un. His father had been the same and she was relieved when he had finally succumbed to the lung disease he acquired from working in the mines. The father had only been 55 years old when he died, but Gladys did not care. He had been a miserable cuss of a man who showed her no affection or regard during their marriage. No, Gladys was under no illusions about her only son, Morris, but she felt powerless to intervene.

Morris arrived early for church, so he could again offer his services as a doorman.

"Oh, Morris," enthused Phyllis, the usual door lady. "You're such a help. I don't know how we managed without you. You do the door then and I'll go and get the trays ready for the tea and the coffee after the meeting. I hear we've a visiting speaker today. Isn't that exciting?"

Morris nodded in feigned agreement and took his place at the door. In that way, he got to hug everyone who entered, including the children. Morris hoped that his particular, favourite family would attend church that day.

Fiona Blake and her three children were regular worshippers at *Waters of Life Church*. The children were little girls: Daisy, Phoebe and Lucy. All were under the age of 10 years and Morris knew that it was only a matter of time before he had his way. Fiona's husband was serving in Iraq and had left her alone with the children. Fiona was a quiet woman who had, so far, politely declined Morris's offers of help with the children.

"Anytime you need help," he had told Fiona with feigned sincerity. "I mean it, anytime at all. Even if you just need to pop to the shop, I can mind the girls for you. Saves you dragging them all out with you," Morris suggested, hopefully.

Fiona smiled, thanked him and said that it was fine, thank you, but she always took the girls with her to the shops. Morris needed a new tactic and was thinking about it when Doreen Dewbury interrupted his thoughts.

"Morris, we're starting."

Morris left his post by the door and went to find a seat. They went through the usual, happy clappy singing routine to which Morris had become accustomed, although he wondered why some of the women felt the need to sing out loud on their own. *Did they think they had good voices? Was that it?* On some days the whole thing reminded Morris of a bad karaoke competition with people vying to be heard. It set his teeth on edge as some of them were truly dreadful, yet everyone would *Amen* and *Praise the Lord* afterwards as if they actually enjoyed it.

Bunch of hypocrites, Morris mused as he studied a small child two rows in front of him. He endured a two-hour-long service. It had taken longer than usual as there was a visiting preacher who got carried away and seemed to feel the need to pray for the entire congregation after he finished preaching. The preacher then made an appeal to the people who wanted him to lay hands on them in prayer. *I would like to lay hands around your stupid throat,* Morris thought, maintaining his fixed smile.

The preacher strode among the people who lined up at the front of the church. He was praying loudly and placing his hands on their heads or shoulders. His voice got louder and louder as a crescendo of religious fervour was reached. The people stood there with their eyes closed and hands raised; some of them were shaking.

Morris watched in a detached manner as, one by one, the people fell on the floor while praying ecstatically. *Oh, for goodness sake,* he thought, crossly. *He's pushing them over. Are they all stupid or what?* The preacher approached Morris, but the latter quickly walked off to the kitchen under the pretence of helping with the tea and the coffee.

"Not me, mate," Morris muttered under his breath. "You're not getting near me."

In the kitchen, Morris was met again by Doreen Dewbury.

"Ah, Morris," she said, pleasantly. "Are you here to help me? You're good."

Morris immediately adopted his church smile.

"It's no trouble at all," he lied. "You know how much I enjoy helping out here. You must say if there's anything else I can do. I'm only too pleased to assist," Morris said with great smoothness.

Doreen was pouring tea from a giant aluminium teapot. At those words of Morris, she stopped pouring and looked thoughtful.

"Well, you know, Morris, we've got a potluck supper next week and we could do with another hand if you feel able," she said, hopefully.

"A potluck supper, eh?" replied Morris with more enthusiasm than he felt. "Well, doesn't that sound swell. What can I do?"

Doreen finished pouring tea before continuing.

"Well, we could really do with someone in here, helping us dish up. Then perhaps if you don't mind, a bit of washing up afterwards."

Morris tried not to pull a face.

"Of course," continued Doreen, "we usually get one of the girls to help wash up. It's really a two-person job. Daisy Blake's a little star for helping us with that task. She's always willing to lend a hand. She's an absolute credit to her mother and what with her father away serving in Iraq . . ."

Morris did not hear any more. Doreen kept warbling on in the background, but he was suddenly lost in a fantasy world where only 10-year-old Daisy Blake and himself existed.

"Count me in!" Morris replied with great finality, interrupting a startled Doreen with the vehemence with which he said the words.

~ ~ ~ ~ ~

On her way to work, Diane made yet another stop at the house of Kirsty Thompson. She had written to say that she would visit in a few days' time, but decided to take a chance and see if she could catch Kirsty at home. Diane was completely taken aback when a man opened the door. She had not yet met Neil O'Grady, but assumed that it was him. Diane smiled and introduced herself.

"Is it Neil?" she asked. "I'm Diane Foster, the social worker who's been putting all the notes through the door. I guess you're getting used to them by now," she said, innocently. "I've left you so many."

Neil O'Grady maintained a neutral expression as he considered Diane.

Then he simply said, "She's not in."

Diane looked perturbed and frowned.

"Oh, that's a shame. I was really hoping to catch Kirsty this morning. Can I ask where's she's gone, Neil, and what time she might be back?"

Neil looked completely disinterested and stared past Diane as he shook his head.

"Dunno where she's gone. She went out first thing with the babby, probably to town, and I don't know when she's back. I'll tell her you called," Neil said and made to shut the door.

Diane quickly spoke up.

"Neil," she replied with some urgency. "It's really, really important that I see Kirsty and the baby this week. Really important," Diane repeated. "Please, can you ask her to ring me on this number as soon as she gets in?"

Diane handed Neil her business card which he took without comment as he closed the door. She walked back to the car feeling frustrated in the extreme. *What were the chances of Kirsty being out,* Diane thought as she got into the car. Meanwhile inside the house, Kirsty Thompson emerged smirking from the kitchen.

"Has she gone?" Kirsty asked.

"She's gone," replied Neil O'Grady. "Good job Daniel was asleep, though, and not doing his usual screaming job," he added, sourly.

Kirsty rolled her eyes.

"Tell me about it!" she agreed. "Stick the telly on," Kirsty added and sat down.

Upstairs, Daniel lay silently in his cot, staring listlessly at the ceiling. He was hungry, wet and cold, but he had learned quickly in his short three months of life that crying was completely and utterly futile.

~ ~ ~ ~ ~

Diane got to her desk 10 minutes later. Immediately, the phone rang.

"Give me a chance!" she exclaimed to the unknown caller before picking up.

"Diane, it's Lorraine," said the voice at the other end of the line.

"Hey, Lorraine, how's it going?" replied Diane. "How's Jessica getting on?"

A small silence ensued before Lorraine continued.

"She's gone, Diane. She's run away."

Diane was still standing up, but slumped down into her chair upon hearing the news.

"I knew it was too good to be true," she said with sadness.

Diane was right. Jessica's track record was appalling. She had rarely managed to stay in a foster placement longer than a few weeks, before seeking out where the action was and running off to stay with one of her newfound 'mates.' Jessica had chronically low self-esteem and craved the approval of her peers at whatever cost. Diane had almost lost count of the number of dubious houses from which she had collected a reluctant Jessica.

"How long's she been gone?" Diane asked, refocussing on the problem and listening to the all-too-familiar tale Lorraine was narrating.

"She stormed out last night, angry because I wouldn't let her go to a sleepover at some friend's house. I didn't know the people, Diane, so I said *no*. When she didn't come home by 11.00pm, I knew she'd gone anyway and, of course, I called the police and your out-of-hours service, but no one could locate her. I thought you'd want to know from me," explained Lorraine.

Diane nodded.

"Okay, Lorraine, you did the right thing. Thanks for letting me know. I'll ring the police for an update and be in touch."

Diane hung up and sat back in the chair, shaking her head.

"Oh, Jessica, Jessica! You really are determined to push me to the limit, aren't you?" she said to herself.

Diane knew full well that she was going to have to take drastic action. She got up and made her familiar way into Glenda's office to discuss the situation.

"We have to do something, Glenda," began Diane in frustration. "Jessica's putting herself at so much risk. We know from police intelligence that she's offering sexual services for drugs and running with a bad crowd again. As a child in our care, we can't just sit back and let that happen to her."

Glenda reflected for a few minutes, balancing Diane's argument with the knowledge that her superiors would most assuredly deny any move on her part to try and obtain a secure order – which Glenda knew was where Diane was going. At 15 years of age, Jessica was a loose cannon. Even if Glenda managed to convince the senior managers to allow Diane to apply for a secure order, there was no guarantee that anything would change.

The local authority's director of social services was a formidable man by the name of Nicholas Bishop. He had a reputation for being a control freak although, it could not be denied, he was good at his job. Bishop had worked his way up from a Level One social worker back in the late 70's, to hold the most powerful job in the county. He answered only to the local government and at 58 years old, he was looking forward to a financially secure retirement. Even if Glenda managed to convince her line manager and the area manager above her, she knew that they would never get past Nicholas Bishop.

Secure orders were notoriously difficult to obtain, requiring a high threshold of risk of significant harm. To deprive a child of his or her liberty was a serious business and not agreed to or undertaken lightly. The kind of order required would, in effect, lock Jessica up for her own safety as opposed to locking her up for committing a crime. If and when a young person was locked away in that manner, the parameters for keeping them secure were so narrow that they were usually released after a few weeks. Such a brief time period was never enough to elicit any meaningful change and usually served to make the young person in question extremely bitter and angry. One, in fact, ended up with a worse situation than previously. In addition, there was the exorbitant related cost which could run into thousands of pounds weekly.

Glenda took a deep breath.

"I know what you're saying, Diane, but there's no way they'll go for it. For a start, it's too costly and knowing Jessica, she'd come out after three months or less and run away again. What we need to do is find her and then talk to her about future options."

Diane threw up her hands.

"What options, Glenda? What does this kid have to look forward to? She's never had a stable home; never. She's been moved from foster home to foster home without anyone successfully bonding with her, to be able to do any real work to help her. If we don't step in with some drastic action soon, she's doomed and you know it."

Glenda knew that Diane was right. She understood all the arguments and had sadly seen it all before as had Diane.

"No, Diane," Glenda replied with firmness. "I'm really sorry, but no. We need to try and work with Jessica on a 1:1 basis and really put some time in with her."

Diane felt defeated, but knew it was a futile argument. She had feared that senior management would never agree to the idea of a secure order, but it did not help Jessica Jackson to be rattling around the system and getting nowhere.

"I don't have the time to spend with her, Glenda; you know that. When am I supposed to spend quality 1:1 time with any of my kids? It's a joke! I hardly have time to look after myself, never mind spend good quality time with the children for which I'm supposed to be responsible."

Glenda could see that Diane was getting close to burnout and was concerned.

"Di," Glenda responded, quietly. "I'll allocate a family worker to Jessica, to do some work with her and take her out a bit. We'll see how that goes."

Diane could feel angry tears forming in her eyes.

"Oh, great," she said with bitterness in her voice. "Introduce someone else new to her, why not?! Yeah, that'll work, Glenda. Great idea!"

Glenda said nothing, but patted the chair next to her.

"Sit down, Di," Glenda said. "Close the door and sit down."

Diane did as she was asked. As soon as she sat down, she dissolved into tears. Glenda had managed enough social workers in her time to know when to be quiet. She let Diane get it out of her system, handing over tissues to her as she wept. Eventually, the sobs of Diane Foster grew silent.

"Sorry," Diane said, blowing her nose. "I'm sorry, Glenda. I didn't mean to be rude to you."

Glenda smiled.

"Oh, good God, Diane; don't apologise! I've had far worse than you can offer. I know you're really stretched and busy, and I know you're still shocked and upset by what happened to Grant Ellis. Maybe, you need to take a few days off – get back some of the hours we owe you, eh?"

Diane laughed a hollow, empty laugh.

"Now that's really a stupid idea," she replied, looking sideways at her manager.

Glenda laughed as well.

"Okay, okay. I concede. I know you won't take time out, but I'm worried about you, Di. I can't have you going off sick or being ill with stress."

Diane sighed.

"I'll be fine, Glenda. Honestly, I'm just frustrated. It's always the same. It comes down to money and resources, none of which we have in abundance. Look, I'm okay now. I'd better get back to it. Jessica's still missing and so is Zarifa Waleed, for that matter – and she worries me more, knowing what she might have gone through. Thanks for the shoulder, I'm out of here."

And Diane went back to her desk where, as usual, the phone was ringing.

Chapter 19

Zarifa Waleed was riding the waves of pain which assuaged her tiny frame. She screwed her eyes tightly shut against the pain, but it was a permanent thing. Without the benefit of painkillers or antibiotics, it was almost inevitable that Zarifa would get an infection in the crudely cut, stitched wound now a week old. The old crone who had so dramatically caused the injury had moved on to other villages which demanded her questionable services, leaving Zarifa in the care of her mother and grandmother.

Nahla Waleed and her own mother had little to offer the suffering child other than sympathy. However, their relief in knowing that Zarifa could now make a good marriage outweighed their concern for her wellbeing. Zarifa needed to pee, but she dreaded making even an attempt as she knew that it would be excruciating. The first time she had tried after the circumcision, she almost fainted with pain. Zarifa's legs were still bound at the knees and the ankles, making toileting almost impossible. However, her mother had held the girl under her arms from behind and encouraged her to squat down, saying that she could still pee if she did it that way. Zarifa had tried, but unbeknown to her, she had been stitched too tightly in that area and thanks to the sharpened twig that the old crone had left in, only the tiniest aperture remained. Zarifa's urine dripped out in minute amounts, its concentrated ammonia burning her fresh wound.

"Mummy, I can't pee," Zarifa cried.

Nahla Waleed explained to her daughter that it would never be the same as before, but she would get used to it. Zarifa doubted that. She could not imagine becoming accustomed to such horrifying agony as she was experiencing. Nahla tried not to think about the absolute terror which awaited Zarifa on her wedding night.

Nahla shuddered at the memory of her own experience. Her private parts had healed into a mass of scar tissue and while she had adjusted going to the toilet and having her period through the miniscule gap which remained, she had been pitifully ill-prepared for the ordeal of intercourse. No one had warned her and nothing had prepared her for it. Nahla's husband, unable to penetrate her, had taken a small penknife and, quickly and deliberately, cut into the scar tissue to allow himself access. The tortuous misery of it all had almost overwhelmed her. Nahla had screamed out loud, only to have her husband's heavy hand clamped over her mouth to silence her as he sweated and strained to relieve himself. From that day onwards, Nahla had lived in abject dread of his conjugal visits. Of course, the scar tissue had re-healed, necessitating the use of the small knife many times over the years.

The next trauma for Nahla had been the birth of her five children, each one of them requiring surgical intervention. And every time after birth, her husband had been right there, insisting that the doctors sew her back up again. Despite all that, Nahla had bowed to cultural pressures and subjected her own daughter to the same misery and anguish as she had been made to endure.

Only now did the knowledge of it all make Nahla weep. She knew that she was effectively trapped. She could never return to England, not at that time; not after what she had allowed Zarifa to suffer. No. Nahla knew that she would be in great trouble if she returned and Zarifa would be taken away from her. So Nahla resigned herself to her fate, but lived in the hope that her husband and the other children would soon join her as he had promised they would.

~ ~ ~ ~ ~

Diane decided to revisit the Spiggots unannounced. She hoped that Janice would be at home without Barry. To her surprise, the plan worked. Despite being two o'clock in the afternoon, Janice opened the door in her dressing gown. Diane could again smell the familiar stench of dirty nappies.

"Hi, Janice," Diane said, brightly. "I was literally passing by and thought I'd pop in and see you again. You don't mind, do you?"

Janice looked around nervously.

"Err, Barry's not here so I'm not sure," began Janice.

Diane was quick to take her up on that.

"I didn't really need to see Barry today, Janice. I thought you and I could have a chat. Won't take long."

Janice took a quick look up and down the street. Diane could almost see the cogs turning as she struggled to make a decision.

"Okay, then. But I can't be long. I've got things to do before Barry gets in from work."

Once inside, Diane noted that things had not improved. The home was untidy, smelly and dirty. Declan sat on the floor playing with an empty cigarette packet. Baby Hayley was asleep on the settee, almost lost among the piles of clothes.

Diane decided to start by taking some personal details from Janice. With Barry's hostile attitude on her last visit, Diane did not have the dates of birth or any other details of the children or the rest of family. Janice did not seem to find such an approach threatening and willingly volunteered the information.

"Is that it for family, then?" said Diane when she had gathered the full names and dates of birth of all the children.

"Well, there's my half-brother, Michael," replied Janice. "He lives with his mum."

Diane sat poised with her pen.

"What's his full name, Janice?" she asked.

"It's Michael Tranter. He's six," came the reply.

"Michael Tranter?" said Diane with great curiosity. "What's your dad's name, Janice, if you don't mind me asking?"

Janice looked slightly uncomfortable.

"Roy," she replied. "Roy Tranter, but I don't get on with him. He abused me and my sister and he's in prison for it."

Diane forced herself to maintain a calm exterior, but her mind reeled at that information. Roy Tranter was a known sex offender. Janice had already said on their initial visit that she had met her husband, Barry, through her father – a fact highly disconcerting in itself. Additionally, there was another known sex offender visiting the home. Diane did not like that one bit. There were too many coincidences and in the middle of it all was a vulnerable young mother and two extremely young children.

"Tell me a bit about your dad if you can, Janice," invited Diane in an effort to understand the tangled web.

Janice could not believe that she had the undivided attention of a social worker who wanted to hear about her experiences. It was like being interviewed again for *Take a Break*. Janice poured her heart out and a worried Diane listened.

"So tell me again how Malcolm Withers fits into the family?" Diane finally asked after Janice had told her story.

Janice was only too pleased to keep on talking, She had never experienced so much attention.

"He knows my Barry through work," she explained. "In fact, he knew my dad as well. They all used to work on the farm at the end of Lower Lane – you know, where the slow kids go."

Diane knew that Janice meant the local educational farm where young people with learning disabilities went to learn simple skills and help with the animals.

"Go on," Diane prompted, her fears rising.

"Well, yeah, they all worked there; helping and stuff. In fact, there were a few of them I knew. I remember a bloke called Derek too: he was me mate Jodie's uncle. Anyway, then me dad got sent down for what he did to me and our June, and a bit later Malcolm got sent down too, but not for as long. Barry visited Malc in prison as he knew he'd been framed. He didn't go see me dad, though; not after what he did to me. When he got out, Malc rang Barry and asked if he could meet me and the kids, so he's been coming ever since."

Diane's mind reeled as she contemplated the enormity of what she had just been told.

"Janice, do you realise we're really worried about Malcolm coming to your house, especially after what he did to those other children?"

Janice shook her head.

"Barry said he didn't do it," Janice replied with vehemence. "He said he was stitched up. Happens all the time."

Diane knew that Janice had been a victim of sexual abuse most of her life, resulting in her having a rather distorted view of it. Diane also strongly suspected that her father, Roy Tranter, had deliberately introduced his friend, Barry Spiggot, to Janice as a means of controlling her. The fact that Janice was only 15 years old when she started a relationship with Barry, 47 years of age at the time, was highly inappropriate and suspect. Diane also knew that Derek Pearson was the uncle of Jodie Pearson: he too had convictions for child abuse. It was a veritable paedophile ring and Janice and her children were smack bang in the middle of most of the known perpetrators. Diane knew that the entire issue would have to be taken to case conference and quickly at that.

"Janice," Diane said, seriously. "I'm going to talk to my manager, but I'm pretty sure she'll say that we're going to have to have a meeting about all this. I'll be in touch. You and Barry will be invited, but you must not allow Malcolm Withers to come to your house. If Barry lets him in, Malcolm Withers is not, under any circumstance, to be allowed with your children if you're not there with them. Do you understand me, Janice? This is serious!"

The eyes of Janice Spiggot grew wide as she contemplated the new and exciting drama in her life.

"Well, I'll have to talk to Barry," she replied, "and I know he won't like it so I'm not sure."

Diane wanted to shake Janice, but instead she reiterated what she had already said. Then Diane returned back to the office, to share the troublesome information with Glenda.

Chapter 20

Jessica Jackson woke up and immediately wished that she had not. She winced at the thumping pain in her head and the intense nausea made her feel even worse. Jessica felt as if she had the flu: her nose was streaming. She looked around, trying to recollect where she had been the night before.

The room was still dark, but Jessica could make out the shape of three newfound friends. They were all huddled in various inanimate piles around the small, dingy room. One of them, a lad of about 20 years old and whom Jessica knew only as Smurf, was groaning. He sat up abruptly and vomited on the floor nearby before lying back down, still groaning.

Jessica searched her memory for a clue as to how she had got there, but it was too hazy. She dimly recalled meeting Smurf and two others the previous night in the underpass on the edge of the estate. The underpass was a notoriously squalid drug haunt, known to all the dealers and the users on the estate. It was a place Jessica had frequented since she moved to Lorraine's house. Although the estate was a good few miles from her new foster placement, it had not taken Jessica long to suss out where the action was and to gravitate accordingly to its sordid underbelly.

The night before, craving a fix, Jessica had told Lorraine that she was off to stay with a mate and given her some bogus name. The stupid woman had gone loco on her and refused to let her out. That was not a new situation for Jessica, so she had simply put on her coat and walked out of the door, knowing that Lorraine was powerless to stop her. She had caught the bus to the Deacon Hill estate and made an initial stop at the house of the girlfriend of Scott Taylor, but no one had been home. Jessica had then met up with her mate, Chrissy, and they made their way to the underpass in the certain knowledge of scoring from one of the dealers down there.

However, all that seemed like it had happened a lifetime ago as Jessica lay back down in the dark and forced her tormented mind to focus. She knew that Chrissy and herself had scored some whizz. Then she remembered Smurf promising them some sort of good time back at his place. Jessica had gone along with him and a few others and ended up at that dive, although Chrissy appeared to have got lost along the way as she was nowhere to be seen. True to his word, Smurf had produced some really good *Charlie* and they spent some time smoking and snorting it, getting high.

"God, I was chalked up," Jessica muttered aloud as she recalled the loud music that she had danced to like a maniac until exhausted.

Jessica put her hand to her head and wished that the pain would go away. She craved another fix and knew it was the only thing that would give her relief.

"Smurf," Jessica whispered, her voice coming out as a croak. "Yo, Smurf! Got any more *Charlie*, dude?" she asked, hopefully.

Smurf lifted his head and quickly recoiled at the sour stench of his own vomit.

"What you say?" he asked, groggy.

"I'm hurting, man! Gimme some more," whined Jessica, wiping her nose with the back of her hand.

Smurf studied her for a moment in the increasing light.

"You think I get this stuff for free, bitch?" he demanded. "You think I'm some kind of fucking charity here? Who the fuck are you, anyway?"

Jessica became fully awake and regarded her newfound acquaintance. Like many of his ilk, Smurf was small and skinny, with the haunted look of an underfed refugee. He had a terrible complexion with several open sores on his face. He was also missing a good few teeth and the ones which had remained were blackened by a lifetime of drug misuse.

"You met me last night and we came back here to party," prodded Jessica, irked by his lack of recollection as to who she was. "You got anything for me or not?"

Smurf laughed, sarcastically.

"Yeah, right," he replied. "I'm all about that."

Jessica felt the gripping pains in her stomach and her headache was reaching a crescendo of agony. She knew that she had to get herself sorted or else she would really suffer. Jessica forced a smile onto her face as she slid over towards Smurf's sleeping bag and put her hand on his leg.

"Well, now," she whispered, "maybe we can come to some arrangement?"

Jessica did not reckon on Smurf's response. He laughed out loud and pushed her roughly away.

"You think I give this shit away to every little whore who wants to open her legs for it? Girl, you're deluded! You're gonna have to come up with something better than that," Smurf challenged.

Jessica was taken aback.

"What d'you mean?" she asked, indignant that her usual advances were spurned by this ugly snake of a drug dealer.

Smurf smiled inwardly.

"Well, now; see? I don't need what you got, but you need what I got. It's all about supply and demand," he replied in a conversational tone. "Now, fortunately for you, my friend, Kenny, here: he wants what you got. And me? I can be the negotiator, helping to bring about a successful transaction, if you get my meaning," Smurf said, finishing his distasteful proposition with a sly wink.

By that point, Jessica's withdrawal was so acute that she would happily have serviced an entire football team if necessary.

"Whatever!" she replied with great irritation as she watched Smurf prod Kenny back into life.

Fifteen minutes later, Jessica closed her eyes and felt the familiar, wonderful feeling of the white powder working its magic. *Piece of cake,* she thought. *Piece of cake.*

~ ~ ~ ~ ~

Liam Powell sat at the table reading *The Sun*. His hairy belly protruded from his pyjama top. Liam scratched his unshaved stubble as he shouted to his partner.

"Bring me some more tea, will you?"

Gemma Powell was in the living room making a half-hearted attempt at tidying up. On hearing Liam's request, she straightened up and marched through to the kitchen where he was sitting.

"What am I, your personal maid?" Gemma demanded. "Get your own tea! I'm busy trying to tidy up. That stupid social worker's coming this morning."

With that, she stomped back into the other room. Liam rolled his eyes and shouted after Gemma.

"Our Morris is dropping by later."

Liam waited for her reaction. Gemma was back in the kitchen in seconds, her eyes blazing.

"I've told you, I don't want that no-good brother of yours here. I can't stand him," she seethed.

Liam stood up from his reading and went to put the kettle on.

"Oh, shut up, woman!" he declared, reasonably. "Morris is not that bad and, anyway, he's offered to babysit so we can go to the pub."

Gemma had already opened her mouth to deliver the next objection, but stopped when she heard that.

"What?" she said, incredulously. "He'll mind the kids so we can go out? What's got into him all of a sudden?"

Liam laughed without humour.

"Dunno," he replied. "Maybe that church thing's doing him some good, after all. Anyway, who cares! We can go and have a few down at *The King's Head*."

Gemma pouted.

"Oh, alright," she conceded, "being as we've not been out in God knows how long. What time's Morris coming?"

Liam had gone back to his paper, but lifted his head to reply.

"About three, I think. And he can babysit on Sunday night."

Gemma nodded, already planning what she would wear, before realising what time it was and started shouting.

"Liam, that social worker will be here in a few minutes, so you better get your lazy arse out of that chair and get dressed."

Diane arrived at the home 10 minutes later and was pleasantly surprised to find it clean and tidy. Liam and Gemma Powell listened to what she had to say and seemed to have a change of heart. They had previously refused to accept that Morris had done anything wrong, but on this day they were accepting of her concerns and agreed with Diane when she advised them not to allow Morris into their home.

"Well," said Diane, taken aback by their cooperative attitude. "I'm pleased to hear you say this. I'll talk to my manager and see if we can close the case as we have no other concerns about you or your children."

Liam adopted a look of self-importance.

"Look, Miss," he said, seriously. "I never did get on with our Morris and if what you're telling us is right, I'll never get on with him again. At first, we didn't want to believe he could do such a thing to kids, but we've thought about it now and you've no need to worry. He'll not get anywhere near our kids. Will he, love?"

Gemma played her part beautifully.

"Not likely!" she exclaimed in mock indignation. "Never coming to my house again."

Diane smiled.

"Well, that's good to hear. Right, then. I'll leave you to it and I'll be in touch regarding my manager's decision."

After Diane left, Liam and Gemma Powell laughed.

"Well, that was easy," bragged Liam with satisfaction. "I'm not having no social worker tell me who I can or can't see in my family," he added, belligerently.

Gemma nodded in agreement.

"I know. Who does she think she is?! I don't believe it, anyway. I mean, I can't really stand your Morris, but he'd never hurt a kid; would he?"

Liam got up from the chair in which he was sitting.

"Course not," he replied, convincingly. "Course not."

Chapter 21

The wailing, ululating cries of the women could be heard across the plains. They lifted their voices and wept as one, all in mourning for the tragic loss of Zarifa Waleed. Nahla swallowed hard in a desperate attempt to quell the bitter tears which threatened as she fought to focus on the sombre task at hand. She felt detached from herself as if she were in another world and another time.

Nahla forced herself to look down at the fragile, pale body of her daughter, Zarifa, who looked as if she was asleep. Her eyes were closed and her skin had taken on a translucent sheen, resembling alabaster. Nahla gently bathed the tiny body which was naked, apart from the coverings required under their laws and which preserved Zarifa's modesty even in death. Nahla's mother stood on the opposite side of the body, mirroring her own daughter's actions. It was only fitting that Zarifa's two closest female relatives attended her in that manner. So far, Zarifa had been bathed only once. She would undergo four more ritual cleansings before being fully prepared for the burial which would take place within 24 hours.

Only three hours earlier, Zarifa had finally succumbed to the raging infection which invaded her tender frame. With no adequate medicines or assistance, Zarifa had been unable to fight it. She grew weak and developed a fever. Her thirst was a furious, insatiable thing which no amount of brackish water could quench. Her eyes had become glazed, her speech incoherent. Zarifa's lips, once soft and pink, had cracked and blackened as the infection coursed unabated through her body, dehydrating her.

In a last ditch effort to save her daughter, Nahla had cut through the bindings which still secured Zarifa's legs at the knees and the ankles. But as her legs fell apart, Nahla had gasped not only at the putrefying stench which emanated from Zarifa's mutilated genitals, but at the sight of the gaping wound itself: Zarifa's genital area was one huge, festering, suppurating injury. Puss oozed from the site of the offensive trauma. It snaked down the sharpened stick like viscous green poison. Despite her lack of medical knowledge, Nahla knew that it was beyond repair. She also realised in desperate anguish that her daughter was lost to her. All that had been left was to sit and hold Zarifa's hand as she bucked and fought the infection through a series of seizures.

Zarifa had taken her final breath in the middle of a particularly violent convulsion which shook her to the core. While it had robbed her of life, the convulsion provided Zarifa with the long-awaited relief from her unnecessary, tortuous suffering. Nahla shook her head at the atrocious memory of it all, but knew that the event would haunt her for the rest of her life.

The washing completed, Nahla and her own mother picked up a simple loincloth, head veil and a loose fitting, sleeveless dress. Nahla dressed Zarifa in the garments before taking the five pieces of simple, white kafan – the ritual cloth specified for Islamic funerals. She sprinkled the pieces with perfume and began the heart-breaking wrapping of the body, binding it with ropes. Both women exchanged silent looks as they carefully wound the kafan around Zarifa. Nahla hesitated when she got to her head. She looked into her daughter's beautiful, now serene, face for the last time, then she stooped down and very deliberately kissed Zarifa on her ravaged mouth. Nahla's tears fell freely onto Zarifa's face and were included in the final wrapping – an eternal testimony to the incomparable grief and guilt that she felt.

The women stood back and considered the small, doll-like mummy that was Zarifa. The girl would remain that way for several hours, so that other family members and villagers could pay their respects. Once that was done, the elders of the village would gather and say the *Salat Al-Janazah;* the prayer for the forgiveness of the dead. Zarifa would then be carried by seven men from the village to her place of burial. Nahla would not be permitted to attend the graveside for that part of the ritual. Zarifa would be placed without a casket in a simple grave perpendicular to Mecca. The funeral service would follow, although there would be no lavish display as that was culturally forbidden. Instead, Nahla would offer a simple wreath to mark her daughter's grave and then there would be a three-day period of mourning – *Hidaad*.

During that time, Nahla would receive visitors who would offer their condolences and sit with her in silent sympathy. The mourning would be dignified and the mother would wear no jewellery or decorative clothing. Nahla doubted her ability to get through the rituals demanded of her, but knew that she had to. She knew that she was responsible for the death of her daughter. She also knew that she would never leave the land of her birth. Nahla bowed her head and wept for Zarifa, for her husband and for her other four children. But she wept mostly for herself, with the certain knowledge that she was now doomed to spend the rest of her days living there as a widow.

~ ~ ~ ~ ~

"I agree with you, Diane," said Glenda Rogers, consulting her laptop. "It's got to go to conference. Give them a ring and see how soon they can organise it."

Diane had just discussed with Glenda the issue of the Spiggot family and their connections to what appeared to be a network of known sex offenders. Diane had also shared her concerns about Barry Spiggot.

"I have no proof, Glenda, but I'm sure he's involved. Look at the evidence! It's all circumstantial, I grant you, but still. He's best friends with Roy Tranter and married Tranter's daughter, Janice, when she was 18 years old, after having a completely inappropriate relationship with her from the age of 15 years when he was 47 years old. He knows Malcolm Withers. Oh, let's not forget Jodie Pearson's uncle, Derek. All of them are known sex offenders. It all adds up to one big headache of a concern. How we tackle it, I don't know," Diane ended.

Glenda looked up.

"Contact the police first and see what they've got on all of them. Let's start connecting the dots. Can you do a genogram? That'll give us a visual of who's who and how they're all connected."

Diane nodded.

"Good idea," she agreed, smiling. "My specialty."

A genogram was a kind of family tree. Diane would draw out all the family members, then place all the other people of interest in concentric circles around them. She would use the diagram with a key of coloured arrows to and from the various suspects, detailing why and how they were involved. It was a simple, but effective, tool in understanding the bigger picture.

"I'll do that later," she said, "but for now I'll ring Jill Fletcher at the Child Protection Team and see if she can give us anything."

Glenda nodded. She knew the potential for innumerable children to be at risk from those men, but they had to have proof and, at the moment, they had nothing but the gut feeling of an experienced social worker. It was usually enough. Diane's gut was rarely wrong.

~ ~ ~ ~ ~

The potluck supper was in full swing. Morris had busied himself in the kitchen dishing up pie and peas, and other assorted savoury treats provided by members of the congregation. His mind was totally preoccupied with the looming responsibility of the washing up and the potential for some fun. *It's about time,* he reflected. Morris had been going to the church for weeks without having anything to show for it. Hopefully, that was all set to change soon. His daydreaming was interrupted by Phyllis who entered his domain with a pile of dirty plates and cutlery.

"Here we go, Morris," Phyllis said, cheerfully. "Clean plates all around. Everyone said how much they enjoyed it, but I'm afraid the hard work isn't over yet."

Morris adopted his familiar church smile.

"I'm pleased it's gone well," he replied. "Washing up's as good as done, especially when I get my little helper," he added, hopefully.

Phyllis looked puzzled for a moment, then a look of realisation spread across her face.

"Ah, of course! Our little superstar, Daisy, will be in to help you soon," Phyllis reassured him.

Morris struggled to prevent himself from smirking in delight. Instead, he continued his duties.

"Ah, well," he replied, "whenever she's ready. There's no rush."

Five minutes later, Daisy Blake entered into the kitchen.

"Hello, Mr Powell," the girl began, politely and innocently. "What can I do to help?"

Sex offender Morris Powell gave Daisy his most winning smile.

"Tell you what, Daisy," he replied with feigned kindness. "Why don't you close the door, so we don't disturb everyone with all the noise of our pots and pans banging about?"

Daisy Blake dutifully shut the kitchen door, unaware that she was sealing her own fate.

~ ~ ~ ~ ~

"Come on, girls," called out Fiona Blake across the church hall. "Time to go home."

Upon hearing their mother's call, Phoebe and Lucy Blake hugged their friends and said goodbye.

"Where's Daisy?" asked their mother as they skipped over.

"I don't know," said Lucy, shrugging her shoulders.

Phoebe stepped in front of Lucy and spoke up.

"I think she's helping Mr Powell with the washing up," Phoebe offered.

Fiona Blake's face clouded over with an emotion unfamiliar to the two girls. Despite her Christian beliefs, she neither liked nor trusted Morris Powell, even though she could not her place her finger on the reason. She simply did not like him and was perturbed to hear that her eldest daughter was alone in the kitchen with him.

"What's wrong, Mummy?" asked Phoebe in concern.

Fiona forced a smile.

"Nothing," she said, brightly. "Nothing at all. Let's go and find Daisy, shall we?"

As soon as the words were out of Fiona's mouth, Daisy emerged from the kitchen. Upon seeing her mother, the girl's face dropped guiltily.

"Are you okay, sweetie?" asked Fiona. "What's wrong?"

Daisy shook her head.

"Nothing," the girl mumbled. "Are we going now?"

Fiona considered her daughter for the smallest time.

"In a minute," replied the mother. "I just want to thank Mr Powell for his hard work tonight."

Fiona Blake went into the kitchen. Morris Powell stood there, leaning against the sink, rubbing his paunch and smiling. Upon seeing Fiona, he looked startled and immediately turned back to the sink to wash up.

"Not finished yet, Mr Powell?" asked Fiona, pointedly. "I thought you'd have got the job done in no time, especially with Daisy helping you."

Morris made a show of drying his hands.

"You know how it is, Mrs Blake," Morris replied, cheerfully. "Always takes longer than you think it would. Don't forget, we had almost 60 people here tonight: that's a lot of pots to wash. Daisy did a super job, though. She's a credit to you."

Then Morris hung up the towel and made his way to the door. Fiona Blake studied him intently.

"Daisy is my pride and joy, Mr Powell, as are all my girls. Not only that, but they are the apples of their father's eyes. Did I mention that he will be back from Iraq next week? Yes, he's got a fortnight's leave. I'll be sure to introduce you to him next Sunday."

Morris pretended to smile.

"Be good to meet him, Mrs Blake. You're a lovely family and I'm sure your husband's a fine man. Steve, isn't it? Well, goodnight," Morris ended as he slid out of the door and into the main hall.

Fiona's eyes narrowed as they followed Morris Powell. She could not shake away the feeling of disquiet that arose within herself.

Chapter 22

Diane picked up the phone which never seemed to stop ringing.

"Hello," she said, trying to also read an email from Jill Fletcher.

"Diane, it's Jill Fletcher. Got some info on your suspected paedophile network. I've sent you an email, but thought I'd also ring you."

Diane sat up and listened intently.

"Go on," she invited with a rising sense of dread. "I was actually just trying to read your email, but got distracted with another call."

"Well, it turns out 10 years ago, your man, Barry Spiggot, used to live in a place called Grenville over 250 miles away in the south. He had a wife and a family there with three children. And guess what? All the kids were taken into care and subsequently adopted due to sexual abuse," said Jill.

Diane immediately felt the goose bumps erupt on her arms.

"You were right, Di," continued Jill. "Barry obviously moved to get away from the stigma and the gossip as it never went to criminal trial. Trouble was, none of the kids made a disclosure good enough for the police in Grenville to take it to the Crown Prosecution Service. It stayed with Social Services. There was a finding-of-fact hearing which determined that Barry had abused all three of his children and they needed to be placed for adoption. His wife was a lot younger than him and although they couldn't prove it, the local authority suspected that she too was party to the abuse."

Diane leaned back in the chair and ran her free hand through her short hair. This was, indeed, vital information.

"Wow! Thanks, Jill. Well done! Glenda's already agreed that it's going to conference, but this puts a different slant on it. I think the best thing is for me to convene a professionals meeting about all the men we have concerns and we share all the available information around one table."

Jill Fletcher nodded in agreement at the other end of the phone.

"Yep, that's the way forward. Let me know when it is and I'll be sure to be there. Meanwhile, I'll keep digging. You never know, there might still be more information on the others."

Diane put the phone down and ignored its immediate demand to be answered once again. Instead, she went into Glenda's office.

"Barry Spiggot has previous history," Diane announced without ceremony. "He has three older children, all of whom have been adopted due to sexual abuse."

Glenda looked up from her desk and despite the seriousness of the information, she smiled.

"Damn, you're good!" Glenda declared with complete sincerity. "I'm going to start calling you Columbo! You said Barry was wrong and once again, your gut instinct was spot on."

Diane felt justified. She had, indeed, felt highly suspicious of Barry Spiggot from the get-go: from the commencement of his questionable relationship with the 15-year-old Janice, to his relationships with, at least, three other known sex offenders. It could not be a coincidence.

Diane allowed herself a small moment of triumph. However, she knew that there was a lot of work ahead and after further discussion with Glenda, a date was set for the professionals meeting whereby all gathered information would be shared and assessed.

"Go for it," said Glenda. "And well done, you!"

Before she could proceed to organise her meeting, though, Diane needed to make a scheduled visit to Kirsty Thompson. She had written to Kirsty saying that she would visit in three days. Today was the day. Diane felt no confidence whatsoever that Kirsty would be at home and knew that if this was the case, drastic action was looming.

Diane got to Kirsty's house on time and went through her usual routine of door knocking, going around the back and peering through the crack in the curtains – to no avail. As on most previous visits, no one went to the door, although the dog went into overdrive upon hearing Diane, treating her to a cacophony of hysterical barking. The social worker waited for five minutes, then had an idea. She went back to the car, got in and drove around the corner. Out of sight, she parked and waited.

Diane suspected that Kirsty was in the house, but avoiding her. If she was right, her idea would pay off. Diane let 10 minutes go by, then returned back to the house on foot, approaching from the right-hand side where she could not be seen from the window. Diane almost held her breath as she knocked again, this time lightly and only three times. She strained her ears, certain that she heard something inside apart from the dog. Then a female voice called out with suspicion.

"Who is it?"

Diane was not, by nature, an untruthful person. In fact, she was the polar opposite. However, this time she bit her lip and reassured herself that it was necessary.

Diane replied, "Avon. I have a free sample for you."

The door opened and there stood Kirsty Thompson. The look upon her face as the realisation of the lie dawned on her was absolutely priceless.

"Hello, Kirsty," said Diane in a level tone. "You and I need to talk."

~ ~ ~ ~ ~

Morris Powell sat in his bedroom feeling invincible. His success with Daisy Blake in the kitchen had been worth waiting for. All the mind-numbingly boring sermons he had sat through, never mind the endless platitudes he endured, had been worthwhile. Morris relived the incident dozens of times and did not grow tired of it.

He had started as Mr Nice Guy, chatting to the unsuspecting girl about church, school and her pet guinea pig, Buttons. Morris then 'accidentally' brushed against Daisy to gauge her reaction. The girl had moved away and said *sorry* as if the contact was her mistake. Morris turned his back on Daisy, to prepare for his first assault. When he faced her again, the child gasped in horror. Daisy had never seen an aroused male before and her mind reeled. She was aware that one should not look under anyone's clothes, so she knew it was certainly rude. She also knew it was wrong. The betrayal of her trust and ensuing confusion was total. Morris had allowed himself the shortest window of time to enjoy the power of the moment. For him, the child's emotional response and her shock were part of his sickening, depraved thrill. Then Morris looked down.

He exclaimed, "Oh, my goodness, Daisy. I'm so sorry! I don't know how that happened. I've got a hole in my trousers which my mum sewed up, but it must have split again. This is terrible, I'm really sorry. Oh, Daisy, don't be upset. It's not your fault, it's my silly trousers."

Morris had then played his ace. He adopted a highly worried look, lowered his voice and whispered.

"You won't tell anyone, will you, Daisy? We would both get into the most awful trouble if you do and, I promise, it was an accident. We don't want your mummy and daddy to know about this, either. They would be very

192

upset," Morris added, slyly. "We won't be allowed to come to church anymore if Pastor Slater found out, so it's best we keep this our little secret. I promise, it won't happen ever again."

Daisy had still not regained her composure. She was breathing quickly and felt hot and sick. The girl was frightened and ashamed at what she had just witnessed. She wanted to be out of the kitchen and away from Mr Powell, but was highly confused. Daisy knew that her mother had taught her it was Christian and right to forgive people. Her daddy had said the same thing and he was a brave soldier, so Daisy was sure he was right – he had said that everyone deserved a second chance. Daisy also knew lots of stories from Sunday School about people being forgiven and allowed another chance, so she was sure it was the right thing.

Very slowly, therefore, Daisy shook her head in response.

"I won't tell," she whispered, solemnly, while her bottom lip quivered.

Morris had almost laughed out loud in relief – he had hooked himself a live one. Instead, he put on a look of gratitude and drummed up some tears in his eyes. Morris chuckled at the memory. God, he was good!

"Oh, Daisy," Morris began fervently, "You're *such* a good girl! I knew I could rely on you. I promise, this will never happen again. I'll go straight home and get these naughty trousers sewn up, shall I?"

From far away, Daisy heard her mother's voice calling her to go home. She turned to leave, but not before Morris called out to her.

"Daisy? Our little secret then, okay?"

Daisy nodded and left the room. Her world had changed forever.

~ ~ ~ ~ ~

Kirsty Thompson resembled a goldfish: an extremely irate goldfish. Her mouth opened and closed repeatedly as she searched in vain for the appropriate words.

"You bitch!" Kirsty managed, finally. "You lying bitch!" she repeated, making to slam the door.

But Diane was on a roll. She boldly put her hand on the door to prevent it from closing.

"Kirsty," she said with firmness, "don't be so ridiculous. I need to speak to you and there is no need to keep avoiding me. You're only making it worse."

Kirsty screwed up her face and spat her words out at Diane.

"Making it worse? How do you reckon that, eh? I don't even know why you're here, sticking your nose in my business!"

Diane realised that Kirsty was not the brightest star in the sky.

"Kirsty, I had a phone call last week from your health visitor. She had some worries about Daniel and it's my job to come and talk to you about it. You remember when I visited ages ago? It's just the same. We just need to talk about how Daniel is, that's all."

Kirsty's eyes were still blazing, but she knew that she could not avoid Diane.

"I'm gonna report you for lying to me," she responded by way of retaliation. "You'll lose your job!"

Diane shrugged as she followed Kirsty into the house.

"I seriously doubt that, Kirsty, but I'll be sure to give you a complaints leaflet before I leave," Diane said in matter-of-fact manner.

Lose my job? she thought as she went into the lounge. *That I should be so lucky!*

Once inside, Diane could see that, like so many of the homes she visited, Kirsty's house was chaotic, untidy and dirty. There were overflowing ashtrays, leftover plates of food, shoes and clothes on every available surface, but no sign of a single baby toy anywhere. Diane felt despondent. *Why could people, at least, not be clean?* she thought, preparing to discuss her concerns.

"Kirsty," Diane began, "your health visitor, Hilary, told me that she was worried because Daniel had a very bad nappy rash and lost weight. I know she made you an appointment for the GP, so tell me, did you take him?"

Diane asked the question despite already knowing from Hilary that Kirsty had not kept the appointment. She wanted to see what Kirsty would say. The latter lit a cigarette.

"Yeah, course I did," Kirsty replied with indignation. "He said it was nothing to worry about and gave me some cream."

"Really?" said Diane with feigned interest. "May I see the cream he gave you?"

Kirsty stopped in mid-drag.

"I used it up," she lied.

"You used it up? The whole lot? Hmm, has it made it better?" Diane continued, determined to press her point.

Kirsty looked irritated.

"Yeah, Daniel's fine now. So is that it?"

Diane was far from finished.

"Not quite, Kirsty. What about his weight?"

Kirsty's irritation changed to boredom.

"Yeah, that was okay too. I dunno what the health visitor was on about."

"Kirsty," began Diane, purposefully. "Which doctor did you see?"

Kirsty stood up abruptly.

"Look, I'd like you to go now. I've told you: I took him to the doctor and that's all you need to know. What business is it of yours who I saw?"

Kirsty began pacing. At that moment, Neil O' Grady entered the room.

"What's going on here?" he asked, petulantly.

"Social worker's here," replied Kirsty with anger. "Yeah, she tricked me into opening the door. Proper lied to me, she did. I'm gonna complain!"

Diane remained calm.

"Mr O'Grady," she replied, politely. "I'm here to discuss some concerns with Kirsty about Daniel. By the way, Kirsty, where's Daniel? I do need to see him as part of my visit."

Kirsty and Neil exchanged glances which Diane recognised as worried looks.

196

"Kirsty," she pressed, "where's Daniel?"

Kirsty's attitude changed to one of bravado.

"Upstairs, asleep. And no, I'm not waking him up. Why should I? It took me ages to get him off this morning and no way am I waking him up for you!"

Diane felt the all-too-familiar warning signs of a significant situation unfolding. She knew that, historically, children had been seriously injured or worse because the social worker took the parent's word that they were asleep or okay. One mother had even gone to the lengths of smearing chocolate over her child's face, to conceal the bruises that she had caused. Diane's something-is-not-right antennae were working overtime.

"I don't need you to wake him, Kirsty, but I really need to see Daniel. We can creep up together and I'll just take a peek."

Neil O'Grady interrupted.

"She said *no!*" he said, raising his voice. "Are you stupid? *No* means *no!*"

Diane considered the situation for a few seconds before responding.

"Kirsty," she said, seriously. "I would not be doing my job properly if I left the house without seeing Daniel. Now, I don't want to get heavy-handed, but if you refuse to let me see him, I have no choice but to contact the police and ask for their assistance. I'm sure neither you nor Mr O'Grady wants that to happen."

Diane waited for the challenge to sink in. It could go in one of two ways and she hoped that it would not end with her being physically thrown out by the unpleasant Neil O'Grady, although she would not put it past him. Kirsty was cornered.

"Oh, for God's sake," Kirsty replied. "Go and see him then, if you're gonna make all this fuss about it."

Diane exhaled.

"I need you to come with me, Kirsty. I can't just go upstairs in your house without you present. Shall we?"

Kirsty Thompson made her way up the dimly lit stairs with a knot in her stomach. Downstairs, they both heard Neil O'Grady.

"I'm not staying here for this nonsense," he shouted, slamming the door behind him.

Diane felt some relief in knowing that he was out of the house, but she also felt some concern as to why he left. Neil O'Grady was not the sort of man to back down from a social worker – not without good reason. As Diane entered Daniel's bedroom, any relief she had felt at Neil O'Grady leaving the house evaporated. The social worker knew that all her concerns about Daniel were justified.

Chapter 23

Jodie Pearson had dreaded this particular day and now it arrived. She had been told to present herself at the Deacon Hill police station at 10 o'clock in the morning, to be interviewed about what had happened to Courtney. Jodie was terrified, not least because Scott Taylor had repeatedly threatened her as to what his mates and himself would do if she told the police the truth.

"Make no mistake, you fat bitch," Scott said, intimidatingly. "You tell them I did this, I'll make you regret it. You'll never see those kids again! Understand?"

Jodie nodded miserably, torn between her inexplicable loyalty to Scott and her undeniable bond with her children. Since her mother, Brenda, had been looking after them, the children were so happy. Jamie did not wet the bed once and Courtney's speech came on a treat. Jodie was allowed to visit the children three times a week, Brenda acting as supervisor. Jodie had been warned by Diane that she could not talk to Jamie or Courtney about what had happened in the kitchen that day and she stuck faithfully to that.

Scott did not ask to see Brandon, so he had not seen any of the children since the incident happened. Jodie's mother was brilliant and kept telling her to just leave Scott and move on, but it was not that easy. Jodie knew that she would probably never get another man; not now. She knew that she was a big lass and what with having three kids in tow, her chances of attracting a decent bloke were nil, especially around the estate. Jodie had reckoned that Scott Taylor was better than no one, but she was not so sure anymore, especially now that he was threatening her.

Jodie went into the police station and nervously told the desk sergeant her name. He smiled kindly and asked her to take a seat. Jodie sat looking at the posters on the wall about domestic violence, racial prejudice and neighbourhood watch. As she was trying to read the poster on domestic violence, a tall, dark-haired man entered and introduced himself as Detective Sergeant Dave Simpson. He asked Jodie to sit down in a small office, then offered her a glass of water which she declined. Jodie was far too nervous to relax and drink. The detective sergeant and Jodie were joined by a fair-haired woman, Jennifer Anderson, who was also a police officer.

Dave Simpson and Jennifer began by asking Jodie to tell them, step by step, what had occurred that day in the kitchen. Jodie trotted out her carefully rehearsed story. It was the same one she had told at the hospital and the one she was almost starting to believe. Both officers looked at Jodie sympathetically, then Jennifer Anderson spoke softly.

"Jodie, why don't you tell us what really happened, eh? We know you're protecting Scott but, honestly, Jodie, is he worth it?"

Jodie did not expect that. She expected to be shouted at and threatened like one saw on the telly. But she was not prepared for people to be nice to her.

Jennifer continued, "Jodie, we know that your little boy, Jamie, isn't it? We know Jamie said to the doctor and the social worker at the hospital that Scott did it. Why do you think he said that?"

At the mention of Jamie's name, Jodie became tearful. She reached into her pocket for a tissue, but Jennifer beat her to it and pushed a box of tissues over to her. Jodie took one, dabbed her eyes and blew her nose.

"I miss my kids," Jodie said with shyness to the police officers. "I really miss them."

Jennifer and Dave exchanged glances.

"We know you do, Jodie," said Jennifer, gently. "That's why it's really important you tell us the truth. Your little girl has a broken arm which, the specialist tells us, was caused by being twisted. It was not caused by a fall. At the moment, there are only two people who could have caused that injury to Courtney: you and Scott. Now, if you didn't do that, there's no reason that I can see why you shouldn't have the children back living with you, although that's a decision for the social workers to make. However, if Scott did that, you need to tell us. I'm sure you wouldn't want him to do it again to another child, eh?"

Upon hearing that she might be able to have her children back, Jodie wavered.

"Can I really get them back, do you think?" she asked, hopefully.

Dave spoke up for the first time.

"That's not our decision, Jodie. Like Jennifer said, that's for Social Services to work out. But in my experience, if we can satisfy ourselves that there is an innocent parent who can care properly for the children, then usually that parent is able to have the children returned to their care. I'm not promising, mind; but it's a possibility."

Jodie Pearson had never done anything of note in her life. She had never been brave and never stood up for herself. She had been walked on and taken advantage of since the age of 10 years. However, despite her failings, Jodie's three children were her world and she had just had enough. She swallowed hard and took a deep breath.

"Scott did it," Jodie said with finality. "He pulled Courtney back to the table when she wouldn't eat her toast and he twisted her arm. He threatened me that if I told you, I'd regret it."

Jodie's words came out in a breathless jumble of apprehension. She was taken aback when Jennifer leaned across and patted her on the arm.

"Well done, flower," Jennifer said. "Now, can you start at the beginning and tell us the whole story?"

When it was over, Jodie felt a huge weight off her shoulders. She knew that she had done the right thing and only hoped that she could get her kids back. She was, however, extremely worried.

"What about Scott?" Jodie asked, nervously. "He said he'd make me regret it if I told you and I'm really scared of him."

Jennifer and Dave looked seriously at Jodie. Dave spoke first.

"Don't you worry about Scott Taylor, Jodie. We'll be going to arrest him later today. Is there somewhere you can go, meantime? Somewhere he won't find you?"

Jodie thought for a moment.

"Well, I could go to me mam's. Scott won't go there. But it's not my day for seeing the kids, so I don't think I'm allowed to go," Jodie said, sadly.

Jennifer stood up.

"Let me go and ring your social worker, Jodie, and we'll see if we can arrange it. It's Di Foster, isn't it?"

Jodie nodded and smiled her thanks at Jennifer. She liked these police officers, they had been nice. Ten minutes later, Jennifer returned looking pleased.

"All sorted," Jennifer said. "Diane's agreed that it's okay for you to go to your mam's today until we arrest Scott. Now, Jodie, make sure you don't let him know about what happened here today. We don't want him disappearing from the face of the estate now, do we?"

It was a relieved Jodie who stepped out of the police station into the cold January air. She walked with a spring in her step in the direction of her mother's house. Jodie had not felt that light inside since, well, she could not recall and those nice police officers had said that she might be able to have her kids back. As Jodie rounded the first corner, though, she stopped in her tracks. There was Scott Taylor's best mate, Shady Green, standing in her path.

"Hey, Shady," Jodie said as calmly as she could, although her stomach was looping the loop. "What's up?"

Shady Green smirked at Jodie.

"Little message from Scott," Shady said, slowly and deliberately. "He said to go straight home. He's waiting for you there."

Jodie looked around wildly for help, but the streets were deserted.

"I can't go now," she began. "I've got to run an errand."

Shady Green stepped closer.

"Maybe, you didn't hear me right?" he said menacingly. "Scott says to go straight home. There was no mention of running any errands."

Jodie did not imagine it possible that she could be so brave. In the blink of an eye, she turned and bolted the 200 yards back towards the police station and almost collapsed in terror on the front desk.

"He's after me!" Jodie said, breathlessly, unaccustomed as she was to running. "Scott's mate, Shady Green, he's after me."

The desk sergeant stood up immediately and pressed a button on his phone. Two officers entered running and after listening briefly to what Jodie had to say, went swiftly out into the street. Minutes later, they returned with Shady Green in tow. He was a well-known, local criminal and did not get far. As Shady was marched through to the back, he scowled at Jodie.

"You're a dead woman!" he threatened.

The police officer gave him a shove.

"Yeah, yeah, Shady. And you're a Columbian drug lord. Get in there, you stupid muppet. Next time, tell Scott Taylor to do his own dirty work."

~ ~ ~ ~ ~

Diane went swiftly over to Daniel's crib and her stomach tightened as she regarded the baby. Daniel was grey and still. Diane picked him up and his head flopped back. She checked his pulse which was faint and thready.

"Call an ambulance," the social worker said, urgently. "Do it now, Kirsty! Call 999 and tell them you need an ambulance."

Kirsty Thompson stood like a lump, unmoving and with her mouth agape.

"Oh, for goodness sake!" exclaimed Diane.

She handed Daniel to Kirsty and reached into her pocket for the phone.

"Take him downstairs now," she ordered while waiting for the call to connect. "Yes, my name is Diane Foster. I'm a social worker for the local authority and I need an ambulance immediately to number 32, Hill Crest Drive. It's an emergency. The patient is a three-month-old baby who is unresponsive, although he has a pulse. Hurry!" exclaimed Diane as she raced down the stairs after Kirsty.

The ambulance seemed to take forever to arrive although, in reality, it was exactly six minutes. As she waited, Diane wrapped Daniel in a grubby blanket and desperately rubbed his hands. The baby boy opened his eyes briefly, then they rolled back again into his head. Diane was frantic and thought the baby was going to die right there in her arms.

"What the hell happened, here?" Diane demanded, imperatively.

Kirsty was still standing, looking lost. Diane's question seemed to bring her back to the present, but she just shook her head.

"I dunno," Kirsty replied, lamely. "He was okay before you came."

The paramedics administered emergency first aid to Daniel in the home. They set up a drip and stabilised him as best they could, before whisking him off to *Queen's Hospital* three miles away. Diane followed in her car, with Kirsty. At the hospital, the doctors quickly took charge of the situation, while Diane and Kirsty waited anxiously. The former took a minute to ring up Glenda and tell her what had happened. Glenda was horrified and told Diane to keep her posted. Eventually, a serious looking doctor entered the waiting room.

"Ms Thompson?" the doctor asked, looking from one to the other.

Diane pointed to Kirsty.

"She's the mother," Diane replied. "I'm the social worker."

The doctor directed his gaze at Kirsty.

"Well, Ms Thompson, your son's lucky to be here. He's suffering from serious dehydration and by the looks of it, he's significantly underweight. When did he last take a feed?"

Kirsty looked flustered.

"I fed him last night," she said, defensively.

The doctor moved closer.

"At precisely what time did you feed him, Ms Thompson?" he asked, pointedly.

Kirsty looked uncomfortable.

"I dunno. I reckon about 10 o'clock."

The doctor considered that before continuing.

"Well, he's a very poorly baby and will have to be admitted to the children's ward for further assessment. Ms Foster, a word if you don't mind."

Diane followed the doctor into his office and he shut the door.

"What the hell is the story here?" the doctor began. "This baby was about three hours away from death due to dehydration."

Diane outlined the details of her involvement with the family and her difficulties in gaining access to the home. She told the doctor how she had tricked Kirsty into opening the door that morning and found Daniel upstairs. The doctor shook his head.

"It's a good thing you got in, Ms Foster. Without your intervention, we would have been dealing with a tragedy here."

Diane knew the implications of what the doctor was saying. She asked to use the phone and relayed his assessment to Glenda who responded in her usual, brisk manner.

"Right, Di. Well, Daniel's going to be in the hospital for a few days, I imagine, so that will give us time to seek legal advice. I'll ring the police and let them know, then I'll give Marcus a ring. From what the doctor said, I'm pretty confident that we have more than enough grounds to apply for an order. Keep me posted," Glenda said and went off to ring up the legal team.

Diane knew that it was a serious case of neglect and the police would want to interview both Kirsty Thompson and Neil O'Grady. She also knew that neglect cases were often the most difficult to prove in court as there was not necessarily any visible injury to the child. In Daniel's case, however, the doctor's testimony would be key. Diane returned to the waiting room where Kirsty was pacing the floor.

"What'd he say?" Kirsty asked without real interest. "When can I go home?"

Diane explained to Kirsty that Daniel would be admitted to the hospital until he was well. She also explained that the police would need to speak to Neil and herself about how Daniel was so unwell. For the first time since the day began, Kirsty looked worried.

"Police?" she replied loudly. "Why police? I ain't done nothing wrong!"

Chapter 24

Fiona Blake listened intently to what Daisy's teacher, Stefanie Cooper, was saying.

"I don't know what it is, Fiona, but Daisy's very withdrawn lately and just not herself. We thought it was a bit of bullying as she and Chloe Parker don't always see eye to eye, but it's not that. I spoke to both girls yesterday and they said they're good friends again. Daisy's work is suffering and she appears unable to concentrate any longer."

Fiona frowned as she acknowledged what Ms Cooper was saying.

"I've noticed too," the mother replied. "Daisy's really quiet at home and isn't playing with her sisters in the same way she used to. I've asked her, of course, but she keeps saying it's nothing."

Stefanie Cooper consulted her papers and nodded.

"Well, Fiona, we'll keep an eye on Daisy and let you know if we come up with anything. You do the same."

Fiona left the meeting with an uneasy feeling. She decided that she would ask Daisy again that evening, to see if she could get to the bottom of what was clearly upsetting her daughter. Meanwhile, Daisy Blake sat listlessly picking at her school lunch.

"Want to play skipping later?" asked her best friend, Sasha.

Daisy shook her head without looking up.

"Nah," she said, "I'm not bothered."

Sasha tossed her blonde curls back over her shoulder and ran off to see if Amy Webb wanted to play. When Daisy got home, she was surprised to find her mother sitting at the living room coffee table with a plate of biscuits and a drink of juice waiting. Not that it was unusual – her mother was always baking and cooking. It was just that Fiona did not usually sit there with it in the living room.

"Hi, Mum," Daisy said in a flat tone of voice.

Fiona smiled at her eldest daughter.

"Hello, darling," she replied. "How was your day?"

Daisy gave a small shrug.

"It was okay, thanks," replied the girl, warily.

Fiona took a deep breath.

"Daisy, honey, come sit here. I need to talk to you."

Daisy looked around.

"Where's Phoebe and Lucy? Why are they not here?"

Fiona patted the sofa cushion by her side.

"Your sisters are with Auntie Heather," the mother replied, "so you and I can have a little chat."

Daisy looked uncomfortable.

"About what?" she asked. "What are we chatting about?"

Fiona steeled herself for the distasteful subject that she knew she had to broach.

"I can't help noticing," she began, "that you've been really quiet lately. Ms Cooper's noticed it too. Anyway, I'm worried about you and when I had a long think about it, I kind of feel you were okay until the day of the potluck supper in church. You remember? You helped Mr Powell in the kitchen to wash up that day."

Upon hearing the name of Morris Powell, Daisy turned pale. She shook her head vehemently.

"Nothing happened," the girl blurted out. "Nothing."

Fiona Blake closed her eyes against the tears which threatened as she took her daughter's hand.

"What did he do, Daisy? You need to tell me. What did Mr Powell do?"

~ ~ ~ ~ ~

Steve Blake whistled as he packed his kit. He had spent three, long months in the notorious Helmand Province of Iraq and was more than ready for some leave. He was due to fly out of Lashkar Gar airport at dawn the next day and would be home by evening to see his family.

Steve was a hardened veteran of many battles. He was the captain of his unit and responsible for up to 120 men under his command. It was his fourth tour of duty and, he hoped, almost his last. Steve would spend two weeks with his family before returning to Iraq for a final tour.

The captain allowed himself a small smile at the prospect of Fiona's great home cooking and the hugs of his daughters. Like most fathers, Steve Blake idolised his little girls. He may have been a big-shot army captain out in Iraq, but at home he was putty in his family's hands, much to Fiona's chagrin.

"Steve," his wife would reason with that look in her eyes. "I've said it's bedtime and that's all there is to it."

Steve would look to his daughters who, in turn, would stick their bottom lips out pleadingly.

"Daddy," they would say almost in perfect unison. "Daddy, please! Just five more minutes."

Steve would crack and look apologetically at his wife.

"Just five minutes, Fifi," he would plead.

Fiona would try looking stern, but Steve would see the crinkles at the corner of her mouth and eyes as she too cracked under the unfair assault of pouting lips and teary eyes.

"Oh, alright," she would concede. "But no more."

And the girls would all dive bomb him with shouts of *Yay, Daddy*, and they would snuggle up for a big hug together. Steve's smile broke into a positive grin as he anticipated seeing his beloved family again.

~ ~ ~ ~ ~

The shoulders of Daisy Blake were still shaking from her now silent sobs. She clung to her mother, burying her head deep into Fiona's chest as she wept. Fiona Blake had continued pressing Daisy about what had happened in the kitchen at church, but it was not until she reassured her daughter that she would not be in trouble that Daisy cracked.

Fiona listened in silent horror to her daughter's account of what had taken place that day in the kitchen. It all came out in a garbled rush: words tripping over words as Daisy let it all go. When it was over, Fiona held Daisy for the longest time, rocking her back and forth, smoothing her hair and cooing to her. Words of comfort, reassurance and love. Daisy knew that it was going to be okay.

"Will you tell Daddy?" the girl finally asked, her eyes swollen and red; her voice thick with tears.

Fiona's eyes clouded over as she stared into the distance.

"You can count on it," she said softly, stroking Daisy's face. "Daddy will most certainly be hearing about this."

~ ~ ~ ~ ~

Scott Taylor sat in Jodie's house and wondered where she had gone. He knew he could trust Shady Green to deliver his message. *Where was she?* Scott was about to ring Shady's mobile when there was a knock at the door. *What's she knocking for,* he thought, annoyed at having to get up out of the chair. He pulled the door open.

"What you knocking f . . ," Scott began, but the words froze in his mouth.

Instead of Jodie, he was facing two burly police officers.

"Scott Taylor?" one of them said. "You're under arrest for an assault on Courtney Pearson on or around the 15th January."

The rest of their words were lost as Scott's mind refused to accept what was happening. *She shopped me!* he thought, incredulously. *The fat cow actually shopped me!*

For once in his life, Scott went without a fight. He was too shocked to do anything else. He had never thought that Jodie had it in her to do such a thing.

~ ~ ~ ~ ~

DC Jill Fletcher looked around the table of professionals. It was a good turnout.

"Good morning, everyone," Jill commenced. "Shall we do introductions, then get started?"

The introductions were short and to the point. Diane was there, of course, as was Glenda. Also present were representatives from the police, probation and the managers and staff from the educational farm on Lower Lane. They had all been invited over Janice Spiggot's claims that her father and other known sex offenders had worked there several years ago, and that all of them had access to the vulnerable young people who attended.

"Right," said Jill in her usual, business-like fashion. "We've been doing a lot of investigating into the background of our known offenders: Barry Spiggot, Malcolm Withers, Derek Pearson and Roy Tranter. All of them are known to have worked voluntarily at the Lower Lane farm estate and all of them have had access to several dozen, vulnerable, young people. What is clear is that all these perpetrators have known each other for many years and maintain their contact to this day.

"Roy Tranter is currently in prison for sexual assaults on his two daughters and our enquiries indicate that while Barry Spiggot has not been near the prison, Tranter has been receiving visits from none other than Malcolm Withers who was only released from the same prison a few weeks ago. Obviously, this is of great concern, given the association of Withers with Barry and Janice Spiggot. Other names that have come up as having worked at the Lower Lane farm or knowing the other

214

perpetrators are Dennis Jackson, Nigel Smathers and Morris Powell, all of whom are known to us as prolific sex offenders.

"Jackson is still incarcerated, but is due for release in three months' time. Smathers is nowhere to be found and Morris Powell is living with his mother at the Deacon Hill estate. We have current intelligence which suggests he is in contact with the other perpetrators via email."

Jill paused to allow the information to sink in. Diane was not surprised to hear it all. She knew that Dennis Jackson was Jessica Jackson's father and that she was involved with the Powell family because of their connection to Morris Powell.

"It's like a spider's web," Diane told the group – a comment which was met with several nods of agreement.

Jill continued, "There are other names linked to these men but, at the moment, we don't know who they are or how they're connected. One is called Alan Slater and the other is a man known only as NB. Neither of them have a police record that we are aware of and, obviously, we're working to try and identify who these men are and will, of course, keep you posted. We don't imagine for one minute that NB is using his real initials, although given the arrogance of these men and their imagined invincibility, it's always a possibility that NB are his actual initials. What we do know is that all these men are exchanging indecent images via what they believe to be secure emails and websites.

"However, we have a covert operation known as Operation Firefly. It is slowly unpicking their network and identifying the main players, although we are most interested in the ringleaders. We have reason to believe that NB is one of the big fish and in control of the lesser members such as Morris Powell, Barry Spiggot and other players. To date, we have identified Jessica Jackson as a victim in many of the photographs. This does not come as a surprise, given her history and her father's current convictions. I will be liaising with Social Services and showing them photographs of other children, in an effort to identify them and their whereabouts. We will undertake the continued surveillance of all these men and we will also visit the farm," Jill ended, looking at the site manager, Bill Jacobs.

Bill spoke up for the first time.

"No problem, Jill," he agreed. "Come any time and we'll cooperate to the fullest extent. We are as anxious as you to get to the bottom of this."

Jill nodded her thanks.

"Okay, we'll be in touch to make arrangements to visit. We'll need details of the young people who used to attend when all or any of these men were undertaking their voluntary work, to establish whether or not they've been victimised."

The meeting continued with various tasks being assigned to the professionals. A further date was set for three weeks' time to reassess progress made.

~ ~ ~ ~ ~

Captain Steve Blake scanned the airport for his wife and children. His plane had been delayed by an hour, which only served to heighten his anticipation of seeing his family after having been away for so long. Finally, he spotted Fiona's familiar, red winter coat in the crowd. Alongside her were his three little angels, all wrapped up against the biting cold in their warm coats, scarves and gloves.

"Hey!" Steve shouted as he waved. "Hey there, you guys. Over here!"

Phoebe saw him first.

"Mummy," she squealed, "he's there! It's Daddy," and set off at a run.

The others followed in hot pursuit, not wanting Phoebe to have more hugs and kisses than themselves. Fiona was close behind, laughing as she cautioned her excited daughters.

"Slow down, girls. Save a bit of Daddy for me."

Steve Blake disappeared under an avalanche of arms and legs. He was hugged and kissed and generally mauled, and he relished every minute of it. He scooped the girls up all at once and roared.

"How's my little soldiers?"

The girls laughed in delight. Daddy always called them his soldiers.

"We're okay," they shouted back, knowing what was coming next.

"We're okay, what?" Steve demanded.

"We're okay, Captain, sir!" the girls shouted as they giggled and hugged their father some more.

"That's more like it," Steve grinned as he set them down. "Now, where's that mummy of yours?"

The girls reluctantly stepped aside to allow Steve to take his wife into his arms. They held each other for a long time before the captain held Fiona at arm's length.

"Let me look at you," he said with tenderness.

Steve took a good, long look at Fiona before hugging her again.

"Looking good, Mrs Blake, looking good," Steve said as they walked hand in hand to the car with a gaggle of little girls, all vying for attention, following close behind.

"So," Steve finally said when they arrived and sat down back at the house. "Tell me what's been happening."

Fiona and Steve had spoken on Skype, but that was intermittent and internet connections were unreliable, so he still had lots of news on which to catch up. Fiona told Steve how the girls were getting on in school and brought him up to date on the latest gossip in the neighbourhood. Eventually, after an exciting tea time, it was bedtime. The girls all insisted on Daddy being the one to take them up, read to them and tuck them in. After what seemed like eternity, Steve returned downstairs, smiling.

"I think they've settled," he began.

But his confidence was dashed as a small voice called down.

"Daddy!"

Steve grinned.

"Spoke too soon," he said and went back up.

That happened for four times before Fiona took over and went up to give a final warning as to what dire punishments would follow if the girls did not go to sleep. It seemed to do the trick. At long last, Steve and Fiona sat together: Fiona leaning on her husband's shoulder, her legs curled up underneath.

"Finally," Steve said, putting his arm around his wife. "I get you to myself."

"I missed you, Captain Blake," replied Fiona, her eyes filling with tears.

"Hey, hey, what's this?" asked Steve, brushing a stray tear from her cheek. "I'm here now, don't be upset."

A despondent anguish settled over Fiona like a cloud as she knew that she had to tell Steve what had happened to Daisy. She knew only too well how her husband would react.

"Steve," Fiona began with a deep sigh. "I'm so sorry, darling. But there's something very difficult I need to tell you."

Steve listened in absolute silence as Fiona explained, as quickly and painlessly as she could, what had happened to their beloved eldest daughter. When she finished, Steve's face was set like stone. His mouth was hardened into a thin line and the look in his eyes was terrible. The captain nodded slowly and put his arms around Fiona who was crying with the effort of retelling the awful details of the incident.

"Shh," Steve soothed. "Shh, don't worry anymore. I'm here now, I'm here. I'll sort it out," he said, softly.

Over Fiona's head, Steve's eyes blazed with undisguised rage and hatred.

Chapter 25

Glenda put down the phone. She had spoken to the police and the legal department about baby Daniel. The police had taken all the details and would make arrangements to speak to Kirsty Thompson and Neil O'Grady about the neglect Daniel had suffered. Meanwhile, Marcus Edwards was in touch with the court and had secured a date for an urgent hearing. The only problem was that the county court did not have an available date before a fortnight passed, so he had booked a hearing in the Magistrates Court. This was not a popular choice as the magistrates were not considered as aware and experienced as county court judges. They relied on the clerk of the court for accurate information regarding the law and the presenting case, and the magistrates usually consisted of a body of up to three people who would discuss the matter between themselves before reaching a decision.

Marcus relayed all this information to Glenda who raised her eyebrows upon hearing it.

"Oh, not the Magistrates Court, Marcus! Can't you get us into County? This is a really serious situation and you know how the magistrates can be. It's anyone's guess as to which way the outcome will go."

Marcus adopted his usual sombre manner.

"Glenda, you know I concur with that viewpoint, but I'm afraid there are no available dates in the county court within our timescale. We have to go with the magistrates and trust that we get a sensible bench."

Glenda sighed.

"Okay, Marcus. But I'm not happy and I know Diane won't be, either."

Glenda was correct. Diane was not happy at all.

"The Magistrates Court?" questioned Diane with sharpness upon hearing the news. "Oh, no, Glenda! Remember that case last year, when we thought it was a foregone conclusion and they disagreed, and those two children went home only to be re-abused by their uncle? Can't we get into any county court? Can't we go to another area?" she asked in frustration.

"I completely understand, Di," replied Glenda, sympathetically, "but Marcus said it's impossible, so we'll just have to make as strong a case as we can. To be honest, given what the consultant said, I can't imagine anyone disagreeing with our application for an order."

Diane grimaced.

"Well, we'll see. I've got no confidence in them, but as you say, we'll have to see. Meanwhile, I'll ring the fostering team and see if they have an available carer for Daniel. He won't be discharged for at least a week, so it gives them a bit of time."

Later that day, Diane managed to identify a suitable foster home for Daniel upon discharge. She had not envisaged a problem as babies were relatively easy to place. *That's one thing sorted,* she thought. *Now let's hope we have a good day in court.* As if he just read her mind, Marcus rang at that precise moment.

"Diane," he commenced in his usual, brisk manner, "we have an urgent hearing booked for tomorrow at 2.00pm. Is that going to be acceptable?"

Diane did not have to think twice.

"Whatever you can get is fine, Marcus. Thank you. I'll meet you in court at 1.00pm."

At the other end of the phone, the lawyer nodded.

"1.00pm it is, Diane."

~ ~ ~ ~ ~

Steve and Fiona Blake talked late into the night. Fiona's relief at having her husband at home and being able to confide in him was tangible. She poured her heart out, expressing her disbelief that someone within a church could commit such a heinous act on an innocent child.

"He's an odious, little man," Fiona explained. "He's fat and pudgy, with a stupid comb-over. I never liked him and never trusted him. I should have known better than to allow Daisy to be alone with him in the kitchen but, Steve, I had no idea he was in there! Usually, Doreen or Phyllis do the washing up. This is all my fault!" she exclaimed as a fresh assault of tears overwhelmed her.

Steve leaned over and stroked his wife's face.

"This is in no way your fault, honey," he said, gently. "There's only one person responsible for this and that's Morris Powell. Tomorrow we'll go to the police and report him."

Fiona sat up.

"Yes, we must tell the police. How many other children are at risk from him if we don't? Oh, but what about Daisy? She's gone through so much, I can't bear the thought of her having to give evidence and relive it all. Oh, Steve, I can't bear it!"

Fiona's grief and sorrow were etched in her face.

"We have to, Fifi," Steve reasoned, "we have to. Daisy will be okay. She's a strong, little girl and has us to support her through this. Don't fret anymore, shh. Now let's try and get some sleep."

223

In the peace and quiet of their bedroom, Fiona's emotional exhaustion overtook her and she fell into a sleep like a coma. Beside her, Steve lay staring into the darkness, his face hardened with the information he had just been given and the knowledge of what he had to do. *Fat guy with a comb-over, eh?* he mused. *Okay, Mr Powell. Let's see how you do with the big boys!*

~ ~ ~ ~ ~

Diane arrived early in court. Marcus was already in one of the small anterooms and poring over the papers, deep in thought.

"How we doing?" Diane asked as she entered. "Any sign of the mum yet?"

Marcus looked up and nodded.

"She's here, Diane, and I have to say: she's extremely fortuitously represented. She has, somehow, managed to secure the services of Piers Hamilton-Blake."

Marcus paused and looked as if he were in pain. Then he continued.

"Mr Hamilton-Blake is one of the leading barristers in the country and quite frankly, Diane, we have a fight on our hands. The man is a giant in the field and I'm at a loss as to how someone like Kirsty Thompson managed to get him to represent her."

As it turned out, Kirsty Thompson had just been lucky. The firm of solicitors she had approached in relation to the impending court hearing did not have any solicitors available. What they did have, however, was Piers Hamilton-Blake who oftentimes did *ad hoc* work for them. It just so happened that another case of his had just been adjourned to a later date, thus freeing Hamilton-Blake up to offer his extremely expensive services to Kirsty Thompson – courtesy of the taxpayers, of course.

Diane raised her eyebrows.

"Surely, we don't have anything to worry about?" she asked.

Marcus did not reply.

"Do we, Marcus?" Diane pressed. "Tell me this is a slam dunk! Daniel was hours away from certain death. I don't care who she has representing her, no bench in the land should fail to find in our favour. Surely to God, we can win this one!"

Marcus gathered his papers and regarded Diane with his hangdog stare.

"I wish I could give you the assurance you seek, Diane, but we're in the hands of the magistrates and have a fierce opponent who will make a strong argument in favour of Daniel being returned to his mother's care, with high levels of support."

Diane leapt to her feet.

"What?!" she exclaimed. "High levels of support? You got to be kidding me, Marcus. Her complacency almost killed him!"

Marcus raised his hands in a calming gesture.

"Diane, Diane," he said soothingly, "I'm on your side. As I said, we'll have to wait and see what outcome we can secure, and hope it's a positive one."

Thirty minutes later, they were ushered into the courtroom. There was a bench of three magistrates and Diane noted, to her dismay, that it was led by Justice of the Peace Margaret Forbes. The social worker groaned inwardly. JP Forbes was bad news on two counts: first, she seemed to have an inherent dislike of social workers and almost appeared to regard herself as some sort of champion of the underdog. Second, it was a standing joke within the office that JP Forbes had a penchant for a liquid lunch. Since this was an afternoon hearing, Diane had no doubt that the justice would have partaken of the sherry during recess.

Diane leaned over to Marcus.

"And here's me thinking it couldn't get any worse," she whispered, cynically.

Marcus was the first to make his petition to the bench. All of them listened intently, although Diane fancied that Margaret Forbes was nodding off. Marcus gave an excellent synopsis of the problems the local authority encountered, to date, in getting Kirsty to engage with them: the missed appointment at the doctor's; the avoidance of the social worker, and so on and so forth. Marcus spoke about the concerns of the health visitor regarding Daniel and Kirsty's failure to take her advice. He summed up by retelling in dramatic style, the events which had led to Daniel's emergency dash to *Queen's Hospital* where he remained in critical, but stable, condition.

"I repeat, Madam," Marcus said, emphasising the point. "Had it not been for Ms Foster's persistence, we would have a very different and tragic outcome to this series of events. In light of the overwhelming evidence of serious neglect, I conclude there's no other sensible option than to place Daniel in a place of safety in foster care until further assessments are undertaken."

The bench nodded as one and thanked Marcus for his summation.

"Mr Hamilton-Blake," invited Margaret Forbes, "if you please."

Hamilton-Blake stood up importantly and paused for effect.

"Your Worships," he began, "I concur with my learned colleague here that this is, indeed, a serious situation. However, I put it to you that it is serious in the complete lack of support this young mother has had from Social Services and other professionals."

Hamilton-Blake pointed to Kirsty who sat looking suitably downcast in her seat beside him.

"This is not a bad person. Inexperienced as a mother, yes; but a bad person, no. What Kirsty Thompson requires is not to have her only child taken from her care, but for those professionals who seem hell-bent on pursuing this course of action, to offer her the intensive support she clearly requires to be a better mother. Ms Thompson readily and freely accepts that she was ineffective in caring for Daniel. However, this was due to her lack of experience, not her lack of care or interest in her first-born son. Her health visitor clearly told the social worker that she felt Ms Thompson was suffering from postnatal depression, yet my client received no support in that regard. Ms Thompson would welcome the intervention of professional help. In fact, she informs me that she has asked for advice and none was forthcoming."

Upon hearing that statement, Diane almost leapt out of her chair and would have done so had Marcus not physically restrained her by putting a hand on her arm.

Piers Hamilton-Blake continued, "Ms Thompson has further advised me that she was, in fact, at home on the days the social worker said that she would visit, but no one went to the home. She has, in short, been let down by the very people who sit here today and petition you for her child's removal into foster care. My client has not been given a fair opportunity to prove herself as a mother and begs the court for that chance. If Daniel were returned to her care, I would suggest a comprehensive package of support, with regular visits to the home and the input of the children's centre. Of course, there would be a thorough parenting assessment, along with other interventions as the local authority saw fit. Your Worships, I accept that Daniel Thompson lies in the hospital today in critical condition, but argue that he and his mother have been failed by professionals who allowed it to get to that point. If the court pleases, I strongly petition for Daniel to be returned home to his mother and to be afforded the support she has been sorely lacking to date."

There followed an hour of further argumentation back and forth before the bench went to consider its verdict. Diane sat with Marcus in the anteroom.

"Why do I feel so nervous?" she asked. "I mean, this should be so straightforward. I cannot believe how much Kirsty Thompson lied in there, saying she was home for my visits. What a load of rubbish! As for that barrister of hers: well, he should be ashamed!"

Chapter 26

Fiona Blake opened her eyes and closed them again. She had woken up with a headache from crying so much. She reached out for her husband and despite the headache, smiled as Steve took her hand, holding it as they lay there.

"Hey, gorgeous," Steve said as he sat up. "Man, it feels good to sleep in my own bed and wake up next to my beautiful wife."

Fiona sighed at the enormity of their situation.

"Are we going to church, Steve?" she asked with hesitation.

Steve's face clouded over.

"Not today, honey; not today. Let's just spend some time together and explain to Daisy what we need to do about the police, then maybe we go to *Frankie and Benny's* later for a treat, eh?"

Fiona felt relieved. She could not have faced church and certainly did not trust herself to come face to face with Morris Powell.

"Okay," she agreed, "that's what we'll do."

Fiona snuggled back down, luxuriating in having Steve back with her again. However, their peace was short-lived as, minutes later, all three girls barged into their bedroom with cries of *Daddy* and piled onto the bed in one giant tangle of arms and legs. Fiona laughed at their antics.

"I give up. They're all yours, Captain Blake. I'll go make breakfast."

An hour later, calm had been restored and the five of them sat together for a late, leisurely breakfast.

"What are we doing today, Daddy?" asked Phoebe, always the leader of the pack.

Steve grinned at Fiona.

"Well," he replied, drawing the word out as long as he could. "Mummy and I thought we might take you all to *Frankie and Benny's*, but then we thought you wouldn't like that at all."

There was an immediate outcry and chorus.

"Daddy, we love it there!" said the girls as they registered their protests.

Steve held his hand up.

"Okay, okay. I surrender. *Frankie and Benny's* it is. But first, Daddy has to run a little errand."

Fiona glanced up at Steve quizzically.

"Errand, honey? What errand?"

Steve looked mysterious and tapped his nose with his finger.

"Aha!" he said, "It's a top secret mission which only daddies can know about, but it might just involve bringing home some chocolate and sweeties."

This had the effect of setting the girls off again into a babble of voices as they shouted their preferences.

"Oh, can I have a *Crunchie* please, Daddy?" asked Phoebe.

"And please, may I have a *Flake?*" added Daisy with enthusiasm.

230

Steve adopted an intense look as he thought about their requests.

"And what about you, little miss?" he asked Lucy.

Lucy frowned as she gave the matter some serious thought.

"A whole bar of *Galaxy*," she finally announced.

"A whole bar!" exclaimed Steve. "Okay, I'll see what I can do. Is that alright with you, Mummy? What would you like?"

Fiona regarded her husband with suspicion.

"I'd like my husband here with us," she replied with emphasis. "What are you up to?"

Steve shrugged his shoulders.

"Chocolate run," he said with a wink. "You have no idea how long it is since I tasted *Cadbury's Whole Nut* chocolate and I'm afraid if I don't get some within the hour, you may not be able to live with me."

Fiona shook her head.

"Oh, you're impossible!" she declared. "Go on with you and bring me some *Revels*," adding with a grin, "a big bag."

~ ~ ~ ~ ~

Morris Powell was disappointed to find that Daisy Blake was not in church that day. He had hoped to follow up on their little encounter and reiterate the importance of keeping it a secret. One could never trust those little brats not to blab.

Morris drank his post-service coffee and tried looking happy as he joined with the inane banter which inevitably followed the meeting. Finally, he could escape and get home. Morris consoled himself with the fact that he was going to babysit for his no-good brother later that evening. He smiled indulgently at the thought of what could happen.

Morris made his way to the bus stop, taking his usual cut through the little alleyway down the side of the co-op. It saved him five minutes and a good half-mile walk. It was unfortunate that this particular way was often frequented by gangs of youth who would inevitably make fun of his comb-over, but he was used to it and ignored them.

Morris stepped into the alley and noted with relief that the way was clear. No kids there to make fun of him, today. Just one guy, one man, walking towards him purposefully. As Morris approached, however, the man stopped and seemed to be waiting for him. Sure enough as Morris drew level, the man smiled.

"Morris Powell?" the man asked. "Hey, Morris, it *is* you, isn't it? Man, I haven't seen you for years. How've you been?"

Morris was taken aback.

"You have the advantage," he replied, confused. "I'm afraid I don't know you."

The man continued smiling.

"It *is* Morris, isn't it? Knew you way back from the mines when we used to work the same shift. God, how long's it been?"

Morris shook his head.

"Well, I'm Morris Powell," he said, "but I never worked in the mines and don't remember you at all. Good day."

Morris made to walk off, but as he did so, the man grabbed him by the arm.

"So it *is* you," the latter said, menacingly.

The man's face had changed and was white with rage.

"Like little girls, do we?" he continued in a strangled voice. "Well, this is for Daisy Blake!"

Morris did not see it coming, so intent was he on trying to work out who this was and what was happening.

Steve Blake's fist connected with the jaw of Morris Powell, shattering it with one blow. Morris fell to the ground and tried desperately to cover his face and body at the same time – to no avail. Steve had made sure to wear his army issue boots. He delivered a perfectly aimed, full-blooded kick to the groin of the offender. Morris screamed in agony as a lightning bolt of pain seared through his private parts. He was still screaming when four of his ribs gave way and his left arm broke under the weight of Steve Blake's unrelenting assault.

"Stop, stop! For the love of God, stop!" Morris pleaded through his injured mouth as he cowered on the ground.

Steve Blake paused for a moment.

"Did you actually mention God?" he asked, incredulously. "You perverted little bastard! God can't help you now. In fact, here's one from Him!"

And Steve Blake aimed a final blow at Morris Powell. He then knelt beside the stricken man, took a firm grip on his head and turned his face towards himself. Morris moaned at the pain of his shattered jaw.

"We've not been formally introduced," snarled Steve, his eyes boring into those of Morris Powell. "I'm Daisy Blake's father and you're the scum of the earth. Touch her or any other child like that again and believe me, I *will* kill you!"

With that, Captain Steve Blake was gone.

~ ~ ~ ~ ~

Gemma Powell looked at the clock and rolled her eyes.

"He's late," she moaned. "You said he'd be here at seven and its half past. Where is he?"

Liam Powell entered the room. He was wearing his best denim shirt and jeans, and had splashed out and put on some aftershave.

"How do I know where he is?" Liam countered. "You know how stupid Morris is, he's no doubt missed the bus. He'll be on the next one, I guess," he continued, considering his reflection in the mirror and wondering why he looked so old.

Gemma sighed loudly.

"He's useless is what he is. Flamin' useless! I knew he'd let us down. First night out in ages and it's gonna fall through. You better get ready to fetch a takeaway as I'm not cooking now," she grumbled.

Gemma did not see Liam pull a face.

234

"I prefer a takeaway any day to your excuse for cooking," Liam muttered under his breath.

Upstairs in her bedroom, a sleeping Jazmin Powell would never know the reprieve that had just been afforded her by Steve Blake. Meanwhile, Steve had returned home and tantalisingly held a large, brown paper bag above his head. Three little girls danced around him trying desperately to reach it.

"Oh, no," Steve said, tormentingly. "The price is two kisses from each of you."

He was immediately besieged and pretended to fall to the floor in mock defeat.

"You got me, you got me," he cried. "I give in."

But it was too late. The girls rained kisses on their father, grabbed the bag of goodies and ran for it. Steve stood up sheepishly.

"They won again," he told Fiona who had entered to see what all the commotion was about.

"You were gone a long time," she commented, looking at her husband intently. "Where did you get to?"

Steve straightened up and looked vague.

"Oh, you know, here and there. I bumped into quite a few people, so it delayed me. Hey, where are those little minxes with your *Revels?* You know what they're like, they'll munch them all if you don't rescue them."

At the mention of her chocolates, Fiona forgot all about her concerns.

"What?! My *Revels*," she shouted in mock horror. "Where are they?"

And off Fiona went in search of her treats, leaving a relieved Steve alone with his thoughts.

Chapter 27

After what seemed like eternity, the bench of magistrates returned to the courtroom. JP Margaret Forbes looked around and Diane noticed that she looked a bit owlish around the eyes.

"Oh, God! Please make the right decision, you old fool," Diane murmured under her breath.

Marcus shot the social worker a disapproving glance and the latter bit her lip as Forbes began speaking.

"This is indeed a worrying and serious matter. We have a baby lying in the hospital as we speak, desperately unwell due to being neglected by his mother who should have afforded him a higher standard of care. However, we are of the opinion that Ms Thompson did not receive the level of support required to deliver acceptable care to her son. It would appear that the local authority failed to recognise her mental state and resulting struggles. Subsequently, they did not offer any viable services which would have enabled her to better meet his needs.

"It is therefore the unanimous decision of this court that Daniel Thompson be discharged from the hospital back into the care of his mother. Furthermore, it is the expectation of this court that the local authority shall provide Ms Thompson with adequate levels of support in the form of a social worker and a referral to the children's centre where a parenting assessment will be undertaken. We will reconvene in three months' time to consider Ms Thompson's progress and make further decisions based on the outcome of the assessments."

Diane stopped breathing. She felt as if a cold hand had just grasped her heart. In peripheral vision, she could see Kirsty Thompson smirking and looking relieved. Meanwhile, Piers Hamilton-Blake shook his client's hand and led her to an antechamber, to better explain what was now expected of her. Diane turned to Marcus, but he could not meet her gaze.

"Marcus," she whispered, exhaling and shaking her head in disbelief. "How in God's name did that just happen?"

Marcus finally looked up from his papers.

"I cannot offer an adequate explanation, Diane. Only that Ms Thompson made a suitably forlorn witness and her barrister made a convincing argument. The bench obviously felt that with the correct support, Ms Thompson can be a good mother, but I fear this isn't over. We'll be back with further representation before the three months are up. I'll make sure it goes before a county court judge and not a magistrates' bench."

~ ~ ~ ~ ~

Shanice Ellis stood up in court, shaking. She had lost a stone in weight since her arrest and looked drawn and pale. She spoke only to confirm her name. The hearing was a formality, after which Shanice was remanded in custody and led to the awaiting security vehicle which transported her back to *Denby Gates Women's Prison*. Despite the grim surroundings of the prison cell along with the rigid routines of prison life, Shanice actually felt safe there. She knew that she would be spending many years behind bars for what she had done and felt genuine remorse for killing Grant. However, prison afforded her the time to reflect on her life and in some strange way, actually relax for the first time in years.

Shanice made some good friends in prison: women who, like herself, had been driven to acts of violence by the sheer desperation of their circumstances. Shanice missed her children, of course, and it broke her heart that she could only see them once a fortnight. DJ had been the worst affected by the outcome. The anguish of Shanice regarding her actions was intensified when she discovered that Tia and DJ had both witnessed the attack. For Shanice, that was particularly difficult to live with and she wept endless, bitter tears in knowing to what she had unwittingly exposed her children.

The children were all receiving counselling for the trauma of effectively losing both their parents and Shanice knew that it would be many years before they came to terms with it – if, in fact, they ever came to terms with such a horrific event. Shanice's mother had agreed to care for the children and was making formal arrangements through a solicitor to apply for special guardianship. Shanice could not have wished for more. Her mother was bereft when she discovered how Shanice had suffered over the years and in the way most mothers do, had blamed herself for not noticing. Shanice stepped back into her cell, exhausted with the emotional stress and gladly accepted a hug from her cell mate, Lara.

~ ~ ~ ~ ~

Ironically, it was the same group of young people who usually taunted Morris Powell who actually saved his life. They came across him lying unconscious in the alleyway, making gurgling noises. One of the young people had the foresight to turn Morris onto his side, preventing him from choking, while another called 999.

In the ambulance, paramedics hooked Morris up to a drip as they raced to *Queen's Hospital*. There the doctors assessed Morris and sent him straight to surgery where they operated initially on his shattered jaw. His left arm was set in a temporary plaster cast, while they waited for Morris to recover from the surgery to his face.

Further surgery would be required to straighten it. Morris also had four broken ribs, a fractured pelvis and a ruptured testicle due to the blunt force trauma to the area. He was, in short, in a fairly bad way.

"Well, buddy," said the doctor as they wheeled Morris out of surgery and into intensive care. "I don't know what you did to deserve this, but they sure did a good job."

A lone police officer was waiting by the bedside when Morris woke up later that day. His jaw had been wired and he could only communicate by writing. The officer was aware of Morris's criminal history and had little doubt in his mind that the incident had been a vigilante type of assault. It was not uncommon on the Deacon Hill estate for the local mafia to dish out their own brand of justice, especially to the likes of Morris Powell.

"So, Morris," began the officer without any real concern. "Want to tell me who did this to you?"

Morris was in so much pain that he could barely focus on what was being said. He tried shaking his head, but the effort was excruciating. Instead, he held the pen that the police officer had given him and wrote.

"Don't know."

The police officer looked at the paper with cynicism.

"Course, you don't," he replied, disinterestedly. "Well, think about it, Morris. If it comes back to you, let us know."

And he got up to leave. But as the officer reached the door, he hesitated and turned back.

"Oh, Morris, the doctor also told me your balls got crushed," he said with feigned sympathy. "What a tragic shame, eh?"

With that the police officer left whistling happily to himself. Back at the police station, DS Dave Simpson was interviewing a truculent Scott Taylor.

"We know you did it, Scott," Dave said, directly, "so save yourself the trouble and make a statement."

Scott Taylor scowled.

"I did nothing," he argued. "Clumsy little sod fell off her chair."

Dave Simpson shrugged.

"Yeah, Scott, keep telling yourself that. I've got two eyewitnesses telling me you did it."

That was news to Scott.

"Two?" he said in surprise, despite himself. "How come, two? There was only me and Jodie there."

Dave smiled.

"You're forgetting, Scott. Jamie was there too and he's a smart lad. No doubt in my mind who a jury is going to believe: you with your fine criminal record and your drug addiction, or an innocent four-year-old who looks like he fell straight out of heaven. Face it, Scott. We all know what happened in that kitchen, so stop lying and man up. Tell us the truth and it'll go better for you. Show some remorse for what you did and we can say you cooperated and hope for a lighter sentence. But, either way, you're going down for this. Only thing for you to decide is for how long."

Dave Simpson knew full well that Jamie Pearson would never be called as a witness, but he was relying on the fact that Scott Taylor did not know that. Scott put his head in his hands as Dave Pearson left the room, giving him time to think.

~ ~ ~ ~ ~

"So, Mr Powell," said the consultant, Dr Zachary Emerson, as he stopped by the bedside. "How are we feeling?"

Morris Powell did not imagine any human being could feel that bad and still be alive. Every bit of him hurt like hell and here was that fool doctor asking how he felt. Morris could not even answer him verbally, so he just lay silently in his solitary bed of affliction. The consultant nodded.

"That good, eh?" he said without compassion.

The police officer had enlightened the consultant as to the likely reason for the situation of Morris Powell. As a father himself, the doctor was not about to waste any sympathy.

"Ah, well, Mr Powell. You can expect the pain to decrease over the next few days," he said brightly. "However, you'll be in here for some time. Is there anyone you'd like us to contact?"

Morris managed to write down the phone number of his brother, Liam, which the consultant took back with him to the nurse's station.

"Decrease the morphine by 2mg," the doctor advised as he passed the phone number to the ward sister.

"Decrease it, doctor?" queried the sister. "But he's still in a lot of pain."

Dr Zachary Emerson smiled in response as he swept out of the ward.

"I know, sister. I know."

~ ~ ~ ~ ~

Liam Powell looked at the phone as it rang.

"Who the hell's that, ringing at this time?" Liam said. "It's gone 10 o'clock."

Gemma scowled.

"Well, if it's that fool brother of yours, tell him to get stuffed."

She was still sulking from her missed night out.

"Pick it up, then!" she continued, bad-temperedly.

Liam answered the phone and Gemma watched in fascination as the colour drained from his face.

"Right," Liam said, quietly. "Okay. Yes, I'll come straight away," putting the phone down.

Gemma stood up, for once genuinely concerned about her husband.

"What is it?" she asked, her eyes wide open. "Who was it?"

Liam picked up his coat.

"It's *Queen's Hospital*," he replied. "Our Morris has been beaten up and he's in a real bad way. I've got to go over there now."

Gemma's concern evaporated.

"Ah, that's why he didn't come around," she responded. "Oh, that's okay. I feel better now knowing he didn't just mess us about."

Liam shook his head.

"Gemma," he snapped, "the man's in a serious condition."

243

Gemma shrugged her shoulders in return.

"You better get off then and see him. I'm going to bed. Don't wake me up when you come in," she said nonchalantly, leaving the room.

Chapter 28

Diane gathered up her notebook, diary and pen, and made her way to Glenda's office for supervision. They had much to discuss, so much had happened since their last meeting.

"How you feeling, Di?" asked Glenda as the social worker walked in. "Any better than a few days ago?"

Diane pulled a face.

"Not really, Glenda. If anything, it's getting worse. I cannot believe everything that's kicked off lately. I don't know where to begin, with it all," said Diane with some despair.

Glenda consulted the list of Diane's cases which was in front of her.

"Right," the manager replied, "we'll begin at the top of this list and work our way down, and see if we can't lighten your load. First off, the Ellis children. Obviously, mum is in prison and likely to be there for the foreseeable future. Grandma has successfully applied for a special guardianship order, so I'm going to transfer the case to the long-term team for them to support her through that process. Then it can be closed. Sad as it is, there will be no more for us to do on that one."

Diane felt a deep melancholy come over her as she thought of the four children.

"Could we have done more, Glenda?" she asked with heartfelt concern.

Glenda regarded Diane.

"Honestly, Di, I don't think we could. We presented it to MARAC as a serious case and you were visiting the home regularly and seeing the children in school. The kids were obviously coached not to say anything as they gave no indication of any problems between their parents. No, Di, it's one of those tragic incidents where enough was enough and Shanice snapped."

Diane nodded.

"I guess you're right," she sighed, "but it doesn't make me feel any better. It certainly doesn't help those kids."

"I know," replied Glenda, "but we need to move on and talk about families we still have a chance of supporting. So, Daniel Thompson?" she said, trying to prompt Diane out of her despair over the Ellis children.

It worked.

"Oh, God! Glenda, where do I begin? It was a nightmare. The stupid magistrates, how *could* they allow that baby to go home? I mean, he's still in the hospital, but he'll be going home in a few days."

Glenda agreed wholeheartedly with Diane.

"I completely understand how you feel, Di, but we need to be proactive on this one. Not that you haven't been that already, but you know what I mean. I want daily visits to the home, either from you, the health visitor or the children's centre, with absolutely every single conversation, phone call, etc., logged for the courts. You and I both know Kirsty won't be able to make the changes required and sad as it is, we need her to fail again so we can take further action. We'll give her support, Diane. She asked for it and she's going to get it. I want the out-of-hours team involved and undertaking visits in the evening too," she said as a final word on the matter.

"Jodie Pearson," said Diane, decisively. "She's doing well now. She made what I believe to be a truthful statement to the police regarding Scott being responsible for Courtney's broken arm, which was borne out by what Jamie said in the hospital. I believe her, Glenda. I don't think for one minute that Jodie did this to Courtney. Her mum's doing a great job of taking care of the kids, but we need to make a decision as to whether or not we can let them go home to Jodie."

Glenda frowned as she considered that.

"Hmm," she mused, "I think for now we'll leave them with Grandma, but we'll allow Jodie to increase her visits. Ring the police and see where they've got to with Scott. If they have enough to prosecute him, we'll consider the children going home with Jodie. However," Glenda added, seriously, "Jodie will need to understand that under no circumstances is she to resume her relationship with Scott at any point in the future, or all bets are off and those kids are back with Grandma."

Glenda and Diane continued discussing the latter's cases. After further debate it was agreed that Diane's colleague, Vicky, would take the Powell case.

"They agreed not to allow Liam's brother, Morris, to visit again," said Diane. "So, hopefully, that's an end to that one. However, I would recommend that Vicky visits the children in school again, to talk to them on their own and see who visits the home before you close it."

Glenda concurred with Diane's plan and ticked the case off her list.

"Where are you with Sharon Lewis?" asked Glenda. "That seems to have gone quiet."

Diane took a sip of coffee before answering.

"She's still refusing to comply with the risk assessment in regard to Michael visiting his dad, so basically it's a stalemate," said Diane. "I don't know how I can move it forward, to be honest. We're pretty sure Roy Tranter is part of our paedophile network. That said, he's not due for release for some years, so I doubt he's a serious contender."

"You can't do anything," said Glenda, decisively, "so we'll close it for now and write to Sharon saying that if she wishes to reconsider, then we can open it up again and do the risk assessment. But you don't have the capacity to be trying to talk her into this. Make sure probation and the prison are clear that Michael is not permitted to visit and as far as I'm concerned, that's the end of it."

Diane's relief was visible as one by one, Glenda made executive decisions about the cases, reallocating those which she could and closing others.

"Right, then," replied Diane, feeling better every minute. "Jessica Jackson's still a worry. She's been missing for two days now and while I know this is not uncommon for Jess, I'm concerned for her safety and wonder who she's running with."

Glenda bit the top of her pen as she thought about Jessica.

"She usually turns up after a few days, though. Right?" the manager asked. "Has she phoned her foster carer? Jessica's normally pretty good about that once she comes to her senses."

Diane knew that no one had heard from Jessica in the two days she was missing.

"No, 'fraid not, Glenda. No one's heard from her. The police are still looking, but they've not taken it that seriously yet as she's always running away."

Glenda sighed.

"Well, there's not a lot we can do, Di. Keep ringing the police for an update and ring around the hospitals now and see if, by any chance, she's been admitted to any of them, although I hope not. Have you rung her known friends yet?"

Diane nodded.

"The foster carer has and I've also been in touch with her old foster carers and they've rung her old friends too, but no one's heard a thing. I'll keep trying, but I hope she's okay."

Glenda consulted her list.

"So who's left?"

Diane knew that she still had some worrying cases to discuss.

"The Waleeds," Diane responded, grimly. "Interpol still have no information on Zarifa or where she might be. I'm sick to my stomach at the thought of what that child may have already gone through," she said with heartfelt compassion. "God only knows what they've done to her over there."

It was indeed a high profile case and Glenda was in touch daily with both the director of social services, Nicholas Bishop, and Interpol regarding the efforts to locate Zarifa.

"For now we have the other children safe and well in foster care. Mr Waleed is being allowed supervised contact once a week, but decisions will have to be made as to the future of the other children. I've been talking to our legal department and while there is no doubt the girls are at significant risk of harm, there's little evidence that the boys would be at any risk. However, we'll argue that if they returned home to their father, he might take them to Sudan. As British citizens, the children have a right to remain in England and I can see that there could be a huge legal argument going all the way up to the Court of Human Rights. It's definitely not a straightforward case, Di. For now I want you to continue with our plans to keep the children in foster care, until we know what happened to Zarifa and the police decide how they're going to proceed with Mr Waleed. Sad to say, but the longer she's missing, the more of a case we have."

"Are we almost there?" asked Glenda in mock weariness. "Crikey, Diane! No wonder you're exhausted. I'm worn out just talking about your workload. Okay, what about little Ruby? How's she doing?"

Diane's face brightened.

"Ah, she's adorable, Glenda! And she's absolutely thriving in foster care. I've got information back from the police. You won't be surprised to hear that our man, Hanif Hassan, has a police record mainly for violent offences and drugs. Most interesting, however, is police intelligence which suggests he's acting as a pimp for several women in the area, so he's not going to be a realistic contender to care for his daughter. He's never really had anything to do with her, anyway, as he abandoned Kelly when Ruby was only a few weeks old. He's kept in touch, but I suspect that's because he's making Kelly work the streets for him, although I can't prove it. I've done an initial viability assessment on his sister as a carer, but that's a total non-starter. She lives about 75 miles away and checks with the local authority in her area have shown that she has two children of her own, both subject to child protection plans so she's no good.

"The one person who might be okay is Kelly's aunt, Nicky. She apparently raised Kelly from the age of two as her own mum, Nicky's sister, died of a drug overdose. She lost touch when Hanif came into Kelly's life, but initial checks are positive. I know we still have to wait for the outcome of the parenting assessments, but I can't imagine Ruby will be going home; not after the injuries she suffered from her mother. I'm hoping that this Aunt Nicky might be a way forward."

Glenda nodded.

"Well, go ahead and start a more in-depth assessment on Nicky and that can run alongside the parenting assessment. You can tell the children's centre to terminate Hanif's parenting assessment as he's never going to be allowed to care for her – not with his record. I'll write to the court and explain why we made this decision and I'm confident they'll accept it. We'll let Kelly's assessment continue and see what the outcome is, but as you say, I doubt she has the capacity to be a good enough parent. We can't ignore the fact that she's already harmed her daughter."

Diane flipped a page in her notebook.

"Finally," she commented with relief. "The last one: Janice and Barry Spiggot."

Glenda allowed herself a smile.

"You've saved the best till last, I see," she said.

Diane groaned.

"I know. This one's so tricky. I've booked a case conference for 10 days' time, so I'll crack on with the report for it, but there's the added little problem of our suspected paedophile ring. I know the police are still gathering information, but I'm going to have to do some checks, to make sure none of the men we know about have any contact with children."

Glenda knew that it was a potentially very serious case and one that could hit the headlines if word got out.

"I want you to make unannounced visits to the Spiggots' home," Glenda began. "Don't go on your own. Take someone with you. Go at tea-time and see if you can catch Malcolm Withers there. I know it's going to be awkward, especially given Barry Spiggot's attitude, but we have to do this. Also alert the out-of-hours team and ask them to make some visits later at night as he may well visit then. For now it's about all we can do. If Withers is found in the home, then we'll take legal advice. Write to parents and reiterate this before conference, please."

Diane scribbled furiously and felt a mixture of excitement and apprehension about the case, given its potential for uncovering a paedophile network.

"Yep," she replied, "I'll get onto it and schedule some unannounced visits for later this week. Well, I think that's it, Glenda. We got through them all," Diane said with satisfaction. "I feel so much better for having a lighter load. I'll meet with Vicky and bring her up to speed on the case she's going to pick up."

Then Diane made a few final notes.

"Well, that's it. I guess it must be coffee time," she ended with a grin.

Glenda grinned back.

"Thought you'd never ask," she said, handing Diane her cup.

Chapter 29

Scott Taylor still had his head in his hands when Dave Simpson returned into the room.

"So, Scott," Dave began, briskly. "What's it to be, son?"

Scott regarded the detective with contempt.

"I wanna deal," he replied, testily.

Dave Simpson tried not to smile.

"We're not in an American television show, Scott. We don't do deals here," the detective explained with patience. "Either you tell me you're the one who broke Courtney's arm and show some remorse about it, and we can hope for a more lenient sentence, or we can do it the hard way. Oh, just so you know, you'll be remanded in custody and those big lads at *Stone Hall*, they might be criminals themselves, but they really don't like people who hurt kids. Mind you, they don't necessarily need to know why you're in there," he finished, allowing the thought to hang in the air.

Scott Taylor was many things, but he certainly was not stupid – he was extremely streetwise. He knew what fate awaited him at *Stone Hall* if word got out that he had broken the arm of a three-year-old girl – it would definitely not be good. Scott looked at Dave Simpson with slightly more respect.

"But you won't tell them, right?" Scott asked with as much bravado as he could muster.

Dave Simpson shook his head.

"They won't hear it from me, Scott; that I can promise you. So what's it to be? I'm guessing it was an accident, eh? She went to get up and you just wanted her to sit down. Is that what happened? I'm sure you didn't mean to break her arm. It was an unfortunate accident is my guess."

Scott knew the game was up. He nodded slowly.

"Yeah, that's it," he admitted. "It was an accident like you said. I didn't mean to hurt her, right."

Dave Simpson slid a writing pad and pen over to Scott.

"Now you can pretend you're in a movie, son," Dave said. "Write it all down for me."

~ ~ ~ ~ ~

Liam stood by his brother's bedside in disbelief. While there was little love lost between Liam and Morris Powell, they were, after all, brothers – and blood ran thicker than water. Liam was aghast at the injuries sustained by Morris. He knew that it would take a long time for his brother to recover.

"Who did this to you, bro?" asked Liam with genuine concern. "Tell me and I'll sort it out! I know a few people, you know."

Morris still could not move or speak, so he took the pen and pad which the nurses had left him within reach and wrote.

"Leave it alone."

Liam looked at the message.

"Leave it alone?" he replied angrily. "Leave it alone?? Are you for real, mate? How can you say that?! Someone needs to pay for this and I can get it sorted for you."

Morris took the pad back from Liam and wrote another message.

"I said, leave it," was all he wrote.

Then Morris closed his eyes against the pain. Liam shook his head.

"It's your funeral," he replied. "I guess you've your reasons."

~ ~ ~ ~ ~

Diane knocked on the door of Kirsty Thompson's house and waited for the dog to bark, but heard nothing. *Strange, I wonder if they got rid of it.* Diane knocked again.

Daniel had been discharged earlier that day after spending a week in the hospital. He had gained weight and recovered from his dehydrated state. There had been a discharge meeting at the hospital and both Kirsty and Neil attended. Diane had, of course, been there and reiterated to them that she would call at 2.00pm, to make sure Daniel had settled back in okay and see if there was anything they needed. Both Kirsty and Neil had agreed to be at home and signed another written agreement which specified that and other points to which they were supposed to adhere. Kirsty had a solicitor present, although it was not Piers Hamilton-Blake who was in court on more worthy matters. The solicitor had spoken quietly and advised her to sign the agreement, to demonstrate that she was willing to cooperate with the local authority and engage with them.

"So where is she?" said Diane aloud.

She tried ringing Kirsty's mobile, but it went straight to voicemail. Diane left a message, explaining that she was at the door as planned and said that she would call once again later on. Then she hung up, frustrated.

"I knew she wouldn't play ball," Diane fumed as she pushed yet another note through the door, before returning to her car and driving angrily back to the office.

Meanwhile, inside the house, Kirsty and Neil gave each other a high five.

"I'm not having no court tell me what to do," declared a poker-faced Kirsty as she turned the television back on. "There's nowt wrong with him and there never was. It was a big fuss about nothing."

Neil let go of the dog which he had held in a vice-like grip to keep him quiet. The animal shook itself and slunk quickly back to its filthy bed in the corner of the kitchen, eager to avoid the toe of Neil O'Grady's boot.

"Right," he agreed. "He's fine. Don't know what all the fuss was about."

Neil lit a cigarette and sat down beside Kirsty to watch television. Upstairs, Daniel began stirring. He had been in a deep sleep as his recent experiences had left him drowsy and exhausted. For the past few days, the baby had become accustomed to someone responding to him whenever he cried. He had been fed and changed regularly; he had felt warm and comfortable. Daniel had been handled gently and spoken to lovingly. He did not know, however, that it was to be the only time in his life that would happen. Daniel was hungry again now so he began crying.

~ ~ ~ ~ ~

Diane got back to the office and was met by Glenda looking pleased.

"What?" said Diane, still angry about Kirsty not being at home. "What's the occasion?"

Glenda took Diane by the arm and guided her into the office.

"The police just rang," the manager began. "Scott Taylor's made a statement. He's admitted to causing Courtney's broken arm although, needless to say, he claims it was an accident. Anyway, he will now be prosecuted for grievous bodily harm and is looking at a custodial sentence. Scott's been remanded in custody and will, hopefully, return to prison after the trial. With him out of the way, I think we can now look at the children having a gradual return home to Jodie, although she'll need a great deal of support. I don't want her going from the frying pan into the fire, setting up shop with yet another Scott Taylor. So do you want to go and tell her the good news?"

Diane gave Glenda a hug.

"About time something went our way!" Diane exclaimed. "Yes, I'll go see Jodie. She'll be ecstatic. Oh, by the way, Kirsty Thompson wasn't home – surprise, surprise!"

Diane was about to leave the office to go and see Jodie when Angie stopped her at the door.

"Phone, Di. It's urgent," Angie said.

Diane turned back.

"What now?" she said in feigned annoyance. "I wasn't quick enough in escaping," Diane laughed as she went back to her desk to take the call.

The social worker listened as the child protection police officer relayed the details she had just been given.

"I'm only telling you, Diane, as I know you had a meeting with Jill Fletcher the other day and this guy's name came up. There's nothing for your department to do as it's an extra familiar case, so we'll be investigating, but thought you'd like to know."

Diane put the phone down and made straight for Glenda's office. She knocked briefly and went in.

"Guess what?" Diane said.

Glenda put down the phone, delaying the call she was about to make.

"Hmm," she said, "you won the lottery?"

Diane shook her head.

"No, better. You remember the professionals meeting we had the other day regarding the paedophile network? You recall they mentioned Morris Powell? Liam Powell's brother who I'm involved with? Well, anyway, the police just rang to say that they've had a complaint from a family who go to the *Waters of Life Church* on the estate. Apparently, Morris Powell has been attending there and indecently exposed himself to a 10-year-old girl. Now, get this: Morris Powell is, as we speak, in *Queen's Hospital* after having been seriously beaten up."

Glenda opened her mouth to speak, but Diane stalled her.

"No, hear me out," Diane insisted, "that's not all. This girl's dad is an Iraqi war veteran who just returned from Afghanistan. The police have put two and two together and suspect he may be responsible for putting Powell in the hospital. How's *that* for news?"

Glenda leaned back in her chair and whistled.

"Really?" she said. "Well, the plot certainly thickens. I'm guessing we don't need to take any action regarding the little girl?"

Diane shook her head.

"No, it's outside the family, so the police will deal with it. Nothing for us to do there, but I can't wait to hear if the dad did this. Can't say I blame him, though. Oh, well, back to it. I'm off to see Jodie."

And off Diane went with a spring in her step.

~ ~ ~ ~ ~

Captain Steve Blake opened the door to find two police officers standing in front of him.

"Gentlemen," Steve said, politely, "can I help you?"

The officers looked slightly uncomfortable.

"May we come in, Mr Blake? We need to have a word with you about your recent complaint regarding your daughter."

Steve stepped back.

"Come on in, I'm happy to help," said Steve, ushering the officers into the lounge.

Fiona Blake was about to lay the table for tea when she saw the police.

"Oh!" she exclaimed, startled. "What's going on?"

Steve went to his wife and put a protective arm around her.

"No worries, Fifi," Steve reassured her. "They just have a few things to discuss regarding Daisy."

Fiona looked around.

"Well, Daisy's not here," she replied. "She's out playing with her friends. Shall I call her in?"

The police officers sat down.

"That won't be necessary, Mrs Blake. It's Mr Blake we need to talk to."

Steve and Fiona sat opposite the police officers and looked expectantly at them. One of the officers cleared his throat and began speaking.

"Mr and Mrs Blake," he began, "we know you recently filed a complaint against a man called Morris Powell in relation to an alleged sexual offence against your daughter, Daisy."

Steve and Fiona nodded in agreement. Fiona looked upset at the mere mention of the incident – she had found it almost impossible to deal with. It had broken her heart when she sat with Daisy as the girl stumbled with embarrassment over her words during a video interview with the police. While they had been kind and sensitive to her, it had not lessened the fact that Daisy had to relive the horrific incident. However, that had been, hopefully, the last time as the policewoman who led the interview had reassured Fiona that children were only required to provide a video statement. She had told them that Daisy would not have to be in court if the matter went to trial.

The police officer continued, "Morris Powell has recently been the victim of a serious physical assault and is currently in *Queen's Hospital* recovering from extensive injuries."

Steve Blake did not react. His expression did not change and he sat perfectly still. Fiona was different: her hand flew instantly to her mouth and her eyes widened.

"Attacked?" she said in amazement. "By whom?"

The police officer looked slightly embarrassed.

"Well, Mrs Blake, that's what we're trying to establish. Morris Powell says he doesn't know who attacked him, but we're not convinced he's telling the truth. No offence, Mr Blake, but given the circumstances we need to ask you where you were on Sunday at around 12.30pm. Mr Powell was attacked at that time as he made his way home from church."

Upon hearing that, Fiona's demeanour changed. She jumped up and her cheeks acquired a high colour. Her eyes blazed with anger.

"Are you suggesting my husband did this?" she demanded. "Are you out of your minds?! He's a decorated war veteran who has served this country for years. How dare you accuse him of such a thing?!" Fiona raged. "And as for that man," she continued, spitting out her words, "oh, yes! A fine, Christian fellow he's turned out to be!"

Steve put a restraining hand on his wife.

"It's okay, darling," he said, reassuringly. "The police have every right to ask. After all, I have an obvious motive. Isn't that right, gentlemen?"

The police officers nodded their agreement.

"Sorry, sir, but you do have motive, given the allegations made by your daughter. So, please, your whereabouts?"

Steve made a show of thinking, but Fiona interrupted his thoughts.

"He went to the sweet shop," she immediately responded. "Remember, Steve? You went to get me and the girls some chocolate. I can tell you what he bought if you like," she added, still piqued.

Steve turned to his wife and nodded.

"That's right, I did; yes. I was at the paper shop on the corner. They can verify that and afterwards I came home. We got ready and went to *Frankie and Benny's* for a late lunch."

The officers wrote down Steve's alibi, assured him that they would check it out, thanked him and left. Then Fiona Blake looked directly at her husband.

"What?" Steve said, shrugging his shoulder. "What's up?"

Fiona knew her husband well.

"Did you do it?" she asked him directly. "You were a long time at that sweet shop, Steve. Did you do this? I need to know."

Steve took his wife's face in his hands.

"Do you think I did it?" he said, posing the question back to her.

Fiona adopted a grave, serious look.

"Steve Blake, you know I'm a Christian and you know my thoughts on violence, but I'm also Daisy's mother and I've had to watch that child suffer. Her life will never be the same again because of what that man did to her. If you did do this, all I can say is I'm glad you did and I hope he's in a world of pain. Now, I never want to speak of it again!"

With that, Fiona kissed Steve on the mouth.

262

After a while, she asked, "Do you want coffee?" and returned into the kitchen.

Steve stood there in complete shock. He had not expected Fiona's reaction – not in a million years.

"Err, yeah. Coffee's great," he replied, finally sitting down while still shaking his head in disbelief.

Meanwhile, over at *Waters of Life Church*, the Wednesday night bible study group led by Pastor Alan Slater bowed their heads and prayed for the recovery of Morris Powell.

Two days later, the same police officers revisited Steve.

"We checked your alibi, Mr Blake," said one of the officers. "The owner of the sweet shop confirms that you were in there buying chocolate for your daughters. He said he had quite a chat with you for 10 minutes or more. *Frankie and Benny's* also confirm your being there for lunch, so we won't be bothering you any more in regard to this matter."

The other police officer stepped forward and proffered his hand to Captain Steve Blake.

"Like to shake your hand, sir, if I may. It's an honour to meet someone who's served this country so well."

Steve shook the officer's hand warmly.

"No problem," he replied. "One more tour and I'll be able to retire and be with my family."

The police officer was the same one who had interviewed Morris Powell in the hospital. He held Steve's hand for slightly longer than necessary.

"Keep sorting out the bad guys, sir," the officer said, meaningfully, "if you get my drift."

Chapter 30

Nahla Waleed lay on a bed of grief, weeping bitter tears. One of the village elders had just been to see her and delivered some bad news. Her husband's uncle had recently flown into the country and informed him that her husband, Hafiz, was in police custody and that all her remaining children were now living with strangers and unlikely to be returned to their father. For Nahla, it was too much to bear. The hope that her husband and four other children might join her in country had sustained her and given her a reason to live. What reason did she have now? She had failed, not only as a mother, but as a wife. The shame was too great to bear. She knew what she had to do.

Nahla waited until darkness shrouded the camp. She rose from her bed, pausing only to look for one last time upon her sleeping, unknowing mother. Stifling her tears, Nahla hardened her resolve. Despite the fact that she would be committing an almost unpardonable sin and, undoubtedly, condemning her mother to lifelong dishonour and probably expulsion from the village, Nahla was determined to go through with her plan. She had failed and lost everything – and it was time to pay for it all.

Nahla made her way by touch into the hut set aside for the ritual slaughter of the sheep and the goats. As Muslims, all animals consumed in the village were slaughtered according to the *halal* ceremony. Nahla had witnessed many an animal die that way and it did not cause her undue concern. It was their fate to die in that manner. Why should she worry about a few sheep and a few goats?

Nahla's hand located the sharp knife normally employed in the ceremony. She knew that it was sharpened each time it was used. Its blade was keen and razor sharp. Uttering one last prayer, death came abruptly to Nahla Waleed and more mercifully than it had to her own daughter. Taking a deep breath, she drew the knife across her own throat, cutting down hard into her carotid artery to ensure a swift end.

The elders found Nahla in the morning, in a pool of her own blood. She was buried quickly, without prayers of supplication and mourners. The villagers were forbidden to speak her name ever again. After all, Nahla Waleed had brought nothing but trouble and dishonour to the village. Only her own mother mourned Nahla's passing and lived out her last remaining years as her daughter knew that she would: an outcast.

~ ~ ~ ~ ~

In Millbrook, 3500 miles away, Jessica Jackson was once again returning to herself after a drug-induced stupor. As usual, the obnoxious Smurf was at hand to goad her and torment her.

"Well, look who it is," Smurf mocked as Jessica struggled to focus. "If it isn't our own resident whore, Miss Jessica J."

Jessica squinted against the light.

"Fuck off, Smurf," she said, conversationally. "Make yourself useful and get me something for this fucking headache."

Smurf had been patiently waiting to get Jessica to a certain point and he knew that it was time. He smiled slyly.

"I think you might need something a little stronger this time, Jess," he replied with feigned pleasantness.

Jessica felt confused. She was not accustomed to Smurf being nice. He was a complete troll, only good for supplying her with *Charlie* which he had done for the past three days. It had been a total trip which necessitated her having sex with a seemingly non-stop queue of Smurf's idiot friends. That was of no consequence to Jessica. She had been turning tricks for men as far back as she could recall. It no longer made any impact. However, her cravings were getting worse as each day passed. Maybe, Smurf was right – she needed something more.

"Whatever," Jessica said with indifference as she lay back down in the dirty sleeping bag.

Smurf sat like a wizened alchemist, hunched over a camping stove. He was holding a spoon over the flame: a spoon with brown liquid melting in it.

"Got this for you," he said, seductively. "Make you feel real good."

Jessica felt exhausted and decidedly unwell.

"Just hurry up," she complained. "My fucking head's killing me."

Smurf completed the cooking process and sucked the lethal brown liquid into a syringe.

"Not be long," he promised, knowing that once he had got Jessica hooked on heroin, she would have to work full-time for him to keep herself supplied. "Here we go," Smurf finally said, "hold out your arm."

Jessica did as she was bid, too far gone to care. Smurf slid the needle into the vein in the crook of her arm.

"You've tried the white, now try the brown. Either way, you're goin' down," Smurf chuckled, amused at his own joke.

The drug took less than 10 seconds to hit Jessica's central nervous system. When it did, the results were catastrophic. She had used an inhaler since seven years of age when she developed an allergy to cats which triggered asthma. However, Jessica had never been very good at carrying the inhaler with her. She had been admitted to the hospital several times after an attack. In foster care, Jessica's health had improved and her carers were vigilant in ensuring that she had an inhaler with her at all times – something which did not happen when she lived at home. However, she was now very far from a caring environment and her inhaler was still sitting on the kitchen side of Lorraine Stevenson's house.

No one could have predicted that Jessica's very first experience with heroin would impact her in the way it did. The drug coursed through her veins slowing her breathing, making it shallow and uneven. Within 20 seconds, Jessica was struggling to breathe. Precisely one minute later, she was gasping for air and convulsing on the floor.

"Shit!" shouted Smurf as Jessica fell. "Shit, shit, shit! What the fuck's wrong with her?"

Smurf's counterparts looked on awestruck as Jessica fought for her life.

"Fucking do something, man!" shouted Kenny who, only hours before, had been only too happy to have sex with Jessica for the price of a fix. "She's on a bad trip, you need to help her," he implored.

"What you want me to do, man? Call the police?" asked Smurf, panicking wildly. "We can't have no police in here, we'd be done for."

Kenny searched his addled brain for a solution as Jessica continued thrashing frantically on the floor.

"Ring 999, then leg it," he suggested.

Which in the end is what they did.

"I've got a *Pay-As-You-Go* phone," shouted a skinny girl no older than 13 years of age. "No one can trace it."

"That'll do!" yelled Smurf, dialling 999. "Now run, all of you and remember: none of you were here."

In all, seven young people left Jessica to her fate that day. By the time paramedics managed to find the drug den, it was almost too late. They found the tell-tale drug paraphernalia indicating a heroin overdose, injected Jessica instantly with *Naloxone* and performed CPR – cardiopulmonary resuscitation. Jessica had stopped breathing minutes before the paramedics reached her, but the fast-acting *Naloxone* worked its magic and along with CPR, brought her back from the brink. She was whisked away to *Queen's Hospital* and placed on life support. Jessica was not out of the woods yet – not by a long way.

As it turned out, the 13-year-old who had placed the call was seriously misinformed. The 999 call was, indeed, traced back to her phone. She was back at home in bed when her parents woke her up, stony-faced, as they told her to go with them downstairs since two police officers were waiting to talk to her. The girl crumbled at the first question and gave the officers the names of everyone who had been at Smurf's place. All involved were arrested and charged with drug offences except for Smurf McCarthy who was never seen again. He had known better than to hang around in such circumstances. Smurf had packed up the sordid tools of his trade and left town for good.

~ ~ ~ ~ ~

Diane returned to Kirsty's house on her way home. It was 5.00pm and she was tired and irritable. Despite Glenda having reduced her workload, Diane knew that it was only a matter of time before she was allocated more cases and would be back to square one. Glenda had already collared

Diane on the way out and mentioned two new cases that she wanted her to look at.

The social worker knocked loudly on the door of Kirsty's house, but once again she was met with silence. Diane consulted her watch and waited a few minutes before pushing a tersely written note through the door, reminding Kirsty of the written agreement that she had signed.

"I'll be back in the morning, missy," Diane said out loud.

Then she set off for home knowing that, rightly or wrongly, she would be having a large glass of wine when she got there.

Chapter 31

Kevin West sighed as he consulted the clock: it was 9.00pm and he was only four hours into the night shift. Kevin worked for the out-of-hours team of the locality – a job he considered thankless. He was part of an often unseen team of social workers who managed urgent calls for help when the regular offices were closed. They also undertook what the team considered 'babysitting' duties for high-end cases already allocated to a social worker, but which required additional visits outside regular working hours.

Kevin had been assigned to go and see a family by the name of Spiggot. The social worker suspected that a known sex offender was visiting the home and hoped to catch them out in the evening when the family did not think anyone would visit. Kevin stretched and yawned as he picked up the case notes and put his coat on.

"I'm just off out to see this one," Kevin called to his colleagues who were manning the phones. "Won't be long," he added, reluctantly leaving left the warmth of the office.

Kevin made the short trip to the home of the Spiggots. The house lights were on and he could hear talking coming from inside as he walked up the path. He got his identity (ID) card ready and knocked on the door. A short, bald guy answered the door.

"What is it?" the guy asked, bad-temperedly. "Who the hell are you?"

Kevin explained that he was from Social Services and showed Barry Spiggot his ID-badge. Kevin was about to further explain the reason for his visit when he heard a man's voice inside the house.

"Hey, Barry, got any more beer? There's none left in the fridge."

Kevin raised his eyebrows.

"Mr Spiggot," he began politely, "I'm going to have to ask you to let me come in and assess who is in the house with your children."

That was as far as Kevin got as Barry Spiggot slammed the door in his face. Kevin returned to the office and called the police, detailing the exchange which had just taken place. He explained his suspicions that a known sex offender might well be in the house with two vulnerable children, against the advice of Social Services.

The evening culminated with two police officers visiting the home. They were met by an irate Barry Spiggot and his nervous wife. The police undertook a safe-and-well check, established that the children were in bed asleep and asked Spiggot who had been in the home when the social worker called around. Barry told them that his brother, Terry, had popped by to visit but just left. The police made a sceptical note and took their leave. There was nothing more to do. Kevin sent Diane an email explaining all his actions and the subsequent actions of the police. The email would be waiting for her when Diane returned to work in the morning.

Barry Spiggot had been taken completely unawares by the visit, so he slammed the door in the face of the jumped-up, little upstart of a social worker almost as a reflex. He returned quickly to the living room of his home where Malcolm Withers sat in stockinged feet watching football.

"So where's the beer?" Malcolm asked in mock indignation.

"You need to leave, mate," Barry Spiggot explained. "That was the social checking up and I'm pretty sure they'll call the police. Sorry, Malc, but you need to go and don't let on you were here, okay?"

Malcolm Withers beat a hasty retreat, leaving Barry with one last task before the police arrived.

"Hey, up," Barry said as his brother, Terry, answered the phone. "I need a favour," explaining what he wanted him to do.

~ ~ ~ ~ ~

Neil O'Grady spent the entire evening at the pub. So far he had downed seven pints of *Stella* and moved onto the chasers, knocking back four whiskeys in a row. He was tired of the non-stop nagging of Kirsty Thompson and the endless moaning about that brat of hers. He needed a change of woman – quickly.

Neil had his eye on the bleached blonde thirty-something-year-old at the bar who was wearing a leopard print top. He was fairly confident that she was eying him back, so Neil decided to make his move. He finished the drink in one swallow and sauntered over.

"Hey, there," Neil began in what he felt was a seductive tone. "How you doing? Can I buy you a drink?"

The woman regarded Neil for the smallest moment of time before she burst out laughing.

"Are you for real?" she asked with sarcasm. "I mean, honestly! Do you really think I'd be interested in a loser like you?"

At that moment, a man approached the woman. He was sharply dressed and a whole lot better looking than Neil O'Grady – even he had to concede that.

"Everything okay, darling?" the man asked as he stooped to kiss the woman.

The woman picked up her wrap and drew it around her shoulders.

"Just fine, honey," she replied, "just fine. Can we leave now and go somewhere else? I need a change of air."

The man was all concern.

"No problem, babe," he said with decisiveness. "Let's go."

And he put his arm around the woman's shoulder and led her out of the bar.

Neil O'Grady had never had much luck with women and was used to getting the brush-off. However, the woman's demeaning dismissal of his advances, coupled with the alcohol, made his temper flare.

"Who the hell does she think she is?" Neil seethed to himself. "Too good for the likes of me, I s'pose! Mike, another scotch!" he shouted to the barman, continuing his drinking binge.

It was about half past one in the morning when the barman, Mike, finally called time on Neil O'Grady.

"Come on, Neil," Mike said, firmly. "Time to go."

Neil lifted his head off the bar.

"What?" he replied. "What'd you say?"

Mike applied his energy into wiping down the bar where Neil O'Grady's head had been.

"Come on, buddy. It's time to go home," Mike repeated.

With some effort, Neil struggled to his feet and out of the door. When the sharp February air hit him in the face, Neil doubled over and vomited into the gutter. Five minutes later, he was making futile, fumbling attempts to get his key into the door of Kirsty's house.

Neil eventually managed to make his way into the kitchen, intending to find something to eat. His dog, Tyson, got up from the dirty blanket to greet him, wagging ingratiatingly. Neil O'Grady responded by kicking Tyson in the side, causing the dog to yelp and retreat back to his bed in the corner, shaking and cowering in terror. Neil continued his nocturnal foraging and managed to find some leftover Cornish pasty which Kirsty had bought from *Gregg's* earlier that day. He wolfed it down and followed it with milk straight from the carton. Then he belched loudly and felt better.

"Bedtime," Neil said loudly to himself, making for the stairs.

As he did so, Neil tripped over the hoover which Kirsty always left out. She had not used it, but left it in the middle of the corridor. Neil cursed loudly as he stubbed his toe.

"Stupid cow," he complained. "Why can't she tidy up?"

Neil continued his way up the stairs. Lying in his cot in the second bedroom, Daniel heard the commotion and began crying. Neil O'Grady closed his eyes against the noise.

"Oh, for fuck's sake!" Neil exclaimed as he reached the top of the stairs. "Don't you start on me, you little whiner. You need to learn to shut up!"

With that Neil opened the door of Daniel's bedroom and went in.

~ ~ ~ ~ ~

Diane had got the call at around midnight and was sitting beside Jessica's bedside, holding her hand and talking softly to her.

"Hey, you," Diane whispered. "You gave us quite a scare there, honey. Why don't you come on back to us now, eh? We miss you."

Diane's words were completely genuine. She could scarcely believe her ears when she had got the call about Jessica's dramatic, life-threatening incident. As she was halfway out of the door, Diane had alerted a frantic Lorraine to the situation – she too was en route to *Queen's*. Diane knew what a close call it had been. The consultant had warned her that Jessica could have suffered brain damage due to lack of oxygen to her brain for the few minutes she had stopped breathing.

"We'll know more when she's stable enough for us to do a CAT scan," the doctor had said, consulting his notes.

The consultant regularly saw too many young people brought into the hospital in that condition. Sadly, many of them were not as fortunate as Jessica. Ten minutes later, Lorraine joined Diane by Jessica's side. The two women hugged each other and shed tears for the tragic young woman lying unconscious on the bed.

Lorraine and Diane stayed there all night, sleeping intermittently on the uncomfortable hospital chairs. In the morning, they took it in turns to go for coffee and freshen up in the bathroom. With Lorraine there, Diane knew she had work to do back at the office.

"Will you be okay here?" Diane asked the foster carer.

Lorraine Stevenson had hardly slept all the time Jessica had been missing. She had rung up every one of her friends and walked the streets of the Deacon Hill estate each night in an effort to locate the girl. Lorraine looked at Diane with tired, but relieved, eyes.

"Di," Lorraine said, wearily, "I'm here now for as long as it takes. I'm not leaving her and I'm not giving up on her. You get off. I know you have so much to do."

Diane gave Lorraine another hug and headed home where she had to apologise to an extremely offended Mojo. After feeding him and giving him a fuss, Diane took a quick shower and changed clothes before going back to Cedar House, her eyes ablaze with purpose. She intended to call at Kirsty Thompson's again, but knew that Jessica's situation took precedence over everything else. She would return to Kirsty's later on.

Diane parked her car all awry, such was her urgency to get in to see Glenda. She almost barged into the manager's office and stood hands on her hips. Glenda put down the pen and waited. She knew that this would happen and was expecting it. Diane launched into her carefully rehearsed argument.

"They *have* to give us a secure order now, Glenda. Please, for the love of God, tell me I can apply. She almost died, Glenda, and she's not out of the woods yet."

Glenda had anticipated that argument and unbeknown to Diane, had already spoken to their legal department and to Nicholas Bishop, the director.

"I'm way ahead of you, Di," Glenda replied. "I totally agree. This has gone too far and Jessica's going to need specialised care in a safe, secure environment. I've applied for the secure order myself and am just waiting for Nicholas Bishop to send the signed document. You'll have the go-ahead to apply for your order, Diane. Hopefully, Jess can go straight from the hospital to a secure unit."

Glenda completely took the wind out of Diane's sails. The social worker had expected to have to argue and plead. She had even considered threatening to resign if the director did not agree about her applying for a secure order. Now, Diane stood in front of Glenda open-mouthed upon hearing her words. All the fight went out of her and she sat down.

"Well," Diane began, "I didn't see *that* coming."

Glenda laughed.

"No, I guess you didn't, but I'm glad we have your approval."

Diane felt relieved as she made her way to the desk to check emails. She saw the one from the out-of-hours team colleague, Kevin West, and her stomach tightened as she clicked to open it.

"What now?" Diane said out loud, knowing that it could be any one of her high profile, complex cases.

Diane read the email partly in dismay, partly in triumph. She had known without a shred of a doubt that despite the fact that Kevin had not gained access to the home, it would have been Malcolm Withers inside the place of Barry Spiggot. If nothing else, the visit gave the family the clear message that the local authority meant business and would not tolerate Withers being there. Diane doubted that even Barry Spiggot would be so stupid as to allow Withers to visit again after that.

Diane rang up the police and they advised her that they had no concerns about the children. The police also told her that Barry had claimed it was his brother, Terry, who had been in the house shouting for beer. Diane rolled her eyes.

"Yeah, right. Course it was," she told the police officer.

"Well, there's no point in me ringing to check as, no doubt, he'll only confirm it since Barry will have asked him to lie for him."

"Ah, well, at least he knows we're onto him now."

With that, Diane put her coat on and headed once again on the familiar trip to the house of Kirsty Thompson. Upon arriving, she knocked on the door and felt the usual frustration as she got no response.

"Oh, you're just taking the mickey, now!" Diane said, angrily, as she got her phone out to ring Kirsty's number.

As suspected, the phone went straight to voicemail and all the social worker could do was leave yet another message.

"I know you're in there," Diane fumed aloud as she pushed the customary note through the door. "You're fooling no one."

Diane got back into the car and headed for the office. She was determined to ask Glenda to allow her to try and visit with the police who could, when necessary, gain access to a home.

~ ~ ~ ~ ~

Kirsty Thompson woke up to the sound of silence. She smiled for the first time in days at the unexpected peace and quiet. That was, however, short lived when she realised that Neil O'Grady was, unfortunately, back in bed beside her. Kirsty had not heard Neil return home from the pub the previous night. He must have been drunk as he had passed out on the bed without trying to have sex with her.

"What time did you get in?" Kirsty asked, waking Neil up.

"What?" Neil replied, squinting at the sunlight streaming through the window. "What'd you wake me for, you silly cow?"

"He's quiet for a change," said Kirsty, ignoring Neil and nodding her head in the direction of Daniel's room. "Played me up something rotten last night, he did. I reckon they spoiled him in that hospital and gave in to his never-ending demands."

"No need to tell me," replied Neil sourly. "He was screaming when I got in at two o'clock. Not that you noticed! You were paying him no mind, as usual. Anyway, I went in and told him to shut up," he smirked. "Must have worked, eh?" he said, self-satisfied as he reached for Kirsty's body.

At that moment, they heard a knock at the door.

"Shh," said Kirsty in a hushed whisper. "It'll be the social worker again. God, she never gives up, does she?"

The knocking was repeated. Then the sound of the letterbox, then silence.

"She's gone," said Neil as he heard Diane's car pull away. "Now, where were we?"

~ ~ ~ ~ ~

"I appreciate what you're saying, Di, but we can't just ask the police to go barging into their house without solid evidence Daniel's in there and at risk. In case you've forgotten, we just lost in our attempts to get legal support for his removal. The court isn't going to be too impressed if one day later, we go in, guns blazing, without a shred of evidence of significant harm."

Glenda had spent the last 10 minutes trying to reason with an irate Diane. She knew that Daniel could well be in the home and fully agreed that Kirsty Thompson was undoubtedly avoiding Diane, but she was reluctant to authorise a joint visit with the police.

"Look," Glenda said, reasonably, "I totally agree that you need to gain access to the home. So why don't we arrange for you or someone else to visit again in a while and see if they answer?"

Diane was at the end of her tether with Kirsty Thompson's game playing.

"But, Glenda," reiterated Diane with great irritation, "we both know she's in there and given the recent circumstances, surely we have grounds to ask the police to go with us," she pleaded.

Diane was still begging for action when Glenda took the incoming call.

Chapter 32

Kirsty discovered Daniel's lifeless body at around 11.00am – after Neil and herself had sex for the second time. Her anguished howls brought Neil O'Grady running into the room.

"Call an ambulance!" Kirsty screamed.

It was too late. In the furore that ensued, both adults were arrested and blamed each other. The coroner determined that the time of death of baby Daniel had occurred at approximately 2.00am, correlating exactly with Neil O'Grady's return from the pub. However, it made no difference which one of them was responsible, whether Kirsty or Neil. Daniel Thompson was dead either way.

~ ~ ~ ~ ~

Diane sat in her flat with Mojo winding himself in and out of her legs. The cat was bewildered by the lack of attention and redoubled his efforts, but to no avail. Diane stared blankly at the newspaper.

The headlines screamed:

BABY D, KNOWN TO SOCIAL SERVICES. HOW COULD THIS HAPPEN?

Another paper led with:

SLAIN BABY'S SOCIAL WORKER DID NOT VISIT FOR WEEKS

And on and on and on.

Inside the newspapers, the reporters had, as usual, gone to town with such gems as WE CAN REVEAL and OUR SOURCES TELL US . . . None of it was accurate, of course, but the public cared nothing about that. All they wanted was justice for baby D and a social worker would do nicely for a scapegoat. They all shook their heads in righteous indignation, gave their ill-informed opinions and lapped it up. Meanwhile, in accordance with official procedure, Diane had been suspended while the inevitable Part Eight inquiry took place.

After Glenda had taken that life-altering phone call that day, all hell broke loose. The police had been on the phone with the news that Daniel was re-admitted to *Queen's Hospital,* but was dead on arrival. Diane eventually learned that an autopsy revealed that Daniel had been subject to a violent and horrific attack. Most of his bones had been broken and he sustained two subdural haematomas in the brain. The paediatric consultant and the coroner had concurred that Daniel was, undoubtedly, violently shaken and thrown around like a ragdoll. More disturbing was the fact that Daniel had other, older injuries which indicated that he had been physically assaulted on more than one occasion. Diane had cried until she had no energy left to cry anymore. It was her worst nightmare come true. She felt as if she were in a living hell.

After her suspension, Glenda had visited Diane at home and was apologetic. She tried telling Diane not to worry, but that ship had left the port long ago.

"Honestly, Diane," the manager said in an attempt to reassure her. "The only people to blame here are Kirsty Thompson and Neil O'Grady. We tried to get the court to allow us to remove him, but we lost. You visited, but they didn't answer the door. My guess is that, sadly, Daniel was already gone. Diane, I'm telling you: this will all blow over and when you're ready, you can come back to work."

Diane looked at Glenda as if she had just spoken to her in a completely foreign and unintelligible language.

"Come back to work?" Diane replied with incredulity. "Blow over? You honestly think I can just come on back after this? Glenda, a baby died – a baby for whom I was ultimately responsible! I can't do this job ever again!"

Diane broke down once more. Glenda could only hold the social worker and concede that she was probably right. To make matters worse, in the days following the death of Daniel, the media somehow got wind of Diane's address and now there was an army of vans and reporters converged on her quiet cul-de-sac. Diane could hear them through the drawn curtains.

"Ms Foster, Ms Foster," they bayed. "Is it true you failed to visit baby D prior to his death, despite the health visitor raising concerns with you?"

Others clamoured, "Ms Foster, is it true another child you're involved with has been taken unlawfully out of England?"

It was relentless and went on for days. Diane could not sleep and she did not dare to go out. Apart from Maxine visiting her and bringing her food which she could not eat, Diane saw no one.

As the light faded on the fifth day of her suspension, Diane peeked out of the curtains. The reporters were still there, watching and waiting. The social worker saw the flash of a camera as some sharp-eyed reporter spotted her curtains moving. She sat back down wearily and stared at the line of sleeping tablets that she had just arranged neatly along the arm of the chair. Diane felt tired – so damned tired. The respite promised by the tablets was tempting beyond belief. She had tried being objective, reflecting on her actions over the past few weeks. Was she responsible for this baby's death?

Diane felt overwhelmed with guilt and remorse not only for Daniel, but also for the still missing Zarifa Waleed, Jessica Jackson and all the Ellis children. However, she had not shaken Daniel's tiny body to death. The social worker had recognised the danger signs and taken appropriate action, but it had all been too late. The courts had missed their chance to intervene, but Diane knew that she could not ride the storm. She had done her best and could do it no more.

Diane went over to the compact disc player and deliberately chose Robert Cray's *I Slipped Her Mind* – she could think of nothing more fitting. She sat back down, stroked Mojo one more time and gave in. As Diane closed her eyes for the last time, her final thoughts were of a pair of impossibly beautiful brown eyes and a large, crooked smile.

~ ~ ~ ~ ~

Maxine Montgomery frowned in concern as she listened to Diane's phone ring without being answered.

"I know she's home tonight," Maxine told her husband, John. "Why doesn't she pick up?"

John looked equally worried.

"You know she doesn't like answering in case it's the press," he offered.

Maxine shook her head.

"I said I'd ring her at eight o'clock and she told me she'd be in."

Maxine tried one more time before looking at John.

Then she declared, "Get the car keys. Something's wrong."

The following day's headlines were no less sensational than those which had already appeared before:

SUICIDE ATTEMPT SHAME OF BABY D SOCIAL WORKER

The newspaper shrieked melodramatically. The public felt completely vindicated. Had they not said all along that it was Diane's fault?

Maxine and John reached Diane's place with minutes to spare. Maxine had a key and let herself in. She was met by a frantic Mojo who meowed at her in urgent tones and hampered her progress into the home by darting in and out of her legs.

"Diane," called Maxine as she stumbled over Mojo on her way through the flat. "Diane, its John and Maxine. Where are you?"

They found Diane slumped in her chair. In the background, they could hear the faint strains of blues music. John called 999, while Maxine wept and placed Diane in the recovery position. The ambulance arrived within minutes and the unconscious social worker was given emergency treatment on the floor of her own living room. She was then whisked away to *Queen's Hospital,* the scene of so many of her work dramas.

Diane required medical intervention to rid her body of the toxins she had fed herself, so she was out of it for many hours. She was unaware that, during that time, Maxine briefly left the room to make an important phone call. All she knew was that Maxine was there by her side when she woke up later that same night in intensive care. John had taken Mojo home with him and sat by the phone waiting for news.

~ ~ ~ ~ ~

That same day, Glenda Rogers was interviewing her third agency worker.

"I need someone who can hit the ground running," she explained. "You are, no doubt, aware from the recent media circus that we've had a few problems as of late. We've got a bit of a backlog of cases."

The eager-faced candidate nodded enthusiastically and agreed to start on Monday.

Epilogue

Diane Foster sat at home, staring out of the window at the frost on the trees. She still felt weak and highly emotional as she continued shedding tears every time Daniel came to her mind. It had been two weeks since her suicide attempt and Diane felt ashamed to her core to have done such a thing. Maxine had hardly left her side and cared for her like a mother hen. She made chicken soup, read to Diane and chided her when she wept and blamed herself.

"Now, stop it!" Maxine warned. "Diane, I've told you a million times and I'll continue to tell you: *none* of this is your fault. You tried your level best to get baby Daniel out of that house and you did everything the court directed. As for Jessica, well, the poor lass was on self-destruct from the moment you got her away from her family. They can't say you didn't try, Di. For God's sake, you practically demanded that Glenda apply for a secure order, but they wouldn't – well, not until it was almost too late, anyway. Oh, and don't get me started on the Waleed family! Now, drink this soup, it's good for you," she ordered.

Diane knew that it would take her a long time to heal, not just physically, but emotionally. She had put her heart and soul into that job, and she still could not believe that so many lives had gone tragically wrong. She felt utterly responsible and although she knew in her heart that she had done her best, Diane still felt as though she had failed. The press eventually got bored of vilifying her and moved on to their next victim, but Diane was left battered and bruised by the whole experience.

Maxine left Diane at 7.30pm with a cookery magazine and a warning to go to bed early. The social worker hugged Maxine and cried again when she left.

"Oh, Maxine, what would I have done without you?" said Diane, wiping away her tears.

Maxine hugged Diane back.

"You'd have gone to pieces," she replied flatly. "Now, shut up and go sit down and chill. I'll ring you in an hour."

Ten minutes later, Maxine Montgomery arrived home.

"How is she?" asked John.

Maxine sank down tiredly next to her husband, gratefully accepting the glass of wine he had ready for her.

"She's getting there, but she's got a long road ahead of her," replied Maxine, sipping her wine and savouring its delicate taste.

At that moment, the phone rang. Maxine put down her glass and answered. She listened intently, her face breaking into a wide smile as she did so.

"Yes?" Maxine said. "Okay, that's absolutely brilliant. See you soon."

John looked quizzically at his wife.

"Who was it?" he asked, intrigued.

John was surprised when Maxine burst into tears.

Diane sat down and tried to read the magazine, but found it too difficult to concentrate. She went into the kitchen to make herself a hot chocolate. She waited for the microwave to ping as it heated the milk and thought she heard the doorbell. Diane opened the microwave door to silence it and listened again. Yes, it was definitely the door. But who could be calling on her at that time of the evening?

Diane wondered if Maxine had forgotten something, but knew that she would have called first. Diane became apprehensive. She had experienced a lot of hatred and personal insults after the death of baby Daniel. She was sick and tired of the press hanging around her house, so she hoped that it was not some other reporter wanting her to 'tell her side.'

Diane went cautiously to the door. She made sure that the security chain was on before opening the door a crack.

"Who is it?" Diane called out, anxiously peeping through the gap.

Out in the hallway, a pair of chocolate brown eyes stared back at her.

"Ethan?" Diane exclaimed in disbelief. "Oh, God; Ethan!"

~ ~ ~ ~ ~

After the new agency worker left the office, Glenda turned her attention to the paperwork from Nicholas Bishop. He had agreed to their applying for a secure order for Jessica Jackson. Glenda scanned the document to ensure that there was no information missing. With Diane off work for the foreseeable future, Glenda would have to attend to the order herself.

Jessica was doing as well as could be expected. Thankfully, she had not suffered permanent damage. She could be discharged to a secure unit which would meet her physical, emotional and mental health needs, while addressing her drug issues. Nicholas Bishop had signed the document with his usual flourish, but also attached a yellow *Post-It* to its front. The note was not signed, simply initialled. Glenda stared at the note and felt the hair on the back of her neck stand up.

It read, "Please keep me up to date on this one."

The director had signed it simply *NB*.

About the Author

Freya Barrington is the pen name used by the author for this debut novel *Known to Social Services*. Freya grew up in Lancashire, England with an overriding passion for animals, specifically horses. After attending girls grammar school where English was her strongest subject, the only desire Freya held was to work with her beloved horses. To the dismay of her parents, she went to work in a racing yard.

Realising that this was not a passing phase, her parents eventually encouraged Freya in her chosen career and she went on to work with event horses, show jumpers and hunters, gaining several *British Horse Society* qualifications along the way – namely, the BHSAI, BHSII and BHSI (SM). All this enabled Freya to work as a riding instructress and trainer which she did on a freelance basis. Freya continued working in the equestrian field for many years, eventually running her own yard.

A chance conversation with a friend, however, brought about a change of career for Freya and she moved away from her life with horses, into the unknown world of residential childcare. To her surprise, Freya found that she enjoyed this line of work and progressed to being a full-time foster carer for the local authority. It was during that time Freya first put pen to paper in a creative way, writing poems about the children with whom she came into contact. A short book of poetry was soon published and the proceeds were used to raise money for a local youth group.

It was during her time as a foster carer that Freya came into contact with social workers. Their dedication and expertise inspired her to also train as a social worker, gaining the Diploma in Social Work in 2001 from the University of Derby with an award for excellence in practice. Freya also gained the Post-Qualifying Award in 2007. She is a registered member in good standing with the Health and Care Professions Council (HCPC).

The main area of expertise of Freya Barrington is as a senior child protection social worker. She has been the principal social worker and mentor on a number of teams. Freya has also worked as a foster carer's support social worker, as a court advisor and hospital social worker. Since 2006, Freya has worked exclusively as an agency social worker, with specific focus on working for local authorities that require experienced social workers to offer support where there are staff shortages. Freya's assessments and reports are in high demand, with managers from several local authority areas making specific requests for her to join their teams.

In 2010, Freya moved with her husband, Steve, to the island of Gozo (Maltese Islands). Meanwhile, she continued working in England as an agency social worker, flying back and forth on a fortnightly basis. This attracted comments from colleagues who said they would never again complain about their commute to work! It was during this time that the idea for this book started taking shape, so with the full support of her husband, Freya took a year's sabbatical to write the book.

Freya continues to live in Gozo with her husband, but plans to travel around Europe, looking for a peaceful spot to continue writing the sequel to *Known to Social Services*. More about Freya Barrington can be found at:

- Blog: freyabarrington.blogspot.com
- Facebook Page: facebook.com/FreyaBarrington
- Google+: plus.google.com/107614255402573788705/posts
- Twitter: @freyabarrington

Selected FARAXA Publications

Stories My Parents Told Me – Tales of Growing Up in Wartime Malta are seven stories by Maltese-Australian author Rupert C. Grech, based on actual events during WWII in Malta. Grech skillfully shows the difficult time it was for children and families, where survival was paramount and family ties were what sustained them. The stories are interspersed with snippets of history, factual details and settings for tales emotionally moving, some of which bring a smile to your face. Grech also describes a culture of a time past for a deeply religious, frugal people.

Bonds in the Mirror of Time is a psychological novel by Rena Balzan, Ph.D., translated from the original Maltese by Antoinette Pace. In this novel, love and selfishness are continually in competition with each other, dominating the lives of the protagonists. Why was Nada abandoned by her mother, Erica, when both needed each other so much? Who really was Maris? Why was Claud dating her when, in reality, he loved Nada? The painter, a very reserved individual, was afraid to fulfil himself as an artist. Why? Why did he end his relationship with Erica, the woman who desired to help him succeed at all cost? In this novel,  the human bonding that exists between the main protagonists is not necessarily annihilated by death. On the contrary, the psychological barriers death portrays present a challenge for overcoming them.

The Legend of Amanda Robins is a supernatural thriller for young adults by Maltese-New Yorker, 14-year-old Corrine Annette Zahra. This novel presents a fast-moving, gripping account of the turmoil resulting from the destruction of Magic State, an invisible island north of Australia. Queen Amanda is forced to evacuate her land and send the inhabitants to live with humankind. Her ex-husband, Dylan, has escaped from a prison island with hordes of werewolves and launched a vicious attack. From the streets of New York where new Twin Towers are born, to the White House, Queen Amanda puts all her powers on display. War and intrigue permeate the pages of Zahra's book which should prove un-put-downable for lovers of magical creatures.

A Land in the Storytelling Sea – A North American in Malta by Sheryl Loeffler presents 50 poems and 50 full-colour, original photographs of the Maltese Islands. Sensual, painterly, even prayerful, these poems and pictures deepen into a land of legend and myth; an island populated, past and present, by saints, beggars and pirates, all of whom are blessed by vivid geometries of light. Loeffler portrays Malta as a country awash in splendour and contradiction, a "land where Christians call God *Alla*." This book is quietly pleasurable in its narrative journey and in its subtle, seductive craft.

The Battle Roar of Silence – Foucault and the Carceral System by Meinrad Calleja explores the philosophical rationales sustaining morality, law, punishment and the carceral system as part of the discourse of globalization. Calleja attempts to desacralize the foundations of this discourse using Foucault's archaeological and genealogical study of institutions, knowledge, discourse and power. This is an interdisciplinary study fusing aspects of sociology and psychoanalysis within a philosophical framework, to tender a politically-charged critique of the contemporary modes of domination and power. Calleja correlates the carceral system discourse to political, social and economic antagonisms that have eroded human rights, democracy and freedom. Consumers of this discourse repress the negative features of such a despotic order and suffer in silence. Articulated is the battle roar of silence.

Popular Operas in the Maltese Islands by Maltese, award-winning author Tony C. Cutajar presents the 20 most favourite operas from the time they started being produced in Malta and Gozo up to 2012. Almost all operas were sentimental or tragic, lyric operas. Interesting details about each opera and its composer are given, together with plot summaries. Interactive links to audio/video selections of the best arias are also provided in the ebook edition of this book.

Bormla – A Struggling Community is a landmark, mixed methods study in which JosAnn Cutajar, Ph.D., presents the people's situation in this impoverished, historical city in Malta. Communities living in places stigmatized by policy makers, the media and the general population, develop coping skills to acquire alternative resources for their social well-being. In Maltese society, resources are often deployed by policy and decision makers not cognizant of the differential needs of communities living in different places. Cutajar gives voice to the people of Bormla, brings their needs to the forefront and gives effective recommendations for change.

Ricasoli Soldier – A Novel Inspired by True Events by Maltese-French author Joe Scicluna presents the historical story of Leo Bonanno, a young man who left Sicily in 1806 to enlist as a soldier with the British Army in Malta. The British had just formed the new regiment and recruited many from Albania, Greece, Italy, Russia and Turkey. But the recruitment process was fraudulent, with many becoming enlisted without informed consent. Leo held many hopes, dreams and ambitions of youth, including the desire to become a soldier to better serve his country. Stationed at Fort Ricasoli in Malta, Leo made new friends and fell madly in love with Lisa, a beautiful village girl

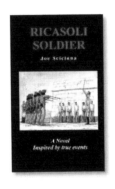

from Kalkara. But all Leo's hopes, dreams and ambitions rapidly turned into a terrifying nightmare and incomparable battle for survival, due to a system of iniquity imposed by a major who was a heartless tyrant.

The Adventures of Joe Fenek by Graham Bayes is the winner of an honorable mention at the 2013 London Book Festival. This book for children presents six stories about Joe Fenek – Joe the Rabbit. Meet Joe and his animal friends Jimmy the rat, Digger the shrew, Tony the rat, Horace the horse, Mario the mouse and Spikey the hedgehog,, all of which share in Joe's adventures around Malta and Gozo.

Strange Tales (Combined Illustrated Edition) by Charles Coyne is a collection of 29 short horror stories, many of which are set in the Maltese Islands. Ranging from Max the doll who ends up being a preternatural killer, through Meinertzhagen the man who turns into a boy after death who tries to entrap his best friend, to Loki the shaman who visits with the dead, Coyne manifests himself a true master at sleight of hand in these tales. Coyne keeps his readers on edge, gripping the seat of their chairs, both during the telling of the tales and in their surprise endings.

Escape: A Supernatural Serial for young adults by Corrine Annette Zahra. I am Tiffany Crooks and with my little sister, Minnie, I live at *The Turville's* with Grandma Crooks and her family. But who, in reality, are the Crooks and the Turvilles? Why does my Grandma Crooks desire, without further ado, to consecrate my sister with blood to the dark sacred even though we are both Christian? Who is the flame-flickered hound? Above all, why did our parents suddenly disappear after they had dropped us off with Grandma Crooks? Where are they now when Minnie and I most need them? Help! What is going to happen to us?

The Philosophy of Desert Metaphors in Ibrahim al-Koni – The Bleeding of the Stone by Meinrad Calleja takes a close look at one of al-Koni's works and attempts to prise out philosophical reflections concealed in the text. A Tuareg by birth, Ibrahim al-Koni is no longer an emerging author. His works have earned him international repute and academic recognition. Themed around a desert context, his novels have been categorized as post-modern, polyphonic, magical or socialist realism and Sufi fabula. In this book, Calleja shows how the desert provides a landscape rich in allusions, while metaphors allow readers to engage in creative interpretation.

Printed in Great Britain
by Amazon.co.uk, Ltd.,
Marston Gate.